DEFIANCE

Book Five of the Legacy Fleet Series

Nick Webb

Copyright © 2017 Nick Webb

All rights reserved.

www.nickwebbwrites.com

Summary: The fog of war clouds everything. Enemies lurk in the shadows, within the very fleet sworn to protect United Earth. Conspiracies and murder abound, and in the background.... The stalled alien invasion lurks. The Golgothic ship has burrowed deep into the core of Saturn's moon Titan, whose mass slowly but inexorably increases. The Dolmasi, once allies of United Earth in the Second Swarm War, now attack us, unhinged and without reason. And all the while, Admiral Shelby Proctor works to answer the most urgent questions of all: what was a piece of the old ISS Victory doing inside the Golgothic ship? And was it Captain Tim Granger's voice that said, "Shelby, they're coming?" And ... are *they* the Swarm? If they are, God help us all.

Text set in Garamond

Designed by Nick Webb

Cover art by Jeff Brown

http://jeffbrowngraphics.com

ISBN-10: 1974591506
ISBN-13: 978-1974591503

Printed in the United Sates of America

For Jenny, L., and C.

NICK WEBB

Prologue

Vilasha Sector, Dolmasi Space
High Orbit over Vilasha-dol
Space Cruiser Khisaga Dolva

It was a small ship, as civilizational threats go.

Vishgane Kharsik, supreme Vishgane of the third auxiliary space fleet patrolling the extreme remoteness of the Dolmasi borders near human space, from his imperious perch in the captain's chair on the highest level of his warship's command center, didn't even see it approach.

The old Swarm carriers had been huge—several kilometers long. But whatever the origin or intent of this newcomer, size was apparently not one of its priorities.

That meant it was weak. If it wasn't willing to project strength and inspire fear at the sight of its ships, then it wasn't worth taking seriously as an adversary. At least the humans knew how to build big. Not as big as the Skiohra, but the largest human ships were still over a kilometer long.

This one was a quarter of that.

No visible guns; another sign of weakness. Vishgane

Kharsik grunted his disdain. For an enemy to swagger into a Dolmasi system and intrude on their space, without so much as revealing its weaponry and strength was not only a weakness, it was an insult.

And it would be responded to in kind.

"Prepare ion fire," he said to the armaments station at his feet. The officers there grunted their acknowledgement.

And then the other ship disappeared.

"Where did it go?" Kharsik bellowed.

The armaments officers looked bewildered.

"Fire!"

"Vishgane?" said one of the armaments officers.

"I said fire!"

A red beam lanced out from the bow of their own ship, and Vishgane Kharsik thumped the side of his chair in approval. The beam extended out into space, hitting nothing.

"Nothing, Vishgane."

Kharsik growled.

And then, a moment after the beam ceased, the world exploded in a blaze of stars and vertigo and rage. At least, that was what it felt like to Vishgane Kharsik. It felt like….

It felt like….

It was nearly identical to the calamity that struck two weeks ago. The disruption of the Ligature that shook his entire people, his entire civilization to its core, wherever they lived, whichever ship they were on. The mental barrage that left an entire people temporarily insane.

He shook his head, struggling to clear it.

"Fire again," he grunted.

"Vishgane?"

"Fire again. Double the power, you kir-*sak*!" he yelled, using the most potent insult he knew. The officer glowered at him, but complied.

The red beam lanced out again, this time shimmering with twice the intensity, and disappeared into the distant background of stars.

"Still nothing, *Vishgane*," said the officer, again letting derision seep into his voice.

That was it. The officer needed to be punished. Severely.

Kharsik pulled out his personal firearm and aimed it at the officer's leg.

He fired. The projectile dug into the scales, and black blood splattered out onto the deck plate. The officer howled in pain and leapt to his feet to face Kharsik.

"You challenge me?" said Kharsik, cooly, though he trembled with the effort at restraint. He never had problems restraining himself—what was wrong with him today?

"Yes, *Vishgane*," said the officer, spitting the title out with contempt.

Kharsik stood up and leapt down to the armaments pit. It should be an easy fight since the officer was at least a hand shorter than he, with smaller muscles, and the hole in his leg seeped black blood all over his uniform.

And short it was, for even as Kharsik toppled the officer and locked his head in a vice grip, preparing to snap the spine, the ship started shaking violently with the impact of weapons fire.

He finished the deed, snapping the neck with precision and dumping the armament officer's body in a heap at the side of the armaments pit. The violent trembling of the deckplate nearly knocked him off his feet as he climbed back up to the command platform.

"What is happening?"

But he needn't have asked, for on the viewscreen in front of the command platform he saw that the other ship had reappeared, closing the gap.

And now it was firing its own weapons.

The beams didn't look terribly powerful, just common ion-assisted lasers, but they sliced into the hull over and over again, and were accompanied by devastating mass-driver slugs. "Why aren't we doing customary evasive maneuvers? Where's the defensive EM shielding on the hull?"

He spun around to the defensive station, only to see the officers there engaged in their own fight. All three were bleeding profusely, and the largest was about to snap the neck of the smallest. "Stop! Stop this instant!" Kharsik yelled.

But they ignored him.

Another inexplicable pulse of rage washed over him like a wave, tugging on his control, ripping at his sanity.

The anger boiled up inside, uncontrollably, raging like a frothing sea on Verdra-dol—his world that, until two weeks ago, had been one of the thriving centers of the Dolmasi civilization.

But now that civilization was dying, which became all too clear to Kharsik as he watched half of the bridge rip away, exposing them all to the deadly vacuum of space. Far down below, he caught sight of the green surface of Vilasha-dol. Would it, too, succumb to the madness that had engulfed Verdra-dol?

And, curiously to the Vishgane, his last thoughts were not

of duty and survival like his long years of training had taught him, but of bloodlust and revenge against the defensive officers that had allowed this catastrophe.

Even as the breath escaped his exploding lungs he wondered if he still had time to leap down into the defensive pit and teach those officers a lesson or two in pain. He looked from the pit, to the advancing ship, back to the pit....

He jumped down, shoving a flailing, suffocating officer aside, and grabbed the weapon controls station for balance. A finger jabbed at the fire control button, and he looked up at the exposed space above him. His ship's red beam slammed into the other ship.

The other ship.

Great Homeworld, he swore. The other ship. It was not Swarm. And it was definitely not like the mysterious intruder from two weeks ago that raped and punctured half a dozen moons in Dolmasi star systems.

It was ... it was *human*.

One final destructive beam from the other ship slammed directly into the exposed bridge, silently vaporizing all his surprisingly discordant thoughts.

CHAPTER ONE

Irigoyen Sector
Near Rivadavia
ISS Independence
Captain's Ready Room

Admiral Shelby Proctor, former Fleet Admiral of the entire Integrated Defense Force of United Earth and its fifty-six worlds, *Companion to the Hero of Earth* Tim Granger, PhD in experimental biology with an emphasis in xenobiology, so-called *Motherkiller* by the Skiohra race, bane of the Swarm, and champion of the senior's division badminton league at Oxford Novum University on Britannia, read the report on the data pad her aide handed to her, and swore.

"Ridiculous. This is utterly ridiculous." She rubbed her painful lower jaw, and glanced over the report again. "This can't be right. We live in the twenty-sixth century, for god's sake. How does this still happen?"

For weeks she'd been receiving regular reports of

instability in Dolmasi society and space, as well as the now nauseatingly regular reports from her contacts within IDF and the UE government detailing corruption and secret kickbacks and back-room deals at the highest levels, as well as numerous rumors of conspiracies far deeper and far more insidious among competing groups within the government—parasites, all of them.

Ever since the mysterious alien ship—the so-called "Golgothics"—had destroyed the planet El Amin in the San Martin system and launched its own ship's core into the crust of Titan in the Saturn moon system of Sol, it seemed the galaxy had exploded. And the betrayal of Admiral Mullins of CENTCOM Bolivar, now CEO Mullins of Shovik-Orion Industries, only added a sense of personal urgency and betrayal to an already ugly situation.

But this new report on her data pad was just too much. She couldn't handle this right now. "Are you sure this is for me?" she waved the data pad at her aide, a tall young man seemingly fresh out of IDF academy. "Please say this is a mistake. You messed up, Ensign. Admit it."

He shifted uncomfortably on his feet, hating to be the bearer of bad news, and replied awkwardly.

"Sorry, ma'am. Doc Patel gave that to me himself, and told me to tell you to report to him immediately. Uh … I mean, respectfully *ask* you to report to him, ma'am."

She tossed the pad onto her ready room desk. "I've got a brewing civil war between us and the GPC—Galactic People's Congress my ass—a few rogue Dolmasi fleets that aren't responding to anyone's hails, a mutinous Admiral Mullins that half of UE's leadership still believes over me, and a moon just a few billion kilometers from Earth that is slowly growing—*growing!*—and Doc Patel thinks he can pull me down to sickbay for a frickin' *root canal?* What the hell is he smoking?"

The aide, Ensign Babu, shrugged and deadpanned: "Cannabis, ma'am. I'd guess cannabis."

She raised an eyebrow at him. While he'd been rather stiff and formal the first week after he'd replaced her former aide who'd died during the engagement with the mysterious alien ship, she was starting to get a sense of the young man, who seemed to thrive on subtly sarcastic asides and snarky comments. To tell the truth, it had gotten her through the past week, what with the steady stream of bad news. His irreverent attitude was a welcome relief from the stark realities of war.

"Dismissed, Ensign," she said, a half-smile still lingering. "Please tell Captain Volz I still want to talk to him asap."

"Yes, ma'am." Babu ducked out the door. Not two seconds later, it opened again.

"Did you forget something…?" she began, still staring down at the data pad.

Captain Tyler "Ballsy" Volz ambled towards her desk and swung the chair around, sitting in it backwards. "Not that I know of."

She looked up in surprise. "Well I'll give that to him. Ensign Babu is fast—I just barely asked him to call you here."

"Oh really? Because I just talked to Doc Patel—he asked me to come up here and—"

She slammed the data pad down. "He's getting *you* to harass me too? *Dammit.*" She stood up and retrieved the teapot and cups from their secured receptacles on the counter in the corner. "Next time you see him, tell him I'll be down there when I'm damn well good and ready, and to stop hounding me. *And* to stop talking to other people about my medical shit."

He grinned, but shrugged. "It's just a root canal, Shelby. Honestly, you'd think he was asking you for a kidney or something."

She gulped the tea down fast, eager for the burn down her throat that would remind her she was alive.

And they *were* alive, against all odds.

They'd survived their confrontations with the devastatingly powerful alien ship, and with the treacherous Admiral Mullins. And somehow, they'd lived.

She caught herself. Not *all* of them.

She still had nightmares about the people she'd lost. Captain Prucha. Pregnant Ensign Flay. Nearly a hundred others. Even one was too many. Just losing Ensign Flay felt like the kind of monumental loss from which she'd never recover. It had been a long time since she'd lost anyone. One might think it would get easier with age, but the opposite was true.

It was harder. Much, much harder.

With age, came the realization that life was fragile, and short.

"I just don't have the time, Ballsy." She set the cup down, and offered him the other, which he declined with a raised hand. "I just received a report an hour ago. The corporate board of Shovik-Orion has declared Bolivar to be a sovereign world, under the direct governance of the Shovik-Orion corporation. Admiral Mullins is now effectively not only the CEO of Shovik-Orion, but the president of Bolivar. Can you *believe* that? That ass-wipe just declared himself president of an entire planet."

"Is that legal?"

"It is now. After Sangre de Cristo was nuked, and after that stolen nuclear missile was launched from our own fighter bay towards Europe, all the worlds are in an uproar. Recruitment for the GPC went up ten-fold overnight." She sat back down with a grunt. "And to keep everything from falling apart, the Senate and President Quimby just signed an agreement with Secretary General Curiel of the GPC agreeing to a nominal degree of self-government for any world that wants it. Which was basically permission for any planet to secede from United Earth, and before anyone realized what a foolish arrangement *that* was, Mullins with his cronies at Shovik-Orion took advantage of it. Bam. President Quimby, allow me to introduce you to President Mullins."

He shook his head in disbelief. "But why would Shovik-Orion do that? They've got lucrative contracts with IDF. Trillions of dollars. We're their biggest paycheck."

"Oh, we're still paying them. We can't just cancel all the contracts overnight—they've designed half our weapons and navigation systems, after all. It would be catastrophic for us if we suddenly decided to kick them all out. Planetary defense systems would fail. All the construction of new starships would halt and be delayed for years while we bid out the contracts again. Even our food processors on board would stop working because their technicians would be recalled, and as everyone knows, you *don't* piss off the foodies. Those machines are finicky, and if I don't get my coffee in the morning, you can bet there will be crimson hell to pay." She grinned, but didn't feel it.

All she felt was impending dread. She'd felt it for two

weeks. And it wasn't because of all the political bullshit. *That* was normal. She'd never served in IDF *without* political bullshit. The dread came from the uncertainty, the not knowing what that final message meant. The message encoded in the alien ship's drilling beam over Titan.

She fell silent, thinking about those words. Volz seemed to read her mind, and said them out loud.

"Shelby, they're coming." He grunted. "Shelby, they're coming, Shelby, they're coming—honestly, Shelby, that could mean anything. It could even be a random chance—it could have been a random pattern and maybe Commander Mumford just read too much into it. Or it could just be a GPC hoax. Get us all looking the other way while they consolidate power on the worlds they control. Or maybe a Russian Confederation plot—they've been quiet for years, and maybe this is what they've been working on. Or maybe—"

She held up a hand to interrupt him. "No. The evidence is in. The data is there. That alien ship was built out of material from the *ISS Victory*. Pieces of it, at least. Commander Mumford did some more tests and confirmed it. I know it's not proof, but it tells me that, somehow, Tim Granger managed to get a message to us before he died. In theory, time would have sped up for him as he was falling into the black hole in the Penumbra system thirty years ago. Maybe he saw something in our future, and somehow ... set pieces in motion to get a message to us? I know, I know," she said, seeing his skeptical reaction. "I know, I sound like a Grangerite." She heaved another sigh. "Look, I'm not claiming he's a prophet or someone ascended to heaven or a higher plane of existence or some bull like that. But Ballsy, the evidence is *there*. How else do we explain this? The tungsten alloy on that alien ship matched that of the *Victory* with ninety-nine point nine nine nine nine *nine* percent certainty, but with isotopics that show it has aged thirteen *billion* years. *Billion,* Ballsy. Thirteen *billion frickin' years!*"

They'd had the conversation several times before and it always went the same way, but he played along. "That's a long time."

"It's almost as old as the universe itself! Just eight hundred million more years, and it would be as old as the Big frickin' Bang." She tossed her hands up in the air in frustration. She was used to dealing with mundane numbers, statistics, data … evidence that always pointed to conclusions based in reality. Not impossible stuff like this. A ghost returning from her past, but traveling through the entire age of the universe to get to her—that was crazyland.

But it was what the data claimed. It's what the data demanded. And as her academic advisor always told her, once upon a time, *trust your data, and it will trust you.*

She wanted to punch her advisor in the face for giving her such a bland bromide. But, dammit, it was true. Data was data, conclusions and implications be damned.

Volz swung the chair back around and sat in it normally. "So, the question is, regardless of who the message is from and how long it took to get to us, is it talking about the Swarm? And *when* is it referring to? Are they coming next week? If so, let's get ready. Are they coming next year? Likewise. Are they coming in a hundred years?" He shrugged. "Honestly, only so much we can do about that."

Silence fell between them as they both considered the

awful possibilities. She finally shook her head. "Who else could *they* be, if not the Swarm? And my gut says it's coming earlier. Not a hundred years. It's now. We have to assume *now*, because if we don't, and they *do* come, and we're not prepared, then we're dead. It's that simple." She stood back up and refilled her cup. "I got another report this morning from fleet Science Division. The earthquakes on Titan are intensifying."

"Do the recon ships and science teams know what's going on down there yet?" Volz balanced a boot up on his knee and bounced his leg nervously.

"No. But Titan's mass has increased by point oh oh one percent since the core of the alien ship penetrated the crust. And just a few days ago a massive EM jamming field appeared around the moon. The recon ships are basically blind now—they have no idea what's going on under the surface, beyond the earthquakes and the increase in mass."

Volz grunted. "Unbelievable." He tapped a nervous finger on the desk. "How is the evacuation of the Saturn system coming?"

"Almost complete," she said, sitting back down with her refilled cup of tea. "It's no small feat to evacuate ten million people from seven different moons. Rhea and Mimas are empty. They're running into trouble with some colonies on Iapetus, though. The locals don't trust IDF down there very much."

"GPC loyalists?"

She chuckled. "Actually, no. Mongolian Amish. I won't even pretend to understand the history on *that* one. But the Saturn moon system should be completely evacuated within another week, and not a moment too soon. Bolivar's moon Ido never exploded, but the debris from El Amin's destruction is starting to affect the next closest planet in the San Martin system. I understand there are a few dozen new massive craters on that planet, and the cloud of debris is only expanding. The domes on Sangre are at extreme risk. San Martin itself should see a drastic uptick in meteor activity in about a year."

"Any risk to the population?"

"Thankfully, no, it won't get *that* bad. Most of the debris is re-collapsing back in on itself. But if *Titan* explodes? Every moon circling Saturn will be virtually razed. The closest ones might even be destroyed eventually, depending on Titan's blast profile. And if there's a chain reaction of moon collisions out there, and by chance one of the larger fragments gets ejected towards Earth's orbit?"

He shook his head in disbelief. "I'd almost prefer to face the Swarm again. At least that was something we could fight against. How do you stop a moon fragment?"

She finished her second cup with a grimace at the burning heat in her throat. "Luckily, that's extremely unlikely. And yet, *something* is going on inside Titan. Let's say it doesn't explode. Then what? What's actually happening down there? And on Ido? And on the half dozen other moons we've discovered that were visited and drilled into by that alien ship before it was destroyed?"

It was an unanswerable question, and they both considered it silently.

Volz started tapping his temple, thinking. "And in the middle of it all, Admiral Oppenheimer orders you to go out to the fringes of known space and look for signs of the Findiri and Quiassi. Two races we've never had contact with. Not even a hint. What's he playing at?"

"He's trying to sideline me. I know it. Send me out on a wild goose-chase for two alien races that we've never met. We've never had *any* intelligence suggesting that they even exist. He's ordering me to go out there and bait them with a meta-space pulse, thinking that they're tied into the Ligature like the Dolmasi and Skiorha are."

Volz shook his head. "That's only going to tick off the Dolmasi and Skiohra."

She could only agree. "And yet, he's also ordering us to use the meta-space pulse against the Dolmasi if they show up in force against us. Thinks that it will disorient them. Make it easier to take them out." She held her forehead in a hand. "I tell you Ballsy, I can't believe it's come to this. The Dolmasi were our allies against the Swarm. And now Oppenheimer is prepping for all-out war with them. What the hell is going on?"

"Do you think he's intentionally antagonizing them? Instigating war?"

She didn't want to answer. She didn't want to say yes. "I can't believe he'd do something so … heinous."

The comm interrupted their thoughts. "Admiral Proctor?" said Lieutenant Qwerty.

"Go ahead."

"Receivin' a distress signal from Mao Prime. They say they're under attack, ma'am." The words came with such a laid-back southern twang that one could have mistaken his pronouncement for an idle commentary on the weather.

She bolted up out of her seat and gripped the edge of the desk. Volz shot her a knowing, nervous look. "Attack? By whom?"

"They claim it's Dolmasi."

Volz gave her a heavy look. "Are you ready to do what Admiral Oppenheimer ordered?"

She returned the look. "Blast them with a meta-space pulse?" and then looked up towards the comm speaker. "Highest alert status, Mr. Qwerty. I'm on my way."

They both stood up and headed to the bridge.

"Orders are orders, Shelby. Especially from Fleet Command. Oppenheimer himself."

She smirked. "I've known other Fleet Admirals in my time. I can say from firsthand experience that they're often full of shit."

He smiled back, even as the red alert lights started flashing. "Don't be so harsh on your previous self. And if I may quote you…?"

"Yes?"

They arrived at the doors to the bridge, and Volz paused before opening the door for them. "Watch your language."

CHAPTER TWO

Orbit over Mao Prime

Lieutenant Ethan "Batship" Zivic whipped his head around, counting the bogeys trailing him, wondering where the hell his backup was.

Five bogeys. He shrugged and gunned his engines, leaping forward through an expanding debris cloud, provided by his previous victim. He could handle five. A quick glance up to the counter on his heads-up display overlaid on the cockpit window told him he was almost a quarter of the way to his goal. Twenty-five out of a hundred and one.

Enemy weapons fire illuminated the cockpit and made him veer left, then right; then he plunged downward towards the atmosphere of the planet before looping even further in a maneuver that outpaced the fighter's inertial cancelers and threw him upward against his restraints with gut-churning force. Well, gut-churning for a mortal.

But he was Ethan Batship Zivic. Heh—Batship. His

callsign was actually Batshit, but Admiral Proctor had ordered all callsigns be non-vulgar. But Batshit was not vulgar. It was descriptive. Normal orbital dogfight maneuvers were for mortals, not batshit crazy people like him. What he was doing was reserved for fighter gods, not fighter jocks.

It wasn't that he thought too highly of himself, he considered as he plowed through a formation of enemy fighters, clipping one on their port thruster and sending it into a tailspin while peppering another with a hundred rounds of fire, blasting it into a fiery explosion. It was that, well, he *was* a fighter god. His own mom and dad had *nothing* on him. Ballsy? Amateur. Spacechamp? Her training records would fall, god rest her soul.

He sailed through the dissipating cloud of glowing dust and debris before immediately looping around and taking a second pass at the formation, which had seemed to only just barely register his presence. Two more explosions coincided with the counter on his screen ticking up to twenty-nine.

His comm headset erupted in his ears. "Ethan, watch your six!" Lieutenant Jerusha Whitehorse was tracking his progress. He smiled—she needn't have worried.

"Way head of you, hun."

There wasn't just one trailing, or two. Four stayed on his tail, matching his every move. He knew they'd expect another gut-churning loop. Instead he was going to commit suicide: turn and face them head on. With a flick of his thumb he cut the forward engines, applied the dorsal and starboard thrusters, flipped the fighter one-hundred and eighty degrees, and reapplied the forward drive at full power. Fifteen g's, which the inertial cancelers managed to regulate to four g's. It was still enough to make him see stars.

But it worked. Another bogey exploded in a cloud of expanding slag and the others veered at the last millisecond to avoid hitting him, crashing into each other instead.

Thirty. Thirty-one. Thirty-two.

Another number below the counter loomed large on the heads-up display. One hundred and one. His goal. The all-time record held by any IDF fighter jock against the Swarm in a single engagement. And he was going to beat it if it killed him.

He soared towards the *Independence*, looped around, and shot up a bogey that had lingered too long in the same course. Thirty-three. A twitch of his wrist sent him careening towards the other capital ship, the *ISS Kobe*, and he let their point defense guns make quick work of his two tails. He grunted—those two didn't count. But another hapless bogey found itself in his sights.

Thirty-four.

He breathed deeply a few times and took a moment to survey the layout of the battle. Besides IDF's two capital ships, the *ISS Independence* and the *ISS Kobe*, at least a hundred other IDF fighters were flitting in and out of the melee, and over two hundred enemy bogeys, based out of four enemy capital ships, loomed large in the background behind the *Independence*, which was unloading everything it had into the nearest one. It was like a fireworks show, and he had a front row seat.

"Remember you've got a squad, Batship," said Whitehorse in his ear. He grimaced, and had half a mind to disable his comm set.

"If they could keep up, I could use them."

"Regardless. They're your team. Depend on your team and

let them depend on you, or you're all dead."

As if to punctuate her words, a dozen rounds from an enemy bogey that came out of nowhere stuttered across his left wing and ripped apart the thruster. "Dammit!" His craft started to spin uncontrollably.

He could pull out of it. He could. The hull of the *Independence* loomed large ahead of him. He had exactly three seconds. All he needed to do was—

Another burst of red streaks connected with the body of his fighter, and the main engine exploded behind him. His craft tumbled hopelessly. There was no pulling out of this one. The *Independence*'s hull approached like a barren gray lunar landscape, punctuated here and there by a port window or rail-gun turret. He wondered what death would feel like. Would it be fast? Did it hurt? How long did one's brain synapses survive a fireball? Enough to feel pain for a few seconds?

Everything went completely black.

He still breathed heavily.

"You should have listened to me," said Whitehorse.

A piercing white light illuminated the front screen, making him wince and cover his eyes. The cockpit simulator opened, and his eyes readjusted gradually to the intense glare of the overhead lighting of the simulator room. Jerusha Whitehorse smirked at him as he pulled himself out.

"Thirty-three, huh? What's one hundred and one minus thirty three?"

He shrugged. "Shut up."

She fell into step beside him as he walked to the prep area. Several towels were stacked next to the bottles of water, and he wiped his forehead with one of them. While not quite as intense as an actual live-fire fighter battle, the simulator could be ... bracing, and even experienced pilots could sweat a liter during a training session.

At least, he assumed a live-fire battle was more intense. He'd never actually fought in one.

"Hey, thirty-three is pretty amazing, Batship. The record in the simulator at the academy is thirty-six."

He shrugged, and gulped down half a water bottle. "Yeah. But Ballsy took out one hundred and one at the battle of Cadiz."

"That was live-fire. You can't compare the two. Apples to oranges. When you compare like to like, you're only three away from the academy record."

He sighed. "Jerusha, look." He turned towards her, and smiled as sincerely as he could manage. "I know what you're trying to do. I appreciate it."

A shadow of exasperation passed over her face. "And *what* am I trying to do?" She folded her arms across her chest. "Enlighten me."

"You're trying to make me feel better. I don't *want* to feel better. I want to blow shit up. *That* will make me feel better. Bam and pew pew and revenge and I just want to punch the shit out of something and for now imaginary bogeys will have to do."

He knew he made no sense. He knew the stuff coming out of his mouth was word soup. But that was ok. All that mattered was getting ready for what was coming.

And what was coming?

War.

"Bull. Look, Ethan, I know she meant a lot to you. I know

it's hard for you. Sara Batak should not have died. And the *way* she died, with that nuke…." She trailed off, the terrible image of the nuclear missile detonating in Earth's atmosphere, vaporizing Sara Batak, the mechanic from Bolivar, was permanently seared in both of their memories. "Admiral Mullins will have to account for his actions some day, but—"

He threw the mostly-empty water bottle against the wall, and it rebounded and splashed all over his boots. "He *killed* her, Jerusha. He *murdered* her. He's not just going to *account* for his actions. No. He's going to pay for them." He grabbed another bottle and ripped the cap off. "And I'm going to make him pay for it. With interest."

"Ethan, I—"

He plowed ahead, interrupting her. "And he's going to find the price to be more than he can afford."

Another smirk. "Done with the cliches yet?"

She had been spending a lot of time with him. Ever since Batak had died. While things weren't the same between them—the romance was long, long gone—he appreciated it, even if he didn't show it. Watching Batak get vaporized in the nuclear blast was … terribly difficult. He thought it was going to send him over the edge. But it didn't. Yet. All it did was harden his resolve, and focus his anger and rage.

And having Jerusha there, talking him through it, encouraging him, hugging him, supporting him—well, it wasn't quite like old times. Those times were gone. But it was nice to have a friend.

She had fallen silent, and stooped over to pick up the water bottle he'd thrown. After she dropped it into the recycler, she turned to leave.

"Jerusha, I...." He swore. "Look. Thanks for being here for me. I ... I appreciate it."

She paused at the door and looked sidelong at him. "It's been less than a month. No one's expecting you to just *get over it*, Ethan. But you need to start remembering who your friends are, and treating them like it."

The door clanged shut behind her.

"Shit," he breathed.

He was about to run after her, but the klaxon interrupted him. The lighting strips along the edge of the floor pulsed red.

"All hands to battle stations," said the automated system. "Red alert. Threat level maximum. All hands to battle stations," it droned on and on. But he was long gone, running towards the fighter bay.

He had no idea what the threat was. No idea who he was about to fight. But he grinned. Finally. He was going to get to break his dad's record.

CHAPTER THREE

Britannia Sector
Britannia
Outskirts of Whitehaven
Nile Holdings Inc. Warehouse

Chris Keen had a hangover, but next-day shipping schedules waited for no man, half-drunk or otherwise. Groaning, he hauled the crate up onto the cart and pushed it along the aisle to the next stop in the vast storehouse. Britannia's sun was a little hotter than Earth's, and Keen felt it, especially amplified by the aluminum roof of the warehouse. He'd lived here for three years now, and he wondered when he'd get used to it. Would he? And worse, the AC was out. Piece of shit AC.

His radio buzzed. "Irish? You there?" His supervisor had called him *Irish* his very first day on the job based on his thick accent, and it had stuck.

He tapped it. "Yeah. What do you want, ya wanker?"

His supervisor grunted a laugh—their friendship thrived on locker-room insults. "Listen, dipshit, when you get done with that order, we've got a special package to put together for a customer."

Did that really require calling him on the radio? "Got it, boss. I'll be there in an hour or so, I've just gotta—"

The supervisor cut in. "No, Irish, I mean a *customer* wants a special order. A *customer*. Like, an actual person is here and wants some shit."

An actual, in-person customer? "Huh. I thought we were a shipping warehouse. Wholesale. All electronic. Do we still take customers? Haven't seen one of them in … forever."

"Looks like it. I guess someone didn't want their order electronically tracked, so they showed up in person. Whatever it is, they've got cash, and we love ourselves some cash, so get your ass back to the office."

Cash. Keen did love cash. And in-person, paying customers, as rare as they were, tended to tip unless they were assholes. And they tipped because if they were there in person, it meant they wanted to be discreet. And customers wanting to stay under the radar tended to ingratiate themselves with the grunts doing the actual work, because it was always the grunts that knew what was actually going on, how to actually make things happen. And if the media or the UE investigators ever come knocking, you want the grunts on your side, staying all quiet-like. Ergo, tips. Big tips.

"Be right there, wanker. And if we make bank this time, drinks are on you at the nudie bar tonight."

His supervisor grunted another laugh. "Irish, if this order pays as much as I think it will, you can buy your own nudie bar tonight."

CHAPTER FOUR

Orbit over Mao Prime
ISS Independence
Bridge

Even with the new trans-quantum drive on the *ISS Independence*, it still took twenty minutes to t-jump across the hundred lightyears out to the Mao system. The journey afforded Proctor the chance to reminisce about the time, thirty years earlier, that the *ISS Warrior* had made a similar mad dash out to Mao Prime to stop an unfolding Swarm attack.

They had arrived too late.

The Swarm had so utterly devastated Mao Prime that there was hardly anything left. It stood as one of the most destructive incidents of the Second Swarm War. Two billion dead. Only a few million remained on the entire surface, scattered across the backcountry, hiding in the hills and mountains, and the habitats in the oceans.

And yet, in spite of the unthinkable destruction, Mao

Prime was also the foremost example of the resilience of humanity. The Chinese Intersolar Democratic Republic—the governing body responsible for Mao Prime—had done a remarkable job rebuilding the cities and encouraging refugees from other devastated worlds to resettle there. A billion people now called it home. It was the shining, cosmopolitan jewel of the CIDR.

And a billion people were now under siege, according to the meta-space distress signal.

"Final t-jump into Mao Prime," said Ensign Riisa.

Proctor nodded, and secured her seat restraint in preparation for battle. On the main viewscreen the blackness of interstellar space gave way to the blue, cloud-dappled orb of Mao Prime. The planet's sun was dawning at the horizon.

And a fireworks show lit up the skies on the dark side of the planet's terminator. Several dozen CIDR cruisers, assisted by a handful of IDF ships, were facing off against a horde of smaller, but deadly, Dolmasi gunships, each like a vicious arrowhead sprouting dozens of eruptions of green weapons fire.

"Tactical status?" she said, gripping her armrests.

Lieutenant Whitehorse scanned her console. "Reading thirty-one CIDR cruisers—that's well over half the Chinese fleet. And IDF's planetary defense fleet out of Cadiz has responded. Ten cruisers and frigates. Captain Pennock is commanding the IDF fleet. Fleet Admiral Sun himself is commanding the CIDR fleet."

Proctor, nodded—that made sense. The CIDR had relocated its fleet headquarters to Mao Prime several years ago, she remembered. "And the Dolmasi?"

"Fifty-eight Dolmasi gunships. Each is smaller than any of ours or the CIDR's, but they pack a punch."

Proctor winced as she saw a CIDR heavy cruiser break apart, then convulse with massive explosions erupting from its core. Three Dolmasi ships pounded into the wreckage with green anti-matter beams. The same main offensive weaponry the Swarm had used. In fact, if she correctly remembered her Swarm history gleaned from limited contact with the Skiohra, that same green anti-matter beam was originally developed by the Dolmasi, only to be later appropriated by the Swarm as the Dolmasi fell under their influence.

"Open a channel to Admiral Sun. And patch Captain Pennock in—he should know what we're planning."

Lieutenant Qwerty drawled a four-syllabled "yes, ma'am," before Ballsy called over from the XO's station.

"And what exactly is our plan, Shelby?"

She shrugged. "At this point we've only got two options. First, get in contact with the Dolmasi Vishgane commanding that fleet, and talk him down. There's got to be a reason they're attacking, and if we can get at the root of the problem with him, then maybe we can stop a war before it even starts."

Ballsy's goatee contorted with a look of *good luck with that*. "And plan B?"

"The usual plan B. Beat the shit out of them." Proctor eyed Qwerty, who gave her the thumbs up, indicating the channel was open.

Half of the main viewscreen filled up with the face of Fleet Admiral Sun, the leader of the CIDR's military and space fleet. "Admiral Proctor, thank you for responding to our time of need," he began, his accent thick. "But is this all you brought? I fear Dolmasi will overwhelm our defenses soon."

"More is on the way, Admiral Sun. Admiral Oppenheimer has ordered our entire Third Fleet out of New Dublin to Mao Prime's defense in addition to what's already here from Cadiz, but it will be an hour or so before they arrive. I was hoping to find a way to get the Dolmasi to stand down first. If nothing else, that will give us some time before the Third Fleet shows up. Have you had any success communicating with the Dolmasi?"

"None. They refuse all hails. And I have not time to attempt further communication. I have already lost three ships, and several more are damaged beyond repair." His voice took on a dangerous tone. "Thousands have died already, Proctor. Do not risk more. I forward tactical plans to you—please assist as you see fit."

The half of the screen showing his face resumed displaying the live feed of the unfolding orbital battle. Proctor swore at the CIDR fleet admiral under her breath, then turned to Commander Mumford at the science station. She didn't want to do what she was about to do. Every instinct inside her said it was wrong, but order were orders.

Damn you, Christian Oppenheimer.

"Are you ready?" she asked Mumford.

"As ready as we'll ever be, Admiral. I haven't had a chance to do live testing—not that I'd know how to do live testing without every being who's attached to the Ligature aware of it."

Proctor nodded. The Ligature—the meta-space mental link shared by every race, every individual who'd ever been controlled by the Swarm—was the only way they knew to catch the Dolmasi's attention, without just killing them. Weeks earlier, a meta-space shunt attached to the nuclear device detonated over Sangre de Cristo had channeled an untold amount of energy into a meta-space spike, which, according to IDF Intel, had had an effect on the Dolmasi: ever since that point there had been unusual fleet movements within Dolmasi space. And Fleet Admiral Oppenheimer had ordered her to use it against them again, intentionally. She'd directed Commander Mumford, the tactical science chief on the *Independence*, to come up with a make-shift meta-space shunt that would let them reproduce the effect, albeit on a much attenuated scale. Perhaps they could catch their attention, or at least distract them long enough to gain a tactical advantage.

It was worth a shot, Oppenheimer had said. She'd protested. But he'd directly ordered her to do it, should there ever be an engagement with the Dolmasi.

That was after his orders to go off on a vain search for the Quiassi and Findiri in some ill-advised attempt to determine their threat status. They were the only two races missing out of the original "Concordat of Seven" of the Swarm, and in all her years in IDF Proctor had seen neither hide nor hair of them. She assumed the orders were meant to simply get her out of the way, and so she appropriately ignored them. "Fire me," she'd said, daring Oppenheimer to get rid of her, just weeks after bringing her back.

But she couldn't ignore two orders in a row.

"Let's try it."

Mumford nodded. "Power level?"

"As high as we can without burning anything out. Even at our highest power we'll still be several orders of magnitude below the Sangre de Cristo incident, correct?"

"About a billion times lower, yes, Admiral. We'd need another nuclear weapon with a meta-space shunt attached to reproduce that level."

She turned back to the screen. Her fingers tightened around her armrests, which she supposed were going to have permanent indents from her grip by the time her tenure aboard the *Independence* was over. On the screen, another CIDR cruiser convulsed with explosions as the Dolmasi fleet tore into it.

"Then let her rip."

CHAPTER FIVE

Sector 52-1267a
Skiohra Generation Ship Magnanimity
Matriarch's Command Center

Vice Imperator Polrum Krull detached the neural interface glove from her right hand, before ripping away the left as well. The rush of voices within her had reached a crescendo, a volume that even she, a grand matriarch of her people, was ill-equipped to handle.

Her children within her body were crying out. Not in unison, as they often would do when presented with an existential threat—which seemed to be happening far more often this century compared to her previous millennia of existence—but as a frantic, disjointed roar. Like white noise. Like static. Each individual voice, each person, each mind within her was most insistent, but combined with the tens of thousands of other equally-insistent voices the conglomerate effect was too much for her.

Something had happened.

"Motherkiller, what have you done?" she whispered to herself. To herself, and to her sixty-two thousand, five hundred and twelve children, each of them living the Interior Life within her body, and who could each hear her every word, her every thought. The mathematicians within her calculated odds of the Ligature failing entirely, the physicists modeled ways to shore it up with focused graviton emitters, the philosophers speculated what existence without the Ligature would even mean, and the lone theologian was convinced that the human god was real and fighting against them. But all of them, to a single person, cried out.

The meta-space pulse had come from the human world of Mao Prime, and she knew, based on her ship's intelligence service tracking, that the *Independence*, Proctor's new warship, had just gone there. And with the pulse had come another rush of madness, of momentary, disjointed, unmanageable and unnameable disunity that tore at the bonds within her. The bonds between her children—between her and them.

It was nothing like the terrible, catastrophic avalanche that had come from the human world of Sangre de Cristo a month ago. She marveled at the irony. A small contingent of her children within her had devoted themselves to studying human history and culture, and she found it almost humorous that a world named after the blood of their Christ had become the epicenter of what she was sure would turn into a galactic struggle. A galactic war. Her theologian child had told her that the original blood of humanity's Christ had been intended to bring unity and peace. This time it brought confusion, division, and war. Plowshares into swords, her child kept repeating, over and over.

This pulse, from Mao Prime, was smaller, but its effect was the same. Disunity. Ripping the bonds between her and her children. As the guardians of the Ligature—not just guardians, but the creators of the link that bound all of them together, both Skiohra, Dolmasi, and every other creature that had been linked to the Swarm—her people were less affected by the trauma of the pulse.

The Dolmasi would not be so lucky. And, even now, through the Ligature, she felt their rage. Their terrible anger.

She felt their lust for revenge.

"Believe me, my children, it will not go unanswered," she said out loud, and through the Ligature, directed the helmsman in the command center to set a new course.

CHAPTER SIX

Orbit over Mao Prime
ISS Independence
Fighter Bay

"Zivic, you're late."

The fighter bay, still half construction zone and half disaster zone thanks to the suicide bomb detonated by that GPC loyalist deck hand, was a hive of activity, made even more hectic since now they had to maneuver around all the construction equipment.

Zivic bit his tongue and tried not to glare at his squad leader. "Was in the simulator. Got here as fast as I could."

His squad leader adjusted the seals on his flight suit and waved them towards the fighters, where the other two pilots in their squad were already waiting. "Got here as fast as I could … *sir.*"

Just count to ten, Zivic. One. Two. Three….

Luckily, Ace, one of his other squadmates, saved him from

saying something he knew he'd regret. "What's the sitch, Hold'em?" she said, clicking her air seals shut on her gloves.

Hold'em—Lieutenant Farrell, the squad leader—ran a finger along the wing of Ace's fighter, as if checking it for dust. As if dust would matter in a life-or-death fighter battle. Zivic wanted to grab him by the ears and shake realistic sense into him. "Dolmasi cruisers are attacking Mao Prime. They've deployed fighters. We're ordered to engage the fighters targeting the IDF cruisers and defensive platforms."

Out of the corner of his eye Zivic saw the scene repeated a dozen times over across the frantic fighter deck: squad leaders running their crews through the tactical situation before they were ordered to deploy. Each answering questions from their squad members that they likely didn't know the answers to. Like Zivic's question. "Do we know anything about the Dolmasi fighters? No IDF pilot has ever engaged one before."

Farrell's face remained stoney. He clearly liked having control of a situation, and not knowing the answer to something—well, in the short time Zivic had come to know his new squad leader, he'd learned that Lieutenant Farrell *always* knew the answer to something, even when he really didn't.

"Correct. We've never engaged them. But I think we can assume that they're more intelligent than the Swarm fighters we've trained against in the simulators, which display more of a hive-mind mentality. As a whole, the Swarm acts together in ways we can't, but it also makes their individual actions and tactics far more predictable and easier to defend against. I doubt the Dolmasi fighters will be anything like that. So for now, we fly like we're fighting human pilots. We've trained against Ruskie fighters in the simulators, so we've had plenty of experience."

Zivic snorted, and immediately regretted it.

"Problem, Zivic?" Farrell pierced him with a glare.

"Well, sim experience is one thing. Actual live-fire experience? That's something else entirely."

Farrell folded his arms. "Do you have a suggestion? Some other way to approach this?"

That caught Zivic flat-footed. He opened his mouth, then closed it, then shook his head.

Farrell looked around the circle at them all. Ace—a small, bony young woman with cold gray eyes (and perky boobs he wanted to squeeze); Bucket—a cheesily-grinning young man who looked just over twenty, but whose goofy grin belied his deadly accuracy and grit in a cockpit; Spectrum—a quiet Thai kid who looked like he belonged in a science lab instead of a fighter cockpit; and Barbie—a tall, lanky, mustachioed man who now raised his hand politely.

"Yes, Barbie?"

"And what if we're wrong? What if those bogeys out there are nothing like Russian pilots? Or Swarm pilots? What's the plan if that's the case?" His thick Australian accent quivering ever so slightly with latent fear. This was a first for them all: live fire with the enemy. And it was showing on all their faces. Bucket and Ace especially—they seemed to wear their emotions on their sleeves more than the others.

Farrell shrugged. That was a rare gesture for a man who always acted like he knew the answer. "We'll find out. Let's move."

CHAPTER SEVEN

Orbit over Mao Prime
ISS Independence
Bridge

"Did it have any affect?" Proctor leaned forward in her seat, staring intently at the ongoing battle on the screen. Mao Prime hung in the distance providing a verdant background, seemingly oblivious to the intense hell that was unfolding far above it.

"Reading ... interesting things from the Dolmasi fleet, ma'am," said Lieutenant Whitehorse. "Right after we transmitted the pulse, there was momentary ... blip, or a pause, in all the Dolmasi movements and tactics. It's almost like each pilot just went haywire for a brief moment before resuming their courses. And after that, their movements became more erratic."

"Erratic? How?" Proctor watched the viewscreen, studying it, tracing out the movements of the ships and fighters. In the foreground their own pilots were blazing towards the main melee.

"Just little things. Veering right when they should go left in a fighter dogfight. One of their gunships started drifting in a slow circle. They're still fighting of course, ferociously, but it's … it's a little different."

Captain Volz had approached Proctor from behind while she stared at the screen. "Do you think we should risk doing it again?"

"I don't know." And a risk it was, she knew. By blasting out that meta-space pulse—even though it was billions of times weaker than the massive pulse generated by the shunt in the Sangre de Cristo bomb, she was playing with fire, just like she'd warned Oppenheimer. Like poking a sick bear with a stick. Would the bear run? Would it fight? Or would it just become terrifyingly unpredictable?

Volz pointed at the *Independence*'s squadron of fighters that was now nearly upon the Dolmasi. "We're out of time. It's either now or never."

Trust the data, Shelby. "No. We have no baseline. We have no idea what we're doing to them with that pulse. In fact, it might even be the meta-space pulses that got us into this mess in the first place. Let's hold off until we're out of options."

"What about Oppenheimer's orders? And I don't know if I like being in a position where we're forced to fight with one hand tied behind our backs. I'd rather be taking the initiative."

She finally turned to look at him. "Me too." She motioned to Lieutenant Qwerty at comm. "Lieutenant, still nothing from the Dolmasi?"

"Nothin', ma'am," he said, his drawl thick and unhurried.

She stood behind his chair, watching him scan the comm channels. "They say you're a polyglot, Qwerty. How many languages do you know?"

"All of them, ma'am."

She looked at him, then did a double take. "I'm sorry? Did you say *all* of them?"

"Well, believe it or not, I have a little trouble with Basque, even though I've got distant Basque relations. And sometimes I miss some of the subtleties between Quechua and Aymara. But, yes, ma'am, all of them."

She stretched for a miracle. "Dolmasi?"

"Sorry, ma'am, we just don't have enough examples of their language for me to do anythin' with it. From the records of the Second Swarm War, I think we've got five lines total of verbal communication, from which I think I know how to say *hello*, and *die Swarm scum, die*.

"Well get on the horn and blast those two things out with everything you've got, Qwerty. That's your new job: learn their language. If, somehow, the meta-space pulse from the Sangre incident disrupted their normal mental processes, then it may also have disrupted their connection to the Ligature, and possibly even corrupted anything they ever learned through the Ligature. I won't pretend to understand how that process works, but the way Granger described it to me, it was like ... knowledge transmitting directly to your brain and imprinting upon it."

Thinking about Granger, she'd trailed off, getting momentarily lost in thought. Where the hell had Mumford gotten on that research? He was supposed to be examining the data from the scans of the Golgothic ship, that had yielded the image of the hull plate deep inside the alien vessel that bore the letters I-S-S V-I-C.

"Ma'am?" said Qwerty.

"What I'm saying is that the Dolmasi may have … forgotten English, since they learned it through the Ligature. And if that's the case, you, Mr. Qwerty, are the most valuable officer in all of IDF. Understood?"

"So…." Qwerty swiveled around to face her. "What I'm hearin' is that you want me to learn Dolmasi? An entire alien language, in just a few days, with no documentary evidence or examples of their grammar, morphology, no comps to other languages, no rosetta stone, no evidence whatsoever that there is even a single Dolmasi language much less fifty regional dialects, and no native speakers I can shoot the shit with?"

"Correct."

He rubbed his hands together. "Sounds like fun. One Dolmasi language comin' right up."

"Admiral," began Lieutenant Whitehorse from tactical. "Our squadrons have engaged the Dolmasi."

She nodded, and sat back down in her chair. "Move us in. Target the capital ships. Relieve some of the pressure the Mao Prime fleet is facing."

She breathed deep, her eyes flashing as the shooting war between her fighters and the Dolmasi began to heat up. "And God help us."

CHAPTER EIGHT

Orbit over Mao Prime
Lieutenant Zivic's cockpit

Zivic barrel rolled. Then swerved. Then looped. He had two bogeys on his tail, but they were persistent. More persistent than any sim fighters he'd faced in the simulators, and more aggressive by far. How was it that a computer training program designed by IDF fighter pilots a generation ago—pilots that had actually been in real dogfights with Swarm bogeys—wasn't realistic enough? Had they intentionally designed the program to treat the pilots with kid gloves, so that when they did eventually face the enemy, they'd be so shocked that any trace of dangerous overconfidence would be laughably unlikely?

Or were Dolmasi pilots just that good? Many times better than any sim Swarm fighter he'd ever faced?

It didn't matter. All that mattered now was surviving.

Hell, not just survive. Dominate. He didn't know his

enemy, but he knew enough. He knew they wanted to win, but he also knew he wanted it more. He swerved, then punched the opposite thrusters to spin out in the other direction before cutting those and applying the dorsal thruster to flip around and blast the nearest trailing bogey.

"Bet you've never seen anything like this, shitwads."

"Cut the chatter, Batship," said Hold'em, the squad chief. "Ace, you've got a tail. Bucket, move in to take the pressure off him. Barbie, back him up. Spectrum, you're with Batship and I—let's take out that squadron at three o'clock."

A chorus of yes sirs, and moments later Ace's tail was destroyed and she joined the rest of them as they bore down on the squadron Hold'em had indicated. They'd sidled up uncomfortably close to a Dolmasi cruiser, but luckily its guns seemed to be preoccupied with a CIDR cruiser off its port bow, and the two ships were exchanging a hail of fire between them.

"Nothing fancy, folks, but let's see if we can't knock a few of these fighters right into their own cruiser. Two birds with one stone. Maneuver Batship One."

Zivic smiled. It was one of the maneuvers he'd taught his squadmates during their training sessions. Hold'em—Lieutenant Farrell—had grumbled a bit, but even he recognized they were genius moves. Hell, it was Ballsy that had taught them to him. Why the maneuvers had never made it into the manuals he didn't know. Probably because they were as reckless as Ballsy himself. And, to a greater degree, Zivic.

He'd show them.

"Batship, take bait position."

"Gee, thanks." But he was grinning. Taking bait position

was fun, in the sense that in the Zivic One maneuver, it was the position most likely to result in a fiery death, as it involved being, quite literally, bait. He shot forward and positioned himself between two bogeys and the Dolmasi cruiser they'd been shadowing. As expected, they darted after him, raining fire down on his bird, though thankfully most of it missed and hit the Dolmasi cruiser behind him. Two birds with one stone indeed.

All the shots missed, except for one, which punctured his port window. He could almost see the spark of a round sail right past his nose through the cabin and out the other window. Within moments all the air in the cabin had been sucked out. Thankfully, his flight suit maintained pressure, and before the rest of his bird got shot up, he erratically looped around, changing directions every split second, in a maneuver that, if he had a co-pilot, would have made him vomit.

"Fellas, if you were thinking of springing the trap, now would be a *fabulous* time...."

He needn't have worried. Simultaneously, from port and starboard, two of his squadmates soared through the melee and blasted the two bogeys trailing him, one of which actually got knocked off course and tumbled end over end until it collided with the Dolmasi cruiser. The other merely exploded.

"Nice shot, Bucket," Zivic breathed into his comm. He couldn't keep the relief out of his voice.

"What, Batship? Sounds like your panties got bunched up a little there," said Bucket, laughing.

Zivic wondered if that's what it was like for the others, thirty years ago. For Ballsy, and Spacechamp—his parents. For all their squadmates, both those that lived and those that died.

If they joked and laughed and horsed around even in the thick of battle, with death all around them. On his tactical screen he saw that out of the *Independence*'s seventy-two fighters, they'd already lost four. Four of his fellow fighters, people with hopes, dreams, bright futures, just gone. Snuffed out by a brief fire and the long relentless cold of space.

Of course they did. How else do you cope? Can't drink in the cockpit. "Well at least I'm not vaginally challenged, Bucket. When's the last time you had any?"

Ace snickered, her higher voice easily cutting over the cross chatter from Bucket. "Please. You're all vaginally challenged, fellas. Now sit back and watch this." She'd strayed a kilometer or so from the squad and had zeroed in on a lone Dolmasi fighter that looked like it was damaged, slowly rotating as if its engines were cut.

"Ace, I'm not so sure about…" began Hold'em.

And Zivic saw it. From below her, planet-side, two other bogeys had been hiding amongst the debris field of a destroyed Dolmasi cruiser, and now shot upward towards her. "Shit." The Dolmasi were essentially mimicking maneuver Batship One, using one of their own fighters as bait. He pressed on the accelerator and shot towards them, firing a storm of rounds, hoping against hope that even at that distance he'd luck out and get in a hit or two.

No such luck.

The two bogeys closed the distance between them and Ace, and soon they were pelting her with their own rounds. Luckily, she'd finally seen them and managed to circle around the disabled bogey. The previously dormant fighter now engaged its engines and swiveled around to face Ace.

"Well this don't look good," she said, before all three fighters caught her in a crossfire.

CHAPTER NINE

Orbit over Mao Prime
ISS Independence
Bridge

"Shelby, our pilots are taking a beating out there. We've already lost seven, with half a dozen others too damaged to do anything other than hobble back here," said Captain Volz, scanning through the damage reports from the fighters and the ship itself.

"What about us? Damage report."

From his expression, the news didn't look good. "Those green beams they're firing at us? Yeah, you guessed it. Same tech the Swarm used."

"But the Swarm got it from the Dolmasi, didn't they?"

He shrugged. "Yes? No? I can't remember. Does it matter? But it's the same anti-matter ion and gamma ray mix. Frothy stuff, this beam. It just cuts right into us wherever it hits. Luckily the hull breach tech they installed on this bird is pretty effective, or half our decks would have vented by now. But those force fields are extremely power intensive."

The deck rumbled again as another Dolmasi cruiser nearby hit them with the anti-matter beam. The green light flashed deadly on the viewscreen.

"Rayna, you there?" Proctor called down to engineering through the comm.

After a few moments, she replied. "Yeah? What is it? Kinda busy here, Shelby."

"How's the power plant, Rayna? How long do we have with our hull breach patch fields?"

"Right now? Maybe thirty minutes. But they keep hitting us at this rate, and that number drops every single time. Our power consumption will match the main power plant output in about five minutes, and our batteries will be tapped just five minutes after that. Whatever you got planned, I'd do it quick, Admiral."

"Just get me those ten minutes, Rayna." The deck rumbled again.

"That's all assuming nothing else goes wrong. They hit a coolant line? Our five minutes goes down to five seconds, real quick-like."

"Understood. Bridge out."

"Admiral," drawled Lieutenant Qwerty, "I'm just not readin' any Dolmasi transmissions. There's no way to decipher a language I can't hear."

Proctor tapped her armrests, weighing their options. The battle was even, and assuming it continued to its finale, would result in a standstill, with both sides destroyed or damaged beyond repair. Before her eyes she was watching years of starship construction get blown away. It would take Wellington Station at Calais near Britannia weeks to repair all the holes that had sprung up in just the *Independence* alone. Holes could be temporarily patched in a few hours, but the damage left behind was severe and systemic. Power systems. Life support. Luckily the computer cores were distributed throughout the ship, but with every battle and every hit sustained, her ship's effectiveness slipped even further.

"Scan meta-space transmissions. See if you can tap into the Ligature."

Qwerty looked up. "Ma'am? I don't know the comm protocols for their meta-space links. Or, at least, our computers don't understand it."

"Treat the link itself like a language, Lieutenant. From what I understood from Granger, it was like a language all its own. Not Dolmasi. Not English. It was a language he *felt* rather than spoke. It was intuitive. I … I'm not sure if that will help you, but we've got to try. If this battle continues, we're all dead. Dolmasi included. And, I think, that will be to no one's benefit."

Qwerty shrugged, but plunged into the analysis. He nodded. "Yeah, there's meta-space transmissions goin' on, all right. And yeah, it's gibberish. Let me see…."

He pressed an earpiece in, as if he was going to listen to the meta-space transmissions. Between IDF ships, meta-space messages were always text-based. The bandwidth was far too low to handle even a simple voice transmission. But maybe Qwerty thought that whatever language the Ligature was mediated by was something that could be interpreted audibly.

He closed his eyes. The deck plates rumbled again and the

ceiling panels shook. On the viewscreen one of the CIDR carriers exploded in a blinding flash as its core went critical. The fire extinguished almost immediately, but the glowing slag of the debris expanded outward, engulfing the nearest Dolmasi cruiser that had been firing on it. Wreckage and carnage littered the space all around the *Independence* and the remaining CIDR vessels and their Dolmasi opponents. The fighters flitted in and out of the capital ships, occasionally erupting into brief fireballs as a pilot slipped up and allowed himself to get pummeled by the enemy.

"Admiral, I—I think I've got something."

She spun around to face him. "Really? What is it?"

"You're right. It's aural. Verbal. Well, not verbal. Not words. But, I think I get it. Well, on the verge of getting it. You're right, this language is nothing like Dolmasi—at least, the six words that I know are nothing like this. And obviously not English, or Russian for that matter. It's ... intuitive and contextual. Hard to explain. Give me a moment, ma'am."

"Lieutenant, you've got exactly one moment to figure this out. Longer than that, and we're fried."

For thirty or so agonizing seconds, Qwerty's eyes glazed over as if he was lost in concentration, listening to the digital buzz that he was playing over the bridge's comm speakers. It wasn't a voice, but a series of tones. Not a song, but it had rhythm and tonality. Frequency variations, pulse durations, wave interference—both constructive and destructive— seemed to contribute to what Proctor could only call a soup of noise.

But it wasn't static. It definitely, without a doubt, was an intelligent communication.

Qwerty opened his eyes.

"Admiral, I—I think we'd better get out of here," he mumbled.

"Why?"

"I—I don't know. I can't translate word for word. But I *feel* like I understand them—their intent."

"What are they saying?"

"To us? Nothin'. To each other?" He swallowed. "Blind, rage-filled bloodlust. There's no intelligence there. At least, no reasonin'. Just pure, unbridled anger and ... hate."

CHAPTER TEN

Orbit over Mao Prime
Lieutenant Zivic's cockpit

Zivic didn't have time to think. No time to reason or weigh the consequences. He only had time to act. "Ace, hold on, girl."

The accelerator depressed to maximum, he pushed his bird forward faster than the inertial cancelers could keep up, and the g forces squashed him back into his seat. The distance between them closed faster than a blink. And then he did something very, very stupid.

With a jarring collision, he clipped his port wing against the wing of the nearest Dolmasi bogey, shearing it clean off. Out of the corner of his eye he saw his port thruster break off and tumble away behind him. "Didn't need that anyway…."

A split second later he punched the starboard and dorsal thrusters to maximum to spin around and boomerang into another of the three bogeys closing in on Ace, and with another screeching grind, his starboard wing clipped the bogey's. He must have dug into the fuel tank and oxidizer simultaneously, since the entire ship exploded in a fireball. Zivic, thankfully, now wingless and without main thrusters, was already clear of the explosion, tumbling end over end towards the third fighter.

It veered out of the way, but a moment later it too exploded in a cloud of debris, and Bucket's fighter sailed through the glowing cloud of slag with a triumphant whoop. "Batship, you alive in there?"

"Yeah. I think. Lost both wings. Sorry, Hold'em, I won't be available for atmospheric maneuvers anytime soon."

Farrell grunted through the comm. "That was an irresponsible move, Zivic. You could have killed yourself and Ace both, and endangered the rest of us as we tried to cover you. And I didn't authorize any Omega maneuvers—"

"Aw come on, Hold'em, that wasn't an Omega maneuver. I'm still alive, aren't I?"

"For now," said Farrell. "Ace? You ok?"

Zivic craned his head around to find Ace. Her bird was shot up pretty bad, but looked intact, for the most part. "Ace?"

She didn't respond.

"Jamie? Ace? Wake up, lady. Come on now...."

With the heat of battle still unfolding all around them, cruisers exchanging withering fire, other fighter squadrons darting in and out of the space between the capital ships in a deadly game of cat and mouse, all Zivic could do was stare at Ace's dormant fighter, hoping against hope she was still alive. That all of the rounds from the Dolmasi fighters had somehow managed to avoid her fragile body at the core of the steel-titanium composite shell of her fighter.

Spectrum broke the silence. "I'm reading a steady, active heat signature. Her engine is out, so I think it's her body. She's alive."

"Life support?" breathes Zivic.

Spectrum mumbled. "Tapping into her bird's system...." The rest of the squadron waited for the diagnosis. "Looks like her life support's battery is low, but intact. She has atmospheric integrity in her suit. And...." He breathed a short chuckle. "I've got a pulse. Definitely alive, but knocked out."

Farrell grunted. "All right. Leave her. She'll either wake up and make her way back to the ship, or we'll send a SAR bird for her later."

"I'm staying here with her, Hold'em. I got no thrusters. You boys go on without me, I'll stay here and fend off any vultures looking to finish her off," said Zivic.

"Roger that. Good luck, Batship."

Zivic watched his four other squadmates, Hold'em, Barbie, Bucket, and Spectrum, soar off to rejoin the ongoing battle, while he tapped his auxiliary thrusters to position him near Ace's dormant bird, and set himself into a slow spin so he could visually see around him in all directions.

And not a moment too soon. A pair of bogeys had noticed his auxiliary thruster exhaust, and had changed course, approaching them.

"Well, shit, Ace. Looks like this is our last stand."

CHAPTER ELEVEN

Orbit over Mao Prime
ISS Independence
Bridge

Lieutenant Qwerty's words sent a chill down her spine. She'd faced the Swarm, thirty years ago, and Granger's description of their motive had similarly chilled her. For months during the Second Swarm War, they could only guess at the Swarm's motivations for the war. That they were conquering territory and worlds was a given, but why? Power? Resources? And it was only after Granger had finally tapped into their collective consciousness through the Ligature that he reported that their true motivation seemed to be not power, not wealth or resources, not strategic planning.

It was simply hate. Dominance. They wanted to rule because they loathed other lifeforms. Loathed their freedom and their cultures and any joy they felt. The Swarm was an other-worldly, other-dimensional species that, from Granger's and the Skiohra Matriarch's descriptions, lived in an almost hellish parallel dimension—a universe not split off from their own, but rather an entirely separate universe that had got its start from the same expanding soup of spacetime from which their own universe had sprung.

And they hated. They hated and conquered and dominated and subjugated and ruled. And where their rule was resisted, they annihilated.

And they did it under the guise of *friendship*, or so they called it.

That Qwerty now felt or understood something similar from the Dolmasi was ... troubling. They'd always been standoffish, ever since the first contact with them during the Second Swarm War. At first they'd feigned they were still under Swarm dominance, even destroying several of the ships in Granger's strike force. But then they switched sides spectacularly during a pivotal battle, turning the tide and allowing Granger, Proctor and IDF to fight another day. Ever since then, they'd been coy, unresponsive, and uncooperative. At best, they were hermits. Inward-looking.

And now, at worst, they had essentially become the Swarm themselves. What had caused the sudden change? Was it really just the Sangre de Cristo incident? The meta-space shunt that had channeled all that nuclear energy into the Ligature? Perhaps reprising that meta-space shunt here had been a huge mistake. She should have waited. She should have doubted the information from Oppenheimer.

"Can you speak to them?"

Qwerty shook his head. "Definitely not. I might be able to create an interface where I can reproduce some of the sounds

I'm hearin', but this is ... complex, ma'am."

"Can you at least ... do something ... say something, that will get their attention? So they'll open up a channel and actually *talk* to us?"

Qwerty shrugged. "At this point, I'd be more liable to say somethin' that will piss them off. There are undertones of meaning here that I'm just not getting. It'll take me weeks to really flesh this out."

She almost snorted. *Weeks*. And he was probably being modest.

"At this point, Mr. Qwerty, pissing them off can't possibly hurt us even more. They already appear quite ... perturbed. Say something. Anything. Get their attention."

He nodded. "Yes, ma'am. I'll try to say somethin' along the lines of, *we come in peace*. Or ... something like that. Might could come out like, *take me to your leader and let me shoot him in the face*. You never know with these first contact type conversations." His tone was joking, but the words were deadly serious. Because they were true.

Qwerty paused, typed some, paused again, and typed a few more commands into an ad hoc translator he'd thrown together at the last second. Shrugging, he pressed the commands that would send it though the meta-space transmitter. "Well, that's that. I'll put it on repeat—"

"No need. Look." Lieutenant Whitehorse was pointing up at one of the viewscreens to the side of the main one at the front of the bridge. Near the opposite side of the planet, another ship had appeared.

A massive ship. A hundred kilometers long. It had a hole on one end, shaped remarkably like the late *ISS Constitution*.

"The Skiohra," said Proctor. "Let's hope they're not going as crazy as the Dolmasi."

CHAPTER TWELVE

Orbit over Mao Prime
Lieutenant Zivic's cockpit

"Not good, not good, not good." Zivic repeated it like a mantra as he watched the two Dolmasi fighters close in. He had nearly zero maneuverability, and zero desire to test whatever that limited maneuverability was against two deadly foes in fully maneuverable fighters.

A quick glance across his controls and the cabin around him yielded nothing. He'd simply run out of options. His luck tank was empty.

But as his dad always told him when he was younger, before they stopped talking to each other, *you can only count on the luck you make yourself.*

"Let's make some luck, Batship," he muttered to himself. His eyes rested on a particular switch far off to one side on his dashboard, and a light went off in his head. "Bingo."

Carefully, very carefully, he angled his fighter slightly to the right, alternating between the dorsal and ventral thrusters, until the rear of his bird pointed straight at Ace's fighter. He flipped the switch and initiated the trigger, hoping the tow cable launcher was not damaged.

It wasn't. With a dull crack he could swear he somehow heard despite his flight suit helmet, the tow cable launched out from the fighter and attached itself magnetically to Ace's bird.

The two Dolmasi fighters were less than a kilometer away, and closing fast. It was far past show time.

"All right you little fuckers, time to see why they used to call me Batshit."

He fired both dorsal thrusters to maximum. The line went taut, and within a second they were rotating, both ships spinning about a common center between them, and quickly picking up speed. The centripetal force threw him down into his seat and slightly to the left—*one of the thrusters must be damaged,* he thought with the small portion of his brain that was still thinking analytically, cooly, and calmly.

The rest of his brain was screaming, *oh shit*! He saw a stream of rounds from the nearest Dolmasi fighter stream past them, and he cut the power to one of the thrusters, which sent the rotating pair of birds careening off in a slightly different direction, different enough so that the stream of fire missed them by just a few meters.

"Batship? What ... what the hell is going on?"

Good. Ace was finally awake. And if she looked out her window to see what was going on she'd probably kill him. "G'mornin', Ace!" He looked out at where his tow cable had attached, right on the nose of her fighter. "Say, you don't happen to have your main drive still online, do you?"

"Yeah…?"

Another pair of streams of fighter fire from the Dolmasi birds, which were now circling them, trying to get a good angle on them. But Zivic kept randomly alternating and adjusting the axis of their dizzyingly fast spin. But one of these times the Dolmasi would get lucky. Or his luck would run out, whichever it was that was keeping him alive.

"When I say *go*, engage your main thrusters to maximum."

"But—"

"No questions! And … GO!"

To her credit, she didn't hesitate. He prepared himself for the whiplash that was inevitably coming, and, sure enough, less than half a second after she'd punched her engines, she'd flown toward the center of their circle and past him with just a meter to spare. When the tow cable went taut again he was moving perpendicularly to her vector, and his bird snapped around. He felt a few joints pop, and he hoped one of them was not his spine.

But the maneuver had done its job—the Dolmasi were completely caught off guard, and right in his sights. He swiveled his gun slightly to correct for his slight rotation leftover from earlier, and let loose a stream of rounds.

One of the Dolmasi fighters exploded.

The other veered off.

And … left. It was gone.

In fact, all the other fighters in the distance were pulling back, retreating towards their cruisers, which themselves were pulling away from the IDF and CIDR vessels.

Retreating?

No. None of them were q-jumping away. And out of the

corner of his eye he finally saw it. Massive, in the distance. The huge Skiohra generational ship. "Looks like the big guns showed up."

"Did you call them while I was out?" said Ace. Her voice sounded faint, like she was half-asleep.

"Don't like it? Then stop sleeping on the job, Ace." He added a forced chuckle, but he didn't feel it—the tone and volume of his voice was troubling to him. And the sudden appearance of that Skiohra ship was ... off. Something was up. First the Dolmasi had gone crazy, and now ... what the hell were the Skiohra going to do?

"Sleep sounds pretty good right now..." she said. The last few words trailed off, as if she indeed had fallen asleep.

"Ace?"

No response.

"Ace! Wake up, girl." He fiddled with his controls, desperate to restart his engines. "Ace! Answer me." The main engine was out. He still had auxiliary thrusters, but they wouldn't be much help in getting both of them back to the *Independence*.

Her groggy voice finally pierced the awful silence of the commlink. "Did I miss something big?"

He breathed a sigh of relief. "Ace, you need to stay awake now. At least until help gets here. You doing ok?"

"I feel something wet. All down my back and legs."

Shit. She was bleeding. One of the bogeys' rounds must have struck her and she was probably bleeding out.

"Mayday mayday mayday. Pilot down. Request immediate assistance," he began, practically yelling the words into his comm.

"Roger that, Batship, SAR bird on its way," came the response from the flight deck. Good. At least she had a fighting chance now.

"Ace? Hang on there, girl. We're going to get the hell out of here. Just stay with me." He paused, waiting for a response. Nothing. "Ace?" More silence. "Ace?"

CHAPTER THIRTEEN

Orbit over Mao Prime
ISS Independence
Bridge

The appearance of Vice Imperator Polrum Krull on the viewscreen didn't surprise Proctor. She'd already recognized the ship. The *Magnanimity*. The same Skiohra ship she'd encountered with Granger aboard the *ISS Warrior* thirty years ago, and the same one she'd seen two weeks ago near San Martin. The same one with a giant, *ISS Constitution*-sized hole in it. Other unrepaired marks of battle scarred its hundred-kilometer-long hull, which seemed to fade away into the distance. She'd never get used to the sheer size of that thing, and regretted not developing the relationship with the Matriarch now sulking on the viewscreen to the point where they could exchange more knowledge. Learn about their ship. Their people. Their society.

War had cut short so many opportunities.

"Motherkiller. Why are you here?"

The words sliced her to the core, just as they had last time she'd seen the Matriarch near the now-destroyed moon of El Amin in the San Martin system. They cut even more deeply, now that she'd lost her assistant, Ensign Flay, whom she felt directly responsible for: she died because Proctor was waiting to issue the order to self-destruct Zivic's shuttle stuck up inside the mysterious Golgothic ship until they'd squeezed as much information out of the sensor scans as possible, and given Lieutenant Zivic more time to get away. That hesitation had cost not only Flay's life, but that of her unborn child. And four other crew members who'd died during that space of twenty extra seconds.

"I'm here because we're under attack. And now I see that the Dolmasi have ceased their attack, coincidentally with your arrival. If I didn't know you any better, Vice Imperator, I'd suspect something."

"Suspect?" Krull gave her best imitation of a human laugh. The diminutive blueish humanoid looked vaguely like an average human in a blue face mask, but she was unmistakably alien, with different customs, mannerisms, and facial expressions that Procter, after half a dozen meetings over the years, had still not entirely figured out. She supposed it would take xenosociologists generations to really understand them, if true understanding was even a possibility.

And yet Krull spoke English, learned through her long connection to the Swarm via the Ligature. So perhaps understanding was not only possible, but inevitable.

Krull continued. "You need suspect nothing, Admiral Proctor. They disengage from the battle because they recognize in us a greater foe. The *Magnanimity* alone is more powerful than all their ships here combined, by a factor of fifty, at least. They disengage because they're waiting to see what happens. Weighing whether they should attack, or pull back and prepare for their next battle."

"Why? Why prepare for their next battle? Why are they attacking us?"

Krull shrugged. An exaggerated shrug, as if she were mimicking the action, knowing that it was what humans did when expressing a lack of knowledge, and yet so over-exaggerated as to suggest the Skiorha's ignorance of the subtleties of human mannerisms. "I was hoping you could tell me. Why are you attacking the Ligature? The human attack on the Ligature at Sangre de Cristo nearly destroyed it. It affected me. Even me. Terribly. To say nothing of what it did to my children, especially those within me. I can only suspect what terrible damage it has caused among the Dolmasi. And here you are, attacking it again. Why?"

"I—I'm sorry, I didn't realize our actions were affecting the Ligature itself."

"Not just the Ligature, Admiral. You were prodding, barreling, tunneling, directly into the Dolmasi psyche itself. All of us—all the beings connected by the Ligature for the last several millennia, are now fully integrated into it. For the Skiohra, for my people, it is natural. It is ours. We invented it. We grew with it and evolved with it over hundreds of thousands of years. But the Swarm stole it, and attached the Valarisi to it, then the Findiri and Quiassi, and finally the Dolmasi and the Adanasi—other humans. The ones you call Russians."

"Are they still connected to it?"

"No." She almost looked like she was smiling, which made her next statement all the more chilling. "All the Adanasi that were connected to it were … purged."

A sick feeling washed over her. "I see."

"Granger alone was connected, and lived. But then he … disappeared. Fell out of contact. Out of range or out of existence altogether."

"He didn't die?"

"Depends on how you define death," she answered, cryptically. "One moment he was there, accessible through the Ligature. Then, he faded. And faded more. Until finally we could only just barely feel him. Hear him. Hear his thoughts like a whisper. Then … nothing. It was too faint. Like a shadow of a whisper, an echo of a whisper. And then … an absence of a whisper, and yet the absence itself was … something."

Proctor repeated the questions she'd asked the Matriarch earlier, at El Amin. "Is he back? Can you feel him now? Has Granger returned?"

Krull laughed. "Of course not. Singularities are one-way trips, I'm afraid. At least, the naturally occurring kind are. And the Penumbran black hole was as natural as they come. A star gone supernova sixty million years ago. Your artificial singularities, yes, they were truly singularities, but they were artificial. The masses involved were minuscule compared to a star, and consequently, they were traversable. Your people, admirably, have ceased research into them—or at least, that's what your government claims. But Granger? No. He went into that black hole, and we haven't felt him since. It took him years, *decades*, to fall towards that event horizon. Even when he was only detectable by microwaves and then radio waves, we could still feel him. But eventually, the wavelength of his radio waves exceeded the dimensions of the event horizon itself, and he fell beyond our ken."

"The Ascension," said Proctor, using the oft-repeated words of the Grangerites. They might be crazy, but at least they had the science more or less correct. Once the radio waves originating as photons coming off the *ISS Victory* and Granger were stretched into radio waves and passed the dimensions of the black hole itself, that meant he'd truly ... *ascended*, whatever that meant. Passed through the event horizon. Gone on to another universe. Or rather, his atoms. Nothing could survive that kind of gravitational stretching. "Krull, two weeks ago we faced the mystery ship. The one some of us called the Golgothic ship. We faced it, and we thought we'd won. Until it burrowed its way into one of our moons, Titan. And now that moon is ... growing. Adding mass to itself, deep inside the crust, or the mantle—honestly our scans are useless so we can't even tell that much."

"Yes, we are aware of the situation. I'm afraid we are just as confused as you are. But I assure you, a substantial portion of my children are working on the problem."

Proctor nodded and continued. "But what you might not be aware of, is what our sensor scans picked up inside that ship right before it blew. It picked out the letters I-S-S V-I-C. Which I believe is part of the hull nameplate of the *ISS Victory*. The ship—"

"Granger's ship," interrupted Krull. "Interesting. Very, very interesting."

"I think, Vice Imperator, that is as big an understatement that I ever heard. But that's not all. We ran the isotopics. The tungsten from that nameplate came from the *Victory* all right, but what was puzzling was that the isotopic signature would indicate that it is … over thirteen billion years old."

Krull stared at her, unmoving, unspeaking. If she thought the claim incredible, she gave no clue.

"You heard me, Matriarch? Did that translation come through? Thirteen billion years. The universe itself is only thirteen point eight billion years old."

"I heard, Admiral. And I have no answer. Black holes are … curious things. Just like with your artificial singularities, there are some of my children that theorize they connect different parts of our universe. I believe your technical term is *Einstein-Rosen bridges*."

"Wormholes."

"Exactly."

"You're suggesting that Granger went through a wormhole?"

"I suggest nothing. To go through a wormhole implies that Granger—assuming he was alive when he went through—went to another location within our universe. Possibly up to billions of lightyears away. If so, we would have felt him through the Ligature—it connects all points in the universe instantaneously. But I have other children that theorize one can traverse the fabric, the boundary, of the universe itself and end up in another reality. The physics are complicated, but solutions to the equation exist that take one to another non-causally-connected universe."

"Which one?"

Krull did her exaggerated shrug again. "There are endless numbers of universes. Reality knows no bounds. We know that the Swarm came from but one of those universes, but that is the extent of our knowledge of any universe other than our own."

"So you're saying that Granger could have gone to the Swarm's universe?" Proctor felt the irrational hope spring up within her, and she inwardly chided herself. She sounded like a deluded Grangerite. *Face it, Shelby, what's lost is lost. Look to the future, not the past.*

"Again, Motherkiller, I'm saying—suggesting—nothing. My children theorize much. They spend their days thinking. I have a small group of five children that are convinced that Granger is indeed a god, like your upstart religion claims. I have another group of four children that solve human word puzzles all day. One child, one of my oldest, is on an endless search for the largest prime number. He's convinced there is one. Children do … the oddest things. I tell you this, these possibilities for Granger's final resting place, only as a way to … what's your term? Brainstorm? I have no idea what happened to him. No idea why a piece of the *Victory* ended up on that alien ship. But I think you're right—solving that puzzle is essential to understanding our other problems."

Proctor sighed. "Like the Dolmasi."

Krull frowned. "No, Motherkiller. The Dolmasi's problems are almost *entirely* human caused. And I have not brought the *Magnanimity* here to save you from the Dolmasi. I've come here to tell *you* to stop. Stop interfering with the Ligature. You play with forces you don't understand—things you can't possibly comprehend."

"Matriarch, I assure you, I have no idea what happened over Sangre de Cristo."

"But you know what happened *here*. At Mao Prime. You've been prodding them. Trying to disrupt them. Keep them off balance with meta-space spikes in an effort to gain advantage over them in battle."

"I … yes," she conceded. "I did so without realizing the long-term consequences. I apologize. But Matriarch, we need help with this problem. If I am ever to have time to divert my attention to the issue of that alien ship that is now transforming Titan into … something else, then I need help with the Dolmasi issue *now*."

Krull shook her head slowly. "Motherkiller, I am not here to fight your petty wars for you. After I help you with the Dolmasi, would you then require my help against your renegade Admiral Mullins? And after that, would you require my help to go finally subdue your pirates and slavers? Or would you like to resume your endless wars with the Russian Confederation? Believe me, Admiral Proctor, there is no end of ways we could help you with war, because that is your nature, and we will not enable it. My people have been preparing for the last thirty years to re-embark on our mission of galactic exploration. There is so much to discover and learn about the universe. About existence and reality itself. The last thing we want is to get bogged down fighting in … human wars."

Proctor felt a surge of jealousy. Galactic exploration. That's exactly what IDF should be doing. Exploring the stars. Meeting new civilizations and building relationships across the galaxy, exchanging knowledge and technology. *Instead, we get jackasses like Mullins and Oppenheimer.*

And not just jealousy. It was a little irritating to be lectured by an alien that enabled the rise of the Swarm in their galaxy, even if that help was coerced.

"At least ... at least help us *talk* to them. If we could only talk to them, get them to see we don't want to fight them...."

"I'm afraid you admitting that you don't want to fight them would only embolden them. They are a ... vigorous race. In your travels I'm sure you've encountered the remains and traces of dozens of civilizations destroyed by the Swarm. But it wasn't the Swarm that destroyed them. Each race the Swarm came upon, it judged. It judged whether they were worthy of incorporation into the Ligature. Into their *family*, as they called it. But most civilizations were found ... wanting. They were judged to be too inferior. And in those cases, the Swarm sent in the Dolmasi. And the result, every single time, was destruction. Complete, utter destruction. I'm afraid your problem is more serious than you thought, Motherkiller. The Dolmasi won't stop until humanity is either destroyed, or they are convinced that you are too strong to conquer. There is no middle ground with them. Up until now they had thought you were too strong to conquer. Apparently that has changed."

A chill up Proctor's spine once more.

"Please, Matriarch. Something ... anything to help us communicate."

Krull hesitated. At least, that was what Proctor interpreted the body language to mean. "I'm afraid, we do not know the Dolmasi tongue."

"Really?" Proctor was genuinely surprised. "But you know ours. You could communicate with the Swarm when they were still here."

"We could. Through the Ligature, we essentially spoke Swarm. We spoke with the Dolmasi in the Swarm communication protocol, again, always through the Ligature. We never had a reason to learn the Dolmasi's language. But humanity? We *had* to learn your tongue. And frankly, it was easy. The Swarm consumed several individuals of your people, and assimilated knowledge of English, Chinese, Russian, French, German, and a few other human languages. And through the Ligature, those tongues were taught to me almost instantly. It was necessary to ease humanity's assimilation into The Family, The Concordat of Seven, as they called it. After the First Swarm War, over a hundred years ago, the Swarm gave us the task of preparing humanity's entry into The Family, and so we spent seventy-five years laying the groundwork. Working behind the scenes, so to speak, to bring you into the Ligature. But that is irrelevant history. What matters now is stopping the Dolmasi, then understanding this new alien threat that is altering your moon Titan."

A thought occurred to Proctor. "Is there a chance the alien ship that burrowed into Titan is Findiri? Or Quiassi? We've still heard nothing about either race, in thirty years of searching."

The reply came quickly. "No."

"Are you sure—"

"I'm sure, Motherkiller, beyond any doubt. They are both a great distance away from us here, and I will speak no more of them."

"Why not?"

Krull looked like she was struggling. "Because. Because, is all. Some latent command by the Swarm, some … thing they implanted in all of us, forbids me from even contemplating them."

How very odd.

Krull continued, "But this I know: the ship that crashed into Titan has nothing to do with them. It is something new. Something we have no knowledge of. And it is not something I wish to become involved with. Neither it nor your Dolmasi problem—"

"But can you—"

Krull interrupted her. "As I said, we will not intervene, but perhaps I can help you communicate with them, as you asked."

"What can you do for us?"

The hesitation was unmistakable this time. What Krull was about to say was clearly uncomfortable for her. "I will give you … the keys to the Ligature."

CHAPTER FOURTEEN

Britannia Sector
Britannia
Outskirts of Whitehaven
Nile Holdings Inc. Warehouse

When Keen finally saw the customer, he did a double take. From the subtext of his supervisor's words, he'd half expected to meet a well-heeled plutocrat. A trillionaire looking to supply his estates with a lifetime supply of … whatever it was trillionaires kept in stock. Booze? Fluff-coke? Women? Nile Holdings, Inc. didn't supply either of those, though Keen was sure it had subsidiaries or corporate partners that did.

He did a double take because the customer had no face at all. Rather, he—or she—wore a mask. Like a gas mask or pressure suit helmet, whose face shield was tinted with a mirror finish.

And the voice.

"Half the amount should have transferred by now, Mr. Joe Rishell. My bank's representative tells me he just made the transfer moments ago."

The voice was almost robotic. Either he had a voice implant, or the helmet was adding distortion to his voice. This person definitely did not want to be found out.

Which meant the payoff would be even higher. Keen smiled. Shit, he'd not only be able to buy his own nudie bar, but his own penthouse in Whitehaven. Maybe even go back to Earth. Get an estate out in Tennessee, or a penthouse in Seattle or New York.

Joe, his manager, checked his hand terminal, and smiled. "Indeed, the transfer is complete." He looked over at Keen with wide eyes, trying not to let the customer see his glee. He passed the hand terminal to Keen and turned back to the customer to go over a few more details.

Keen glanced at the device, which was still connected to the warehouse's corporate bank account.

One hundred million dollars.

Holy shit. Granted, most of that belonged to the company, but, damn, the bonus would be astronomical. And—he checked to make sure ... yep, that included a generous tip. A million dollars each, for him and his supervisor. Five hundred grand for the secretary. That alone would be enough to pay off all his debts and buy a new house there in Whitehaven.

Best ... day ... ever. He cleared his throat. "I'll get to work right away on the shipment, Mr....?" He turned to his supervisor for help with the name, trying to suppress the urge to laugh, grin, shout, to grab the customer by the hand and shake it right off. "Anyway, what're the goods?"

The customer answered for him. "Gallium."

"Gallium?" Huh, interesting. "How much? Ten kilos? A hundred?"

"All of it."

Keen paused for a moment, trying to remember how much supply they had. Basic chemicals, compounds, and elements was one of Nile Holdings inc.'s specialties—they supplied all the government research labs and industrial research partnerships. "Uh ... *all* of it? I think we have over fifty metric tons of the stuff ... I don't know if—"

"All of it."

One million dollars. Plus the bonus, which he still hadn't even bothered to calculate yet. Probably another two million on top of that. "Right away, sir. I'll have it all ready by the end of business tomorrow."

"No. I want it tonight. Stay all day, all night if you have to. That gallium needs to be on a cargo hauler immediately, and not a moment later. Understood?"

He shook his head, repeating the mantra in his head, *three million dollars, three million dollars, three millions dollars....*

"Understood. I'll get it done by the end of the day. Destination?"

The stranger shook his head. "You don't need to know."

Joe Rishell demurred. "Well ... we don't need to know an *exact* location, but the distance will determine what kind of cargo hauler we use. Is this somewhere on planet? Here on Britannia? Or out to Calais or one of the stations in-system? Or Earth? Farther?"

"Farther. That's all I'll say."

Keen shook his head, still repeating the mantra in his head. "Very well, I'll transfer it into one of our long-range haulers. We'll use the *Angry Betty*—she's got the most powerful q-jumpers of all our ships. Get you there in a pinch."

The customer shook his head. "It'll get *you* there in a pinch. This is a delivery. I don't have the time to come along for the ride—I've got ... other things to be doing."

The customer handed him a data pad of others specifications for the order—what kind of container to be used, some kind of dispersal and aerosolization equipment, simple orbital thrusters for the container. Apparently this was to be moved around in orbit for at least part of its journey. Whatever. The money was good. More than good. It was astronomical. The customer could have demanded the gallium delivered in a thousand gold-plated douchebags and neither Keen nor Rishell would have bat an eyelash.

Payday was coming, baby.

CHAPTER FIFTEEN

Orbit over Mao Prime
Lieutenant Zivic's cockpit

The recovery ship was going to be too late. Ace was running out of time. Zivic knew that if the loss of blood was great enough to make her pass out, death was soon to follow.

He had to do something, now.

"Ok, Ace, hold on tight, SAR bird's coming," he said. The backup power cells were still full, and he did something that under normal circumstances might be considered extremely foolish.

He dumped all the reserve power into the auxiliary thrusters. Before he gunned the accelerator, he checked to make sure the tow line connecting him to Ace's bird was still intact. It was. It spanned the twenty meters separating them, taut.

"Batship, we're detecting odd power readings from your —" began the deck hand.

"Tell the SAR that I'm meeting them halfway. More than halfway, if I can manage it…." He gunned the thrusters. The extreme forces shoved him deep into his seat, and he finessed the controls to minimize the whiplash on Ace's bird.

Before he knew it, they were nearly there. Search and Rescue was only just departing the *Independence*'s flight deck, and before he crashed into either of them he swung his hobbled fighter around and used up the last of the backup power cells to slow them down enough for the rescue team to latch onto them.

"Batship, we're detecting you just used the last of your reserves and that you've lost life support—"

"It's ok. I'm on suit life-support. I'll be fine for a few minutes. Just get Ace the hell out of here."

It took far longer than he would have liked, but the recovery vehicle latched onto both of them and gently towed them down onto the flight deck of the *Independence*. He jumped out of his cockpit before the hatch could get even halfway open and sprinted towards Ace's ruined bird.

The recovery team was already pulling her out.

She was a bloody mess.

Shit. Shit shit shit… he repeated in his mind. The medics were strapping her to a gurney and injected her with something before they rushed her out the door. He sprinted close behind, ignoring the searing pain in his ankle—when did that happen? Had he somehow injured himself during the mission? Didn't matter. All that mattered was saving the girl. Being the hero.

Dammit. Was he falling for that girl? What was it with him and falling for women he rescued? Before he knew it they were at sickbay, and he followed them into the surgical ward.

A nurse blocked his path. "That's far enough, Lieutenant."

"But—"

"I *said*," she stared him down, "that's far enough. You did your job, now let us do ours."

The doors shut, and all he could do was pace the wall, trying to peer around the blinds that had been drawn across the window into the surgical ward. Dammit. He was too late, wasn't he?

Sara Batak, dead. That kid he'd left behind on Ido's research station, dead.

And now he was going to lose another one.

CHAPTER SIXTEEN

She knew she was dreaming, but as always, Proctor couldn't stop the familiar sequence from proceeding. It went like clockwork. Inexorable and incontestable.

"That shot is one in a million, Shell," her sister said. And she was right. Shelby peered through her scope at the bird off in the distance, perched on the branch of an acacia tree on the savannah. Its plumage was a wild shade of purple mixed with yellows and fiery oranges. She wasn't even sure if it was a real species of bird—sometimes the simulator got creative. They called it an "elf bird", since it's hooked beak and inquisitive face reminded them of what an elf from certain fantasy novels might look like.

But for now, that bird was real, and she was going to hit it, whether it was two meters away or ... she checked the range finder on her rifle ... two hundred meters away.

She thumbed a few more beads on her rosary, and mumbled the custom prayer she'd come up with for occasions like this on her virtual hunting trips with Carla. "Hail Mary, full of grace, help me shoot that bird's fat face, hail Mary, full of grace, help me shoot—"

Carla grimaced. "I told you to stop that. Mom said it was

DEFIANCE

blasphemous."

"You're blasphemous, Car. You're messing up my shot. In the church of the holy shooting range, that's worse than calling a magazine a clip."

Carla's grimace turned into a sly smile, and she leaned in close to Shelby's ear even as she began to pull the trigger. *"One in a million,"* she whispered.

The trigger pulled. The shot went wide, and the bird flew away with a flurry of flaps and squawks. Purple and yellow feathers drifted down in a cloud to the branch where the bird had been perched. Shelby turned to Carla and swore. *"Dammit, Car! I had it, and you ruined it!"*

Carla giggled, as only a twelve-year-old could. *"It's not even a real rifle. Just adjust the auto-aim controls on the program and get this over with. Come on, I want to go home. I'm feeling tired."*

Shelby scowled. *"In a few minutes. I want to hit that damn elf bird."*

"Stop swearing. You know mom hates it. She'll make you say a hundred more Hail Marys tonight."

Shelby smirked. *"Only if you tell on me again. Come on, Car, I'm fourteen. I can swear all I want."* She settled back into her aiming position, which the computer automatically detected and summoned the purple and yellow plumaged elf bird again. In the back of her mind Shelby wondered what kind of bird it really was. Something exotic, no doubt. Something from the lush savannahs of Britannia, or Cadiz. Those worlds always had the prettiest birds.

It flew in from the canopy of branches to alight on its previous perch, and began preening itself. *"Ok, Car, here we go. One in a million. Prepare to be amazed...."* She bit her lip, repeated her silent, blasphemous prayer again, and squeezed the trigger.

Missed. *"Dammit!"* Shelby pounded the giant fallen tree she'd been leaning against for balance. *"Ok, one more and I'll—"* she turned to her *sister to convince her to stay for another few minutes.*

But Carla was on the ground, sprawled among the fallen brown leaves. Several were caught up in the tangle of her wild hair.

Her eyes were closed.

"Carla? Are you napping on the job? Come on. You're supposed to be helping—"

She trailed off when she saw the trickle of blood coming from the girl's nose. "Car! Carla!" She shook her sister, but she didn't wake up.

And even in her dream, she realized that moment was when the decades of nightmares began.

CHAPTER SEVENTEEN

Earth
Lower Manhattan
United Earth Presidential Mansion

"Agent Pratt, get the hell out of my way."

President Theodore A. Quimby thought himself a Man of the People. Capital 'M', and capital 'P'. After all, when you win your election in a landslide vote, taking forty-nine out of sixty-two worlds and nearly fifty billion votes, it's easy to think people love you. It's easy to interpret the crowds of millions at your rallies as a show of love for you, and not a show of revulsion for your opponent.

And so when the alien ship had shown up last month and thrown his celebrity-filled calendar for a loop, actually forcing him to meet with his generals and intelligence officials, he was beyond pissed. Not just at the modest loss of life and the loss of the *ISS Chesapeake*, but the fact that the secret service now objected to every single one of his usual activities.

No more glad-handing the crowds. No more jogs through Central Park, dropping in unexpectedly at fast food restaurants to grab a burger or curry and a photo op with regular joe voters.

He was the most powerful man in the galaxy. And he was a prisoner.

"Sir," said Agent Carter, "I can't allow you to leave the presidential grounds without your motorcade." He filled the doorway of the presidential mansion's rear exit with his massive frame.

"Bull honky. Malarkey. I'm the goddamn president of United Earth. More people voted for me as their leader in the history of civilization than anyone else. I'll do what I fucking want." He tried to get around him. "Come on, Kal," he called behind him to his body man, Kalvin Quinkert. "We're going on this jog whether Tiny here wants me to or not."

Tiny—Agent Carter—didn't budge, but rather stretched his arms out to completely bar the door. "Congratulations on your life-affirming election victory, sir, but I'm still not moving. Please wait for the motorcade and the rest of the security detail."

Quimby held a finger up to the man's nose. "I'm not going on a run with ten god-damned armored vehicles following me, or with twenty secret service agents that can't keep up."

Before Agent Carter had time to respond, the hallway filled up with presidential aides, followed by his chief of staff. *Goddammit!* "Sir—" Mr. Bird began.

"Can't I get twenty minutes, Mick?"

Mick Bird, the chief of staff, shook his head solemnly. Always so solemn. Like a god-damned graveyard groundskeeper. Why the hell did he hire this guy? Right. His rich asshole of a veep, John Sepulveda the sixth or eight or some bullshit, insisted his cousin get a plumb job. Paying his political debts. "Sorry, sir. It's Fleet Admiral Oppenheimer. He's in your office."

Quimby let out a defeated sigh. "Fine." He allowed Agent Carter to escort him back to the executive office suite, his body man in tow, followed up by Bird and his aides. *Shit, it's like a circus wherever I go.*

When he stepped back into his office, Oppenheimer rose to greet him. Dark circles ringed his lower eyelids. It was clear the head of IDF had gotten little sleep over the past few weeks. "Mr. President, we have a situation."

"Another one?" Quimby collapsed into his desk chair, accepting his defeat. Maybe tomorrow he'd make it out for his run. He bent down to take his running shoes off and slipped the loafers back on. Maybe he could turn back time to three months ago and throw the election to his opponent. Being president had turned out to be awfully … inconvenient.

"Proctor is at it again. Defying orders, going rogue. And this time she's fraternizing with the Skiohra without authorization."

Quimby waved a hand impatiently, rubbing his temple with the other. "Slow down, slow down. Back up. Did the operation work? The meta-space pulse?"

Oppenheimer made a face. "That's what I'm telling you. She's defiant. I ordered her to hit the Dolmasi ships with it, and she did at first, but only at one tenth power before giving up completely and running off to beg the Skiohra for help—"

"Wait, she actually left Mao Prime, tracked down the

Skiohra, and brought them back to the battle?"

Oppenheimer shrugged. "Well, no, not exactly. The Skiohra ship *Magnanimity* showed up halfway through the battle and—"

"That's the same one Granger and Proctor dealt with back in the Second Swarm War, right?"

"Correct, sir. The one the *Constitution* collided with in the war. It showed up, and Proctor started unauthorized talks with them, and convinced them to get the Dolmasi to stand down."

Quimby leaned forward. "So … and help me out here, Admiral … she defused the situation? That sounds like a win to me. Can I go running now?"

Oppenheimer's face seemed to be getting redder and redder. As if he found it beneath himself to be explaining military matters to a civilian. "It means, Mr. President, that the main force of the Dolmasi escaped. They initiated aggressive action against us, and right when we were on the cusp of victory, Proctor let them escape."

Oh god. The dick-wagging. President Quimby folded his fingers patiently on his desk. "So, it sounds like we have a *second* rogue admiral on our hands, except this one seems to be in the business of stopping wars, not profiting off of them. Tell me, have you sacked Mullins yet?"

A pause, and when he answered, his voice was ice. "The situation has not changed, Mr. President." Oppenheimer clearly did not like talking about the Mullins situation. It showed on his face. In his voice. "We can't just relieve him of duty. As the virtual head of Shovik-Orion, the chaos he could cause in all our military systems is unthinkable."

"Would he do that?"

"A month ago I would have said no. I would have said Mullins was a patriot who would never think of doing something so … brazen and callous. But now?" Oppenheimer scowled and folded his arms. "I'm already working on an exit plan—a way to reduce our dependence on the Shovik-Orion-produced military systems, so that when we *do* cut him loose the damage he could cause would be greatly reduced. But, unfortunately, that plan is *years* off. Re-writing software and reverse-engineering almost every system on our fleet ships is no small undertaking. Plus, we have to do it covertly, so the bastard doesn't find out and lose his shit."

Quimby waved a hand impatiently. "Ok, ok, we've discussed this all before. Why are you here? Explain to me why I don't get to go on my run today."

"Proctor. As I said, she—"

"Yes, yes, she's a defiant bitch. But she's a war hero, Christian. She's earned her right to be a free-range admiral."

"Not when she endangers the mission!" Oppenheimer was clearly getting agitated.

"And what mission is that? Winning the war against this new alien threat? The … the Golgothics, or whatever their name is? I think her track record on winning wars of alien aggression is already quite established by now. In my first intel briefing I learned that it was actually Proctor that tracked down the last Swarm ship over twenty years ago and annihilated it. Now, tell me, can I go on my run?"

Oppenheimer sighed. "Mr. President, I think it's time I … laid it all out for you." The admiral talked like a man at the poker table about to reveal all his cards, and unsure that his bet fit the hand. *This ought to be good.*

"You mean you haven't laid it all out for me before now? You realize I'm the god-damned commander-in-chief, right?"

"It's because it's more of a hunch. But somewhat based on raw intel. Highly classified intel. A month simply isn't enough time to brief you on *every* piece of intel we have, or on the incredibly complex details of our history with the Swarm and its attendant races. You see, I believe the new alien ship, the Golgothics, was ... sorry, let me back up." He stood and started to pace. "When the Swarm hit us the first time over a hundred years ago, it was simple. Aliens attacking us, we fight back, and, for no apparent good reason, they give up. They leave. We win. But then ... thirty years ago, they came back."

Quimby nodded. "That's well understood, I thought. The orbital cycle of the black hole in the Penumbra system with its red-dwarf companion opened the meta-space ... uh, rift, into whatever universe the Swarm came from. Every hundred and fifty years. Except the Russians at the time, headed by President Malakov, opened it prematurely with the artificial singularity tech, giving us the gift of Swarm War Two. My dad was president of the Senate at the time. Told me all about it."

"Correct. But you're leaving out some of the history. In Swarm War One, it was just the Swarm. It was simple. One enemy. Everything was clear cut, apart from the usual political and diplomatic bullshit with the Russians, Chinese, and the Caliphate. But in Swarm War Two, all of the sudden the Dolmasi show up. A race that claimed to be under the control of the Swarm, until they *coincidentally* figured out how to free themselves from Swarm influence. And then, wouldn't you know it, the Skiohra show up a month after that with some sketchy bullshit story about how Granger's actions at the battle of New Dublin somehow magically freed *them* from Swarm control as well."

Quimby hesitated. "I … hadn't heard that part. How did he do it? Granger, freeing them from the Swarm?"

"Doesn't matter. Has to do with the interaction between the Ligature—the meta-space link all the Swarm-affiliated races used to talk to each other behind our backs—and the Russian singularity tech. Something about mixing quantum mechanics —what the Ligature depends on—with general relativity, which governs the singularities. But the important part that stands out to me is this. When the Skiohra showed up, they told Granger that the Swarm family was made up of not one, not two, not three, but *seven* races. The 'Concordat of Seven,' they called them."

Quimby grit his teeth and gripped the edge of his desk. "Why isn't this common knowledge? Why wasn't I told?"

"I'm telling you now. You're a new president and, frankly, there's just a lot of shit to catch you up on. Takes time, Mr. President. And if we were to tell the general population that there were *seven* alien races out there, my god, can you imagine the panic? It's bad enough with just the Dolmasi and the Skiohra lurking out there. Good thing they generally keep to themselves or things would be worse."

Yes, definitely should have thrown the election. Quimby leaned back in his chair and kicked his feet onto his desk. "So … who are the rest of the seven?"

Oppenheimer held up his fingers as he listed them off. "One, the liquid Valarisi, who we used to think of as the Swarm but just turned out to be a race the Swarm had corrupted and controlled, and who are now completely extinct, thanks to our friend Shelby Proctor. Two, the actual Meta-Space Swarm, we call them. The beings who extended their influence though the Penumbran black hole and took over the Valarisi thousands of years ago. Three, the Skiohra. Four, the Dolmasi. And five, the Adanasi. That was the Swarm's name for us. Humans. At least, the humans they brought under their control. Mostly the Russian high command at the time."

"Shit," Quimby breathed. "And are ... are they *still* under Swarm control?"

Oppenheimer scowled, as if he were lecturing a child. Quimby made a mental note to replace the asshole at the earliest opportunity. "Of course not. The Meta-space Swarm is gone. Granger sealed the Penumbra link permanently with a bunch of President Avery's anti-matter bombs. And the Russians did what Russians do best—there was a huge purge right after the war. Malakov basically disappeared the entire high command and replaced them. You can probably guess where the old ones went."

"Siberia?"

"Or worse, Canada. Anyway, that leaves two races. The Findiri, and the Quiassi."

"Who are they? Where are they?"

Oppenheimer finally stopped pacing and turned to face the president. His look was grave. "We ... don't know."

"What do you mean, *we don't know*?"

"We don't *know*, but I have my suspicions. Allow me to lay them out for you." He pulled out a holo-projector data pad and began displaying a slick, flashy presentation on the wall of his office. High production value. It almost seemed Oppenheimer had scripted the entire conversation. At least, his half of it, and he seemed to know in advance what Quimby's responses would be, and the president felt played because of it. *Dammit, don't they know who the hell I am?*

"No, stop. I'm not sitting through a whole presentation. Just give me the conclusion. Get to the point, Admiral."

Crestfallen, Oppenheimer clicked the projector off and cleared his throat. "Long story short, I ordered Admiral Proctor to get out to the periphery sectors to investigate a few leads related to my suspicions about the Findiri and Quiassi. She refused. And given her actions at the battle of Mao Prime, I have reason to suspect that ... she is under their influence."

Quimby laughed. "Impossible. *The* Admiral Proctor? The quote unquote *Companion of The Hero of Earth*? Under the influence of some alien race? I don't mean to go all Grangerite on you, Admiral, but if it ever got out that I was somehow against Proctor, I'd lose half the votes on Earth, San Martin, Britannia, and half a dozen other worlds. There's not that many actual full-on-crazy Grangerites, but she's damn popular. Even more-so now that she's been called back into service. Don't tell me you're having second thoughts about bringing her back? As I recall, it *was* your idea."

Oppenheimer grunted at the reminder. "I didn't anticipate Shelby being so ... stubborn. I thought I could control her more than—"

Quimby snorted. "Control? Ethan it took me four wives to figure out you can't control them."

The fleet admiral made a face. "Mr. President, with all due respect, Proctor and I are not married, and your many marriages are nothing like—"

"Of course you are. You're married to your job, Christian.

Everyone knows it. And by extension, with Proctor, it's like you are now dating an ex-wife of yours, loving and hating every minute of it. Fighting, re-opening and rehashing old arguments, gossiping about each other behind their backs ... please don't tell me you two are fucking...."

Oppenheimer was turning red, and Quimby couldn't tell if it was from embarrassment or anger. Good. Let him feel both —it gets the control back where it belongs: with Mr. President. The admiral started to protest, but Quimby held up a hand to stop him.

"Kidding, Christian. Take the stick out of your ass. Look —it sounds like we both have similar problems. We each have a rogue admiral on our hands. Consider this my official permission to go do something about yours, while I go handle mine."

The meaning of his statement began to dawn on Oppenheimer. "You mean, I can relieve Proctor?"

"Of course not. Politics, remember? But you can ... *persuade* her to follow your lead. As long as I don't hear about it. Besides, I've got a rogue admiral of my own to put in his place. This one is above your pay grade, I believe." He stood up, and with a knowing glance to Quinkert, his body man, the kid immediately left to go gather the president's personal belongings for a quick interstellar trip.

"What are you going to do? I told you, if we piss him off and Shovik-Orion decides it no longer wishes to service our starships—"

"Don't shit your pants, Christian. I got this. I just won the biggest election in galactic history, remember? I persuade people. I get them to think we're on the same side. It's what I do. He'll find I can be *very* persuasive. And in the end, he'll back off, and he'll think it was *his* idea."

He walked out of his office leaving the admiral behind. The other man's face clearly looked like he wanted to talk more, but Quimby both didn't care and also wanted to leave the impression that he was the alpha dog: driving the conversation, in control of the situation. It would piss the admiral off, sure, but then Quimby would heap some public praise on the asshole and puff up the blustery, shallow ego. It's how he neutered and controlled the most powerful political leaders that ended up endorsing him. Play them like fiddles. Their fragile egos were his piano.

"And where are we going, Mr. President?" asked Quinkert.

"Bolivar. To have a few choice words with Mr. Mullins."

And what were those words going to be? Hell if he knew. He had a day-long interstellar voyage to figure that part out. Shoot from the hip—that's why people loved him. Maybe a few beers would be all it took to loosen Mullins up a little. Or giving him a fat payoff. It worked for him before.

Or give him a planet. Shit, whatever it took. He sure as hell wasn't going to be a sideshow to some megalomaniac admiral. Much less *three* of them.

CHAPTER EIGHTEEN

Orbit over Mao Prime
ISS Independence
Bridge

There was an unwritten order of things. Every social situation, every locale where humans gathered into social structures—there were always law codes and regulations and rules, and inevitably, there was the stuff that happened under the table. And in the military, Proctor mused to herself as she walked into the bar, that "under the table" stuff often happened right there on top of the table in full view of everyone.

Like the bar itself. She smiled lopsidedly at the name stenciled on the archway to the converted storage room near the fighter bay: Futwick's. She knew there was a joke in there somewhere—she knew for sure there was no crew member named Futwick aboard the ship.

She flipped a chair around at a table and sat in it

backwards. Captain Volz was already there, glass half empty—usually she would have said it was half full, but such were the times. She noticed several other officers and pilots stand up in respect once they'd noticed her, and she waved them back down—the unwritten order allowed the existence of the unofficial bar next to the fighter bay, but the written order still required standard courtesy and protocol.

"Ballsy. Been here awhile?" She indicated his half full glass, while simultaneously catching the attention of the barkeeper, who this shift looked to be one of the fighter deck hands.

"Less than two minutes." He held the glass up and gulped the rest of the beer down. "It's been a hell of a day. Did the last of the Dolmasi ships finally leave?"

She nodded. "A few of them hung around, staying well beyond Mao Prime's moon, but they finally q-jumped away. Polrum Krull finally saw reason and agreed to keep the *Magnanimity* in the system until the last Dolmasi ship left."

"And the *Independence*? What's our itinerary?" Volz waved at the deck hand to hurry up.

"Admiral Sun from the CIDR fleet asked that we stay awhile—at least until the *Magnanimity* leaves. The Skiohra make them nervous, and Sun thinks I've got cachet with them. That if I'm around, the Skiohra will behave themselves."

Volz grinned half-heartedly. "They don't step out of line with the Motherkiller around."

She shot him a glare. "That was uncalled for, Ballsy."

"Sorry." Volz looked sheepish. She wondered if that glass was his first. Though by the unwritten order, the drinks they served there had to be lower alcohol content than usual. The deck hand finally came over with another glass full of the watered-down beer for Volz and looked at her questioningly. She glanced at his name tag. Rydberg.

"Ma'am?"

"Coffee. Cream and sugar, please. And yeoman Rydberg?"

"Ma'am?"

"*Extra* strong."

By the look on his face, he knew what *extra strong* meant. She couldn't officially be asking for Irish coffee, after all. He saluted and retreated behind the bar to prepare her drink.

"I assume you'll speak at the memorial service?" Volz downed another half of his new glass.

She paused several moments. Sighed. "Of course. How many pilots? Did Sanders make it? He was in intensive care earlier…."

Volz shook his head. "No. Batship just told me he passed. The burns were too extensive. Lost too much blood."

Proctor held her head in her hands. "Damn." She didn't even notice the deck hand place the coffee in front of her—it was there when she finally looked up. "How many?"

"Nine."

She gulped several swallows of coffee, relishing the burn, welcoming its fire and the accompanying warmth of alcohol. She could have been one of the nine—any of them could—but for now, she was alive, and she savored it, all while feeling the pain of losing her people. People who were her responsibility. People who wouldn't go home to their kids and wives and husbands and parents. "*Damn*," she repeated.

"Death is life, Shelby. We've all got to go. Question is when. At least those folks went out for a cause, and went fast. We can only hope for as much for ourselves."

"A cause? And what cause was that?"

He didn't have an answer. They sat in silence for a minute. She glanced over to the table next to them full of enlisted men and women—mechanics, by the looks of them and nodded a greeting. They gave nodded salutes back. "Batship? Which pilot is that?"

"My son."

Proctor's eyebrow went up. "I thought his was Batshit."

Volz grinned—good, they needed something to laugh at, so she'd laugh at whatever he found funny. Anything to distract them, even for a moment, from the awful realities of war. "It was, until you tamped down on the, quote, *potty-language* two weeks ago."

"Ah. Batship." She glanced back up at the sign on the wall. "Futwicks." She shook her head. "You people. Pilots. Fighter jocks. There's not a rule or regulation you people won't sidestep around."

Volz grinned even wider. "If we didn't, there'd never be places like Futwicks."

She raised her cup. "And god bless you for it."

Volz looked sidelong at her, stroking his stubble goatee—another unwritten rule: officers in war could look like whatever the hell they wanted to, as long as they got shit done. "You could have just changed it all when you were Fleet Admiral, you know."

"And why would I do a batship stupid futwick thing like that?" She sipped the coffee, feeling the Irish whiskey finally kick in a little bit.

Volz grunted. "No more of this sidestepping rules shit. Just have it all out in the open, you know?" He finished his second, and final beer—the deck hand had caught his attention with a questioning glance, but Volz waved him off.

"Absolutely not."

"It happens anyway, Shelby. May as well be up front about it. I mean, come on," he waved an arm around towards the storage bay-turned pub with a look that said *gotcha*. "Here you are."

She sipped another mouthful. "Here I am, and I wouldn't have it any other way. Ballsy, I never had kids. But I had my little brother and sister and nieces and nephews, and I've commanded thousands of twenty-something kids over the years. And the one thing I've learned about humans—young people in particular, is that they, we, *have* to rebel against something. It's in our blood. It's our evolutionary and cultural heritage. If we're not rebelling against something, by god we'll soon find something to rebel against. And I, for one, would far prefer to channel that rebellion into something beautiful like Futwick's than something terrible like … whatever you people would do if this place were officially sanctioned."

"A fight club?"

She smirked. "Don't push your luck, Captain." She downed the last mouthful. "It's human nature. Defiance. Rebellion. It's what gave us Magna Carta. It's what gave us the American Revolution. The French Revolution. The women's suffrage movement. It's what gave us the People's Accord that ended the First Interstellar War. On and on and on. It's what gave us bloody Tim Granger and the defeat of the Swarm."

At the mention of the name, the mood went darker.

"But they're back," Volz said.

"We don't know that."

"*Shelby, they're coming,*" he quoted to her.

"That could mean anything."

He stared her in the eye. "Or, it could mean exactly what we think it means. Exactly what we *know* it means."

"I know. Dammit, I know. But Ballsy, *thirteen billion years*. How the hell is that even possible? It flies in the face of all reason."

"Tim always did have a knack for flying in the face of reason. You could say it was his defining quality."

Proctor snorted. "His defining quality was being a crotchety old man who grumbled. Constantly."

"And now he's a god," Volz added with a smile. "How ironic."

"I think not. Sounds like the Old Testament god to me. Grumpy old man who grumbles all the time. Destroys a few cities. Sends a few plagues. The usual."

"The question is, taking the Granger-as-god fantasy a bit further," he stared down into his empty glass. "Is he the Old Testament god of wrath and vengeance? Or the New Testament god of salvation and redemption? After all, we've got several moons with holes bored into them, the *ISS Chesapeake* destroyed, hundreds, no, thousands of deaths already—"

She cut him off by leaning in. "This is classified top secret. Tau twenty. But you should know. You know the moon in the Jakarta sector? Tal Rishi?"

"Yeah. Uninhabited system, right? Except the Golgothic ship hit Tal Rishi with its beam while no one was looking?"

"Right." She downed the last of her coffee. "I just heard a few minutes ago. It's gone."

He looked up suddenly. "What do you mean, gone?"

"Gone. Disappeared. The whole moon."

"Debris?"

"None."

Volz puffed air in exasperation. "You're the scientist, you tell me. Is that possible?"

"No."

"Let me get this straight. A thirteen billion-year-old message from Granger. A piece from the *Victory* just as old as the message. Now an entire moon just ... poof ... disappears. What the bloody hell is going on?"

She shook her head. "I wish I knew. Believe me, Ballsy, I wish I knew." She was half-tempted to wave the yeoman over to refill her cup. But the slight buzz she felt was enough. With the Dolmasi out there, ready to spring on an unsuspecting system at any time, she had to stay ready for duty. "It's like my mom always said, they come in threes. The bad things. The deaths, the catastrophes—whatever. They come in threes. My question is, after Granger's message, and after Tal Rishi going missing, what the hell could follow that up?"

A shadow passed over Volz's face, and he looked like he wanted to say something. But he just played with his cup.

"Out with it."

"You've had way more than *three*, Shelby. Are you doing ok? I haven't heard you talk about Danny even *once* since you learned he was dead."

"We don't know for sure he's dead." She said the words, but they sounded hollow even to her.

Danny Proctor. Barely twenty years old. Oldest son of her younger brother, almost like her own son since she had helped raise him over the past ten years.

And he was gone. Just months after finally achieving his dream of captaining his own starship, a merchant freighter named the *Magdalena Issachar*. But an unknown ship had intercepted it over Sangre de Cristo in the San Martin system, boarded it, killed Danny's crewmates, and detonated the freighter's cargo: a stolen nuclear missile, destroying one of the domed settlements on Sangre.

They found Danny's charred space suit a hundred kilometers from the nearest domed settlement several days later.

"If you say so, Shelby. When you're ready to talk about it, I'm here. I haven't lost a child or a nephew like that, at least, not exactly, but if you want to talk…."

"I don't. Not yet."

"Fair enough." He spun his cup a few more times. "Oh, Lieutenant Qwerty reports he figured out a new Dolmasi phrase as he listened in on their Ligature comm traffic when the Skiorha showed up."

That caught her interest, and made her glad that Volz had the good sense to change the subject. "Really? What?"

He cleared his throat dramatically. "Ohhhhh shiiiiiit."

She laughed. Ballsy could still make her laugh, after all those decades. "Well tell Mr. Qwerty to keep at it. I want a full Dolmasi dictionary by the end of the week."

"And Commander Mumford is still working on the analysis of the sensor readings we took of the Golgothic ship before it plunged into Titan. He's having a hard go of it—honestly, he needs more people. An actual science team."

She nodded. "I might still have some sway at IDF

Sciences. I'll see if I can't pull some people in. Besides, I've got a few other things I want them to look into. I want our own people looking into the science of the meta-space pulse and its interaction with and effect upon the Ligature. I want some extra eyes on the data we got on the *Magdalena Issachar*—just to confirm what Admiral Tigre's folks are telling me. And...." She paused, considering. "And I want to take another look at the black hole data. I know, I know, our top scientists have been studying the Penumbra black hole for three decades. But ... I just want to ... I don't know. Take another look. Study the interaction of those anti-matter bombs that Tim piloted into that thing with the meta-space link the Swarm supposedly used to enter our universe. There are issues of causality and interactions between quantum physics and general relativity physics that I'm not one hundred percent clear on. And I also want—"

He started laughing.

"What?"

"You know who you sound like? President Avery. Especially when you mentioned her anti-matter bombs. She had dozens of different secret projects going on at once. Probably still has several of them going on right now, even though she's been out of office for twenty-five years. The whole anti-matter bomb project—the *Mars Project*, she called it, to confuse the Russians about what it actually was all about— was secret right up until we finally used them on what we thought was the Swarm's homeworld, and then again a day later when Tim ran a few of them into the Swarm's end zone like he was rushing with a football. But was that all Avery was working on in secret? I bet she had a dozen other things up her sleeve in case those bombs didn't work. You're the same. Always thinking twenty steps ahead."

"Are you making fun of me?"

"No. I'm complimenting you. I guess I'm just saying that … with you on our side and back in the game, as bleak as things seem, I can't help but think that our enemies have a freight train headed straight at them. A freight train called Shelby Proctor." He lifted up his glass and tipped it towards her as a toast, and tried to drink before he remembered it was still empty.

"Well I'll be a lot more at ease when we know what the third thing is," she said, circling back. "A message from Granger, a moon disappearing, and then…."

As if on cue, her comm beeped. She shot Volz an unnerved look, and pulled her hand terminal out of her pocket. "Proctor," she said.

"Admiral, a small freighter is approaching and is requesting permission to dock."

Her brow furrowed in mild surprise. "Commercial freighter?"

"Affirmative."

"Permission denied. We don't have time for whatever they—"

"I told them that, ma'am. But … well, she says her name is Fiona Liu. Was really insistent that her name get passed to you."

Fiona Liu? Proctor's eyes bulged out. Her spine ran cold. *Oh my god.*

Volz mouthed to her, "*Who the hell is Fiona Liu?*"

She replied into her hand terminal. "Permission granted.

Shuttle bay two. I'll meet her there." She stood up and rushed for the door. Volz followed close behind.

"Who the hell is Fiona Liu?" he repeated.

She didn't even pause as she responded. "His girlfriend. Danny's dead girlfriend."

CHAPTER NINETEEN

Orbit over Mao Prime
ISS Independence
Sickbay

Zivic paced. Back and forth past the door to the surgical ward, stopping every now and then to peer in through the window, past the blinds, through the small half-centimeter gap between them and the window sill. Wait, were they done? Or were they just taking a break? He saw the surgeon step back from the operating table, frustration covering his face. His front was wet with blood.

Dammit, dammit, dammit....

"You're hopeless, you know?"

He spun around at the sound of the voice. He didn't know whether to smile or glare at the voice's owner. "Look, Jerusha, she was hanging by a thread out there. If we had have been ten seconds later...."

He turned back to peer through the window, while she

sidled up next to him. "How is she?"

In truth, he had no idea. But the fact that they were still operating had to be a good sign, right? "They've been in there for two hours."

"That's good, I suppose. If things were beyond hope, they'd have stopped by now."

He leaned his head onto the window and closed his eyes. "I lost Sara Batak. I didn't realize how hard I'd fallen for her, and then when she died so suddenly, it just … I was just … completely floored. And now, saving Ace only to have her hit by a stray bullet…."

She grabbed his shoulders and twisted him to face her. "Zivic, listen to me. You've got to stop this. Look, I know you. We nearly got married, remember?"

He managed a half smile. "Yeah. What do you say … give it another shot?"

She held a finger up to his lips. "Shush. I'm not joking around. Just listen. You've got a … problem, Zivic. You've got this image of yourself as this knight in shining armor, riding in to the rescue to save the damsel in distress. Which is fine. Whatever motivates you to do your best in battle and complete the mission … whatever. But you're taking it too far, Zivic. You saved Batak, you fell for her, and she died. You had *me*, Zivic. You had *me* right in front of your nose, and you couldn't commit. It wasn't until after I'd left that you realized what you'd lost." She smacked her forehead. "Oh my god. I just realized."

"What?"

"You. Your problem is that you only want what you can't have. Once you saw you couldn't have me, that's when you went off the rails, trying to impress me or whatever you were trying to do with that stunt that killed your mom and stepdad—"

"Stop—"

"And then Batak. You rode in to the rescue. You started having a thing going, and then she was taken from you abruptly. Unfairly. And so you lionized her in your mind. Set her up on this angelic pedestal. You convinced yourself that it was a sure thing between the two of you, when the truth is you barely knew her. There was no basis for a relationship there. Saving the girl doesn't *get* you the girl. You understand that, right?"

"Just stop—"

She didn't let go of his shoulders. "And now, Ace. You're just smitten with her, aren't you? You saved the girl, and now she might die, and so you're pining over her."

"I am not."

"You are. Admit it. Why else are you here?"

He felt his face getting red. "Because she's a comrade. Pilots look out for each other."

"Really? Then why aren't you with Bucket? He got hit too. Didn't you know that?"

"He did?"

"Yeah. He just got out of surgery. Took a bogey's round right through his shoulder. Missed his aorta by an inch. But you didn't notice because you're hung up … over the girl."

His mom, Spacechamp, always told him when he was a teenager that lies hurt. But the truth hurt much, much worse. And listening to Whitehorse made him cringe. Made him angry, because he recognized the truth in the accusations.

She somehow read his mind. "Look, I'm not saying this to accuse you, or hurt you, or even to stop you from pursuing her."

He faked another half-smile. "Gee. Thanks?"

"I'm only saying this to help you, Zivic. I hate seeing you get hurt. Over and over and over again."

"I'll be fine." He breathed deep and set his shoulders square. "Really. I'm fine, Jerusha. Maybe I do have a thing for her. Maybe not. And yes, I'll go check in on Bucket in a second. But I just had to know how she was doing. I can't keep losing people like this." He smiled again, this time a little more genuine. "I'm fine."

She let go of one shoulder, but squeezed his other, and smiled. "One more thing you should know, Zivic."

"What?"

"Ace has a girlfriend."

He couldn't mask the expression creeping onto his face. "Wait, what?"

Whitehorse started to walk away. His expression had apparently told her enough. "You really know how to pick 'em. Just a comrade, huh? Aw, shit, I shouldn't have told you that—you only want what you can't have, which means now you're going to fall for Ace even harder."

He scowled. *Dammit!* "Come on. Let's go check on Bucket."

"I'll take a rain check," she replied, backtracking through the door back into the main ward. "I've got to get back up to the bridge. Tell him hi for me."

He watched her start to leave, and saw beyond the door that the main ward was full of wounded from the skirmish with the Dolmasi, and that Bucket, his fellow pilot, was indeed laying bed-ridden in the corner, an IV hanging above him.

"Wait, Jerusha. Do you know the stats? From the battle? How many did I get?"

She eyed him, then glanced down at her data pad that she kept with her at all times. "Lieutenant Ethan Batship Zivic. Confirmed kills…" she looks back up at him. "Eight."

"So … not one hundred and one?"

"Not today, Batship. Maybe next time." She turned and retreated back to the main ward.

He followed her out, and parked himself in a chair at Bucket's bedside while Whitehorse left sickbay. "Maybe next time, Batshit," he said to no one.

CHAPTER TWENTY

Orbit over Mao Prime
ISS Independence
Shuttle Bay

The freighter looked new, and if Proctor didn't know any better she might have thought it was actually an IDF supply ship, based on its aggressive angles and pockets that looked like they might have at one point housed weapons. If it was once a military ship, all identifying marks had been removed. She wondered what she'd find if she had a tech crew examine the transponder data files. Perhaps the ship was stolen from IDF and repurposed as a private cargo freighter.

The freighter's hatch opened. Proctor waited in the shuttle bay's anteroom, watching on the monitor as the freighter's ramp descended and the squad of marines positioned themselves to greet the visitor. And, of course, check her for weapons, bombs—anything that would pose a threat to the admiral or the ship.

She stepped down the ramp—at least, Proctor assumed it was a she. The figure wore a mask, almost like a vacuum-rated flight suit. A corporal shouted some orders to her, and she raised her arms. The marine stepped forward and frisked her, checking her pockets, then waving a scanner over her body.

Several minutes later the marine turned to the camera and nodded. Proctor pressed on the comm. "Bring her in here, Corporal."

The door to the anteroom slid open and Liu walked through, accompanied on either side by a marine, along with one ahead of her and two behind.

Proctor stood in the center of the room facing her, arms folded. When the guards finally paused, forcing Liu to stop several paces away, she noticed that not only was the other woman's helmet still on, but the oxygen was flowing. That set alarm bells off in the back of her mind. Contingencies and possibilities started to play out in her mind's eye—was the woman going to gas them all? Is that why she was still wearing her helmet?

No, the marines's scan was thorough—they would have detected something like that. But, Proctor remembered, her dead nephew's former girlfriend *had* worked several years as an IDF Intel field agent. If she was planning something, it was likely to be undetectable.

"You're not dead," said Proctor.

Liu, rather than respond, started fiddling with her helmet, releasing the clasps and thumbing the oxygen flow off. The marines nearby raised their weapons and swung them up towards her, making her freeze.

Proctor waved. "No, go ahead. Take it off."

The helmet came off. And Proctor gasped.

Most of her face looked like it had melted. Her hair was gone. The only picture she'd seen of the woman was the one in her service file, essentially an unsmiling mug shot. The woman standing before her bore little similarity to that picture, except for the unsmiling part. In fact, Proctor wasn't sure if it was the ghoulish effect from the melted skin, but it looked like Liu was either snarling, or grimacing.

"Oh my god," said Proctor. "What happened? That looks recent ... oh," she added, the pieces suddenly falling into place.

Admiral Mullins had said Liu was dead. Killed in the blast at CENTCOM Bolivar that was supposedly meant for her—for Proctor.

But he was wrong. Or lying. Because clearly, the woman standing in front of her was not dead. Though it looked as if she may have been at one point.

"My apologies, Admiral. The helmet keeps the environment around my face at optimum temperature and humidity, and flows trace amounts of antiseptics and regrowth hormones across my skin. It's a compromise—it allows me to be up and moving and not in a hospital bed."

Proctor couldn't help but stare at the ruined face. "I can't imagine any sane doctor would let you out like that. A month in the hospital, at least."

"Like I said, compromise."

"The doctor let you out?"

Liu's glare was cold and hollow. "The doctor would have killed me, Hippocrates be damned. He was Mullins's man, after all."

"You work for Mullins," said Proctor. It was a statement,

not a question.

Her scowl darkened. "Worked," clarified Liu.

Pieces of the puzzle shuffled in her mind. Proctor assembled them into one solution, then shook them up into another. But the problem was that she still lacked key pieces. "Mullins tried to kill *you*, not me."

"Oh, I'm sure he wouldn't have minded if you'd died too. He claimed to like you, but as a field agent, I was trained, extensively, on how to tell when people are lying. And I'm pretty sure Mullins doesn't like you in the slightest."

Every one of her words looked like it pained her, like the act of speaking was pure torture. Proctor imagined stretching that ruined skin into speech, the bare muscles and tendons forming tortuous words, was pure hell.

"Why would Mullins want you dead?"

Liu finally smiled. In her mind, Proctor could almost hear the other woman's skin crackle with the strained motion. "Because I know too much. I know far, far too much."

CHAPTER TWENTY-ONE

Orbit over Mao Prime
ISS Independence
Armory

Marine Number Two checked his assault rifle one final time, and then felt his vest to make sure he had the two extra magazines. He nodded to Marine Number One.

Marine Number Three and Number Four gave him the thumbs up. They were all ready.

They were nameless. *Marine Number Two* was his name now. He needed to be untraceable, without history. And no commanders—they were operating solo. At least, that was the story if they were, in the event that everything went tits-up, captured.

But the little pouch on his chest would be the insurance against *that* unhappy possibility. He tapped his own and nodded to Marine Number Two's chest pocket. "We just received the go-ahead. You got your Goodnight Moon?"

"Ain't Goodnight Moons. They're *Goodnight Sons*. As in, goodnight, son, you're dead."

The gravity of the statement weighed on him, but he knew what he was getting into. He signed up for it. Danger was the name of the game in this line of work, and for his employer—well, death was a small price if they achieved what they came for.

Marine Number One nodded. "All right. Let's get this show on the road. Four, get to Engineering. Three, Shuttle Bay. Two, with me."

They could hear the other marines training through the wall. The training simulator had a firing range, and the rest of the men were lingering there, as usual. That's where this group of marines tended to linger after their training session was done. Firing big guns was therapeutic after all, and they were at war—they deserved every bit of *therapy* they could get.

But it was show time. The signal indicated they needed to act quickly, and so they left the training simulator's locker room, stalked out into the hall, and locked the door behind them.

CHAPTER TWENTY-TWO

Orbit over Mao Prime
ISS Independence
Sickbay

Proctor had finally convinced the newcomer to go to sickbay, which Liu acquiesced to on the condition that the admiral accompany her, which was perfectly fine with Proctor, since the former IDF Intel agent seemed to be at the center of recent events.

"How is she, Doc?"

Patel had shooed Proctor out of the examination room when they'd first arrived, and now the doctor had finally emerged ten minutes later with a scowl covering his face.

"Really, Shelby? Doctor-patient confidentiality." He snapped a glove off his hand and into the recycle receptacle.

"Cut the bullshit, Doc. Didn't stop you from telling both Babu and Ballsy about my frickin' tooth. Technically, she's dead, according to IDF records, so legally you're fine on a technicality. But even if you weren't, I can invoke—"

He waved his still-gloved hand. "Oh, stop. You sound like a first year ensign, threatening to quote regulations at me. Your concern for her would be touching if I didn't know that you've been avoiding me like the plague for the past two weeks."

"Stop changing the subject. It's a damn root canal—it can wait until after the apocalypse." She sighed in exasperation. "Look, Patel, we've known each other a long time—"

Patel had finally snapped the other glove off and was washing his hands. "Yes, since I interned on the *Chesapeake* thirty years ago. And you were as stubborn then as you are now." He turned the water off and flicked his hands mostly dry before wiping them on his scrubs. "And since I know how stubborn you are, I'll save us the time." He looked up toward the ceiling, as if about to talk through the comm. "Patient notes, Lieutenant Fiona Liu, preliminary examination. Patient displays extreme third degree burns over approximately fifty percent of her body, as well as lacerations and contusions consistent with a detonation or other explosive event. Rudimentary medical attention has already been administered, though at this late stage of recovery patient will likely require extensive skin grafts since scar tissue has already formed—"

Proctor held up a hand, "But Doc, what about her supposed death? I need to know if she's telling the—"

While she spoke, the doctor glanced all around the room, turning every which way, without looking at Proctor. The message was clear: you're not here.

"Must be ghosts in here…" he grumbled. "Continue patient notes for Fiona Liu. Patient also shows trace amounts of experimental compound HG dash one eight six two, suggesting that at one point she may have either intentionally or unintentionally slowed her heart rate down to approximately two beats per minute and entered a state of limited consciousness, for what reasons I can't fathom. Other than the burns and the superficial tissue damage, patient is otherwise in excellent health, consistent with a normal twenty-eight year old woman. Recommended recovery regimen: skin regrowth hormones—probably Dermigen Five A, given patient's youth, as well as Dicyclopropithol for inflammation. Acetemeniphene for pain management."

Proctor nodded. "Thank you, Doc."

He jolted and snapped around towards her. "How the hell did you get in here?"

She smiled and pat his arm as she opened the door to the examination room where Liu was waiting. "Nice, Patel. I promise you can rip this damn tooth out soon. You know, as soon as we save civilization. Again." She pulled the door shut behind her.

"He's ... odd," said Liu, once the door was closed.

"Yes," agreed Proctor. "You have no idea." She pulled a chair over and sat across from the former intel officer. Her dead nephew's girlfriend. Former girlfriend? She realized she had no idea what exactly was the nature of their relationship, whether it had ended or was, in fact, progressing by the time Danny had died. "Ok. Talk."

"What first?"

Trust verification first, she thought. Proctor realized she needed to give her a few questions that she already knew the answers to, just to make sure Liu was telling the truth. It was no guarantee against deception, but ... it was something. "How did you escape? How did they think you were dead?"

Liu nodded. "When the blast hit I already suspected Mullins wanted to get rid of me. I had guessed too much about his plans, and that unnerved him. So when the blast hit—it knocked me out for several minutes, I think—but when I came to I swallowed a Goodnight Moon—"

"I'm sorry, a what?"

"A Goodnight Moon. It's a little pill they used to give us in the service for … contingencies. Lowers your heart rate to almost nothing. Most of your cells go into temporary hibernation. But you actually stay partially awake—just enough to be aware of what's going on around you, and enough where you can force yourself to snap out of it if you're in danger. So basically when the ER doc on Bolivar looked at me, he pronounced me dead, and when no one was looking I bolted. Grabbed the first ship I could find and got the hell out of dodge."

So, at least that checked out. Proctor had feigned ignorance on the Goodnight Moon pill, but she knew very well that its active ingredient was, as Doc Patel put it, compound HG-1862.

Proctor leaned forward. "Fiona, I understand you were … involved, with Danny Proctor. My nephew."

Liu's expression hardened. "I was."

She asked the question she wasn't really sure she wanted an answer to. "Tell me. Was he GPC? Was my nephew a terrorist?"

"Terrorist? Danny? Of course not. He was sweet. And kind. I—I'm ashamed to say it, but—" She grimaced. "Mullins … assigned me to infiltrate the GPC, and Danny was my way in. It started off that way, but after I got to know him, well, my training went out the window. I got involved. It was pretty steamy there for a few months before we decided to pull back a bit."

"So, you used my nephew to infiltrate the GPC?"

She answered immediately, not a trace of shame on her face. "Yes."

She was a professional, Proctor could give her that. "And? What did you learn?"

"That the GPC is basically what it claims to be. They wear their intentions and goals on their sleeve. Nothing underhanded going on. What they say is true: they're working for independence from UE for whichever world wants it. There are a few affiliated groups who are more ... militant, and mostly outside of Secretary General Curiel's control, but the GPC itself is on the up-and-up."

"And Mullins? What does he want?"

Liu's face looked cold at the mention of the name. "Mullins? War. He wants war."

"Why?"

Liu blew out a puff of air in exasperation. "Hell if I know. He didn't exactly give me the bad guy monologue before he tried to kill me."

"But you have a better idea than anyone right now of what he's after. Speculate."

Liu closed her eyes. "Mullins is ego driven. I mean, he wants money and power just as much as the next guy. But Mullins thrives on being the guy at the top. He needs it. Craves it. And so he's positioned himself through his connections as an IDF admiral, to being not only the head of Shovik-Orion, but essentially the strongman of Bolivar. They've got a president, of course, but he's basically Mullins's puppet. And, through his leadership at Shovik-Orion, he fancies himself the strongman of not only Bolivar, but every world where Shovik-Orion has a major presence, which, in the Irigoyen sector and the sectors close to it, is at least seven or eight planets. Many of the new colonies were essentially funded and started by Shovik-Orion."

Proctor leaned back in her chair. "So. Mullins wants to rule his own little empire like a petty tyrant."

"Oh, not just that. War is profitable, Admiral. For a company like Shovik-Orion, which supplies UE, IDF, and GPC, and a good portion of the Chinese, the Russians, and even the Caliphate, a war—especially one on the scale of the Second Swarm War—is the biggest profit-making engine they have. So not only is he probably trying to set up his own little empire with himself at the top, he wants to fund it off the backs of everyone else, and if he has to start an intergalactic war to fund it, and if, in the confusion of said intergalactic war, he manages to get his political dominance officially recognized, since IDF, in their need for a regular stream of supplies from Shovik-Orion, won't do anything that might piss him off and cut off the equipment for the war effort…."

Proctor shook her head. "What a big, ugly mess." She paused to process all the information. The implications. The possibilities. "How is he doing it? I assume this mess with the Dolmasi is his fault. And, most likely, the alien ship that slagged a bunch of our moons."

Liu shrugged. "I think, but I'm not sure, that Shovik-Orion has a secret research arm. A black projects division. And

I'm pretty sure that they've been doing banned artificial singularity research involving meta-space shunts."

"The shunt. My god..." murmured Proctor. If true, that was terrifying, devastating news. Artificial singularities, developed by the Russian Confederation and used by the Swarm during the last war, had wreaked terrible, unthinkable destruction. The possibility that someone might be developing the technology further....

"At least, I did hear Mullins talk about a shunt at one point, though at the time I didn't know what he meant?" She posed the statement as a question.

Proctor weighed how much to tell the other woman. She wanted the conversation to be a one-way street, but she supposed that throwing Liu a few bones might spur her memory, or possibly garner trust. "The bomb over Sangre De Cristo. It was more than just a nuclear device. Half of the energy was ... shunted, into meta-space. We think it's what was responsible for both summoning that alien ship, and for driving the Dolmasi crazy, among other things." Proctor pointed a finger at her. "That's *highly* classified, by the way."

Liu smiled. "I'm dead, remember? That means I've either lost my clearance, or have a higher clearance than you." It was a small joke, accompanied by a small smile, but the gesture was appreciated. Though Proctor wondered if the former intel officer was performing psy-ops on her.

"Admiral?" The speaker in the ceiling blared with the drawled voice of the comm officer, and Proctor lifted her head to answer.

"What is it, Lieutenant Qwerty?"

"Ma'am we just picked up a highly targeted meta-space

signal. Was basically pointed straight at us—very tight confinement beam—spatially, at least."

Proctor raised an eyebrow. "Source?"

"That's just it, ma'am, it looked like it came from nowhere in particular. I almost thought it came from Mao Prime's moon, but then I checked the numbers and that's not quite right. It's like it came from slightly *above* the moon, from our perspective, at least."

"Have you decrypted the message?"

"No, ma'am. Workin' on it."

She nodded, and stood up, offering a hand to help Liu. "Understood, Lieutenant. Please keep me informed."

Liu followed her out the door into sickbay proper, where Doc Patel was waiting.

"Thank you, Doctor. I need to borrow your patient for awhile. Don't worry, I'll have her back before the end of the day."

"Ma'am?" said Liu. Procter realized she hadn't told Liu what she wanted her for.

"We've pulled some research on Shovik-Orion recently. I want you to look it over and tell me what you think."

Liu nodded.

The sickbay doors opened, and Proctor's security detail came in. Damn, they were good. Knew exactly when she was ready for them. She gave them a quick nod—which they returned—and she looked back to Liu. "Please come with me." She noticed Liu was still looking at the marines, a strange expression on her face. Recognition?

When Proctor turned back around, the marines had leveled their assault rifles.

And pointed them straight at her.

CHAPTER TWENTY-THREE

Britannia Sector
Britannia
Outskirts of Whitehaven
Freighter Angry Betty

The *Angry Betty* was a beast. An ancient, cobbled-together, heavy, rickety, barely-functioning beast of a cargo hauler. But it was dependable, and its q-jump engines were the best out of all the tiny fleet of ships that Nile Holdings, Inc. had, at least at the local warehouse Keen worked at.

The gallium—all fifty tons of it, enough to fill a cavernous steel storage container the size of a small house—sloshed as the *Angry Betty*'s thrusters ignited. As instructed, he'd arranged for special dispersion equipment to be installed on the container and the orbital thrusters attached. He assumed the customer would control it remotely, but that was not information that was forthcoming from the strange man, and Keen was not going to risk asking. Nothing was going to stand in the way between him and that pile of cash. And all the hookers and booze that pile of cash would fund.

"Whitehaven spaceport traffic control, this is the *Angry Betty*, cargo freighter with Nile Holdings, Inc., registry number oh-five-seven-charlie-dash-sixty-four-thousand-and-one-dash-zed-five. Requesting permission to enter orbit."

The comm radio scratched with the reply from the control tower several kilometers away. "Acknowledged, *Angry Betty*. Destination?"

"Proprietary."

In truth, he still had no idea. All the customer had said was, "*far.*" And besides, it was none of traffic control's business.

"Acknowledged. Just confirming you're actually leaving orbit and not sticking around. That's all we care about here."

"Affirmative, traffic control. I confirm—*Angry Betty* will be leaving orbit."

A long pause. "*Angry Betty*, you're cleared for orbital insertion path Whitehaven Delta Six. Your launch window begins in two minutes and extends for ten more. Safe travels."

"Thank you, traffic control, *Angry Betty* out."

He flipped the comm off, engaged the main engines, and minutes later the *Angry Betty* was screaming like a bulbous, heavy, unwieldy banshee out of Britannia's orbit. The green continents were visible below through the thick atmosphere, and the white snow-packed peaks near the coast glistened in the morning light.

When I come back, maybe I'll buy a frickin' mountain....

He plugged the tiny data pad the customer had given him into the receptacle on the nav computer, and moments later the system informed him of an impending q-jump. He settled back into his chair for a long nap—the customer hadn't told him how many jumps the journey would require, and he'd worked all night putting the order together, so it was time to catch up on some sleep.

And dream of his new country estate. And the women. And the booze. And the pool. And the race car. And the mountain. And the tropical island. How much could a few million buy? He wasn't sure, but he was about to find out.

CHAPTER TWENTY-FOUR

Orbit over Mao Prime
ISS Independence
Sickbay

Proctor stared down the barrel of the gun. She wondered briefly if it was seconds from going off, or if this was an arrest. An illegal arrest—unless Mullins had managed to not only convince Oppenheimer, but President Quimby and the chairman of the joint chiefs himself. She supposed that, technically, Oppenheimer had the authority to arrest her himself, but given the political situation….

Dammit, her mind was rambling. It was something that tended to happen when faced with death. Her animal brain took over, and, as it turned out, her animal brain was a scientist who thought a lot. And the animal brain, in spite of the gun pointed towards it, couldn't stop thinking about Liu's suspicions about the new artificial singularity research program. If there was anything more frightening than an imminent bullet to her brain, it was the possibility that the technology behind the artificial singularities was being improved on in some unthinkably destructive way.

"Admiral, you'll come with us. Immediately," said the marine. His eyes drilled into hers unflinchingly.

She inclined her head slightly, signaling to the comm system that she was about to speak. "Proctor to bridge."

The marine smiled.

She tried again. "Captain Volz, this is Admiral Proctor. Please respond."

Silence. The marine twitched his gun slightly towards the door. "I don't think they'll be sending help, ma'am. Come with us. Now."

She grit her teeth, put her hands on her hips, squared her jaw, and said matter-of-factly, "No."

The other marine swore and advanced on her, grabbing her by the upper arms and shoving her towards the door. "We don't have time for this, ma'am," he growled.

Doc Patel, who had been hanging back, trying to present as small a target as possible, made his move. He lunged for the marine holding the gun still pointed at Proctor's chest, trying to jab him with a meta-syringe, likely full of a tranquilizer. How he'd managed to get one loaded during the brief confrontation she could only guess—did he just keep one in his pocket at all times, as a precaution? She made a mental note to buy him a beer later at Futwick's.

The gun cracked.

Patel stumbled backwards, grasping at his chest.

He fell.

Blood was erupting from a hole in his scrubs, pulsing with

each heart beat. But with each pulse, the flow lessened. His face, at first terrified, relaxed and went blank as he died.

The gun moved back to her, and the marine nodded towards the door. "Admiral? Now."

CHAPTER TWENTY-FIVE

Orbit over Mao Prime
ISS Independence
Bridge

Volz leaned over the comm station, peering at the console in front of Lieutenant Qwerty. "The signal had to have originated somewhere. What about the satellites orbiting the moon? Can we access them somehow and go through their comm logs?"

Qwerty shook his head. "I doubt it, Captain. Even under normal circumstances, those satellites are Chinese, and even though we've got treaties that would let us look through their logs, the paperwork would take months. And they just fought off a … you know … alien invasion. I don't think CIDR's in a talky mood just yet."

Volz rubbed his temples. "Fine. What about our IT boys? Surely we can hack in? Don't we have a ten trillion dollar cyber-security budget?"

Lieutenant Whitehorse, sitting nearby at the tactical station, mirrored Qwerty's head shake. "Negative, sir. First off, cyber-security isn't the same as cyber warfare. Second, hacking into a satellite is trickier than you might think. Even UE satellites. We've got backdoors into *those*, as you know. But CIDR satellites? Those things have something like fifty nested firewalls. The Chinese really, really, *really* don't want people hacking into their satellites."

"I bet Admiral Sun will give us access. I mean, we *did* just help him fight off an invasion of their capital…."

Whitehorse shrugged. "CIDR military folks are skittish. I'm sure he'll say something like, 'yeah, you saved our planet an hour ago, but what have you done for me *lately*?'"

Volz had had enough. "Fine. I want to know where that meta-space signal came from. Now. Give me some options, people."

Mumford raised a finger. "We could rule out the CIDR satellites, at least. Just interpolate their positions when the signal was sent, and then—"

Qwerty interrupted, "But meta-space signals have such a long wavelength, it's almost impossible to nail down the source, spatially, at least not without a great deal more triangulation than we—"

"Yes, yes, but that would at least rule out the ones on the other side. I mean, how many CIDR satellites could there be around Mao Prime's lifeless, uninhabited moon?" Mumford asked.

"Fifty-seven," said Qwerty.

Mumford looked crestfallen. "Oh."

Volz balled up his fists, ready to pound something.

Something just felt ... off, about that signal. That it seemed to originate from empty space, and that it was, unusually for a meta-space signal given their large wavelengths, targeted directly *at* the *Independence* in a tight beam, and encoded. If he was honest with himself, he felt like someone had just painted a large set of crosshairs on the ship. It was irrational, but that's what it seemed like.

"Move the ship. Get us into a higher orbit. Geosynchronous. And begin t-jump calculations to get us out of here at a second's notice."

"T-jump heading, sir?" said Ensign Riisa at the helm.

"Any heading. Just a few light seconds away—I'd still like to see what's going on here if we have to hightail it."

"Aye, aye, sir," she replied, but then furrowed her brow. "Sir? I'm not getting a response from the engines."

Volz jolted upright. The alarm bells went off in his head. "Come again?"

Riisa shook her head in frustration. "The status board says they're online, I ... I just can't access them."

Volz raised his head toward the ceiling. "Bridge to engineering. Rayna? What's going on? Are the engines down?"

Silence.

"Captain...?" Lieutenant Qwerty's face had started to drain of color. "All comms from the bridge are out. In fact, we've lost control of just about every system, as far as I can tell."

Volz spun around to the entrance to the bridge, and pointed at the two marines stationed there. "Seal the bridge. Now. Protocol Firestorm."

The marines, to their credit, sprung into action. They knew

what Protocol Firestorm meant: that the ship had been compromised, and that their job was to lock the bridge down and keep intruders out at all costs. The doors, already shut, now locked into place and bars extended from hidden sleeves to seal them tight. Volz could almost hear the ventilation system shut down, switching over to a local emergency backup—if any intruders had planned on gassing them, that avenue of attack was closed, too. The bridge was now hermetically sealed.

"Captain...? This is strange." Ensign Riisa looked up from the nav console. "The ship's power plant is ... well, operating normally, but there's something strange about the phase of the containment envelope. It's ... pulsing. Semi-regularly."

Volz strode over to see what she was talking about. Sure enough, on the console, he watched the readouts from the power plant waver. The phase kept on changing—something that would have absolutely no effect on the performance of the power systems, or any effect whatsoever. But it was....

"Code." Volz waved Qwerty over. "Lieutenant, read this for me."

Qwerty sprung out of his chair and watched the pulsing of the phase envelope on Riisa's console. "It's Morse, alright." He had a momentary sense of deja vu, remembering how, just a few weeks ago, a thirteen billion year old message had been transmitted to them using the same archaic code. *Shelby, they're coming*, encoded into an alien weapon, using Morse, of all things.

Qwerty started reading the words as they were spelled out by the engines. "Engineering taken. Intruder target is sickbay, shuttle bay." He looked up. "Then it repeats automatically."

Volz felt like someone had hit him in the gut. With a half-ton hydraulic wrench. "Sickbay—that's where Shelby is. They're going for the admiral."

CHAPTER TWENTY-SIX

Orbit over Mao Prime
ISS Independence
Engineering

Rayna Scott loved her engines like her children. At least, that's what she thought—she'd never actually had a child. Real children screamed far too much. Diapers, bottles—ain't no one got time for that shit. Give her a hydro-wrench, diagnostic kit, a few spare power couplers, and she'd be happy for life, tinkering with her beloved friends—her real children.

But now something threatened her child, and she was about to go mother-bear on their asses.

"Have you locked out bridge control yet?" said the burly marine. The assault rifle he held, aimed idly down at the floor, looked far more interesting than anything he was saying, so she addressed her reply to the gun itself.

"Yep. They're as stuck as stripped machine bolts."

The marine nodded, and whispered something into his

headset. While he was distracted she keyed in the rest of the modulation sequence into the power plant's cycle, struggling to remember the Morse code. Given the events of the recents weeks, it *should* be something the bridge crew would recognize. Maybe. Humans could be forgetful, though. Not like her machines.

"What are you doing?" said the gun. Or rather, its owner. But so much easier to converse with the machine. The beautiful, deadly machine.

"Just making sure the engines don't explode while the bridge crew is locked out," she glared down at the gun, imagining a rigid mechanical mouth where the magazine joined up with it. The trigger guard was like a tiny eye, with the trigger itself a raised eyebrow, making the rifle look surprised, especially with the marine's finger stuck squarely through its eye socket.

"Well hurry it up, then get back in there with the rest of the engineering crew," said the gun's meat sack, waving over to her office off to the side of the engineering bay where her people were locked up.

"Patience, dearie, don't rush an old lady. You might get more than you bargained for," she mumbled at the gun, finishing the code sequence and setting it to auto-repeat.

She overheard him whisper again into his comm headset. "Engines secured. Working to clear path to shuttle bay." Good thing he thought she was a deaf invalid. One last set of adjustments to the morse signal….

There. She turned toward the gun, looking down to address it. "Will that be everything, Mr. Firearm?"

"No. I want you to lock out all the doors leading to the

hallway outside the shuttle bay, except for the one leading from sickbay and engineering."

She shrugged down at the gun. "I assume you want me to release the locks and clamps on one of the shuttles, too?"

The marine snapped his finger, and waved a hand down in front of her eyes. "Hey. Eyes up here. Stop that, it's creeping me out."

She kept her gaze steady on the rifle's trigger guard, staring it down, eye to eye. Damned if she would be the one to blink first. "I'm so sorry to hear that. You should really think about getting your owner some counseling. Seems he's intimidated by the granny." She gave the trigger guard a small wink. A little joke between friends.

The marine, clearly exasperated, shook his head. "Just ... just get the hallways locked out. Now."

She turned back to the engineering command console and began entering commands, the corporal watching her every finger tap very, very closely. "You know, dearie, I've shit bigger things than that owner of yours...." She needed to turn that exasperation into something more ... potent.

"*What* did you say?" Out of the corner of her eye she saw that the marine's face was going red.

She finally flashed her eyes up to meet him, momentarily. "Not talking to you. Butt out." She turned back to stare the trigger guard in the eye. "If it might help him, I know a doc who specializes in *low T*, if you catch my meaning."

Her fingers worked independently of her mouth, and out of the corner of her eye she saw that the marine's eyes had drifted from the console to her. And they looked angry.

"What ... what did you say?" he repeated.

Her fingers worked. Her mouth worked too. "Just saying, dearie," she said, addressing the gun. "If your owner really wants some help, the doc is fantastic. Low T is an epidemic these days, they say. Some young men have taken to waving around fine upstanding rigid boom sticks like you to compensate for the flaccid stick down under, if you catch my meaning." She gave the trigger guard another knowing wink.

"Shut your mouth and work."

Her fingers worked. And her peripheral vision told her that the marine's jaw was clenching, his brow furrowing, his eyes squinting. His mind most likely weighing the prospect of how good it would feel to knock an old lady upside the head, versus calming down and completing his mission. Hmm … looks like he needs a bit more encouragement.

"I was friends with a big boom stick like you, once." Her fingers worked. Her mouth worked too. "I rode him. Oh, man did I ride him. His equipment was … finely crafted. Expertly engineered, if you catch my meaning." She winked at the trigger guard again. "Not like," she nodded upward, "*you* know. I know, I know, you'd rather be held by a big, strong man and not a flaccid boy—"

Boom. That got him. He reached out and firmly grabbed her face in one of his massive hands, wrenching it up to stare her down. And in that moment, she made her critical move. Rather, her fingers did. The commands were entered in, even as the spittle accompanying his threat sprayed her cheek. "I … said … shut … your … mouth … bitch."

One last tap of her finger. Done. His eyes still locked on her, she nodded quickly. "Fine. You're a big strong man. I cower. Please oh please don't hurt me."

He glared at her, but released his grip. "Finish. Now." He jabbed a finger at the console, and she bent back over to complete the sequence he'd demanded.

"Almost there…." A few more taps, and he scrutinized the screen to verify. "Done. All doors locked out, with manual overrides remotely disengaged. All except for the hallway leading from sickbay and engineering."

"Good." He traced a finger along the screen, nodding in confirmation that she'd done as he commanded—which of course she had. No sense in pissing off a kid with a gun, after all. He tapped his headset and whispered into it again. "We're ready down here," he said.

She smiled. *More ready than you know, dickwad.* She glanced at the trigger guard, its eyebrow still looking surprised at the finger jammed through the eye. "You have a nice trip now, dearie. Don't forget to call."

CHAPTER TWENTY-SEVEN

Orbit over Mao Prime
ISS Independence
Deck 12, Hallway B

Proctor walked slowly, carefully down the hall, mindful of the assault rifle aimed at her back, her mind racing to figure out a plan. Clearly, there was some element within IDF that had enough reach and influence to convince a handful of her marines to, in effect, stage a mutiny.

There was only one answer. Admiral Mullins. Probably with the backing of Fleet Admiral Oppenheimer. Without tacit approval at the highest levels, the marines probably wouldn't be risking their lives or careers in such a brazen move. She'd never, ever, known a marine to perform his duty dishonorably, so they simply must be loyal to what they considered a higher authority, which, technically, Oppenheimer was. And Oppenheimer, with his toady, the late Commander Yarbrough—god rest his traitorous soul—had probably staffed the

Independence with loyal people before she even arrived to take command.

"Faster please, Admiral," said one of the marines, with a nudge of the rifle to her back. Well shit, at least the kid was polite. Marines always were, even when they were about to kill you.

Except these simply couldn't be marines. Marines were loyal. To think they could participate in a mutiny was ... almost unthinkable. Maybe they had stolen uniforms? And guns? And ID's? And somehow fooled their commander and the biometric identification system? Shit. If they weren't marines, the conspiracy ran deep. Hell, it ran deep even if they *were* marines.

She exaggerated her limp. "Working on it, Corporal. Still nursing the injury from the *last* assassination attempt, mind you. Give an old lady time to heal before you try taking her out again."

Another nudge with the rifle. "We're not here to kill you, Admiral. Just to take you to a ... safer location. For your own protection."

"Right," she said. "And our passenger too? Sounds a little too coincidental to me." She didn't need to look behind her to know that the other marine was ushering Fiona Liu along the hallway behind them. Though what the marines knew about her background ... and training ... Proctor wasn't sure.

"That's enough talking, Admiral."

They came to the utility stairwell and the marine nudged her down. Apparently taking the elevator lift was too much of a risk for them, which meant that they hadn't locked down the entire ship.

Which meant that she could count on her people to attempt a rescue.

She kept her senses engaged on every detail around her—almost effortlessly, given the amount of adrenaline pumping through her blood—looking for the opportunity, for any sign that a rescue was underway.

But as they progressed down the stairs, through the next hallway—the shuttle bay was just one more stairwell away—she knew she couldn't rely on someone else for a rescue. She needed to do something *now*, or she'd soon be at the mercy of Mullins. And given his recent megalomania, she wasn't entirely sure he wouldn't just airlock her, and write off the incident as a horrible wartime accident.

She could easily duck into the enlisted mess up ahead. Swing around the corner, yank the assault rifle out of her marine's hands as he advanced around the corner to follow her.

Stupid. She should know better. The marines were far better trained than to be taken in by some amateur attempt like that.

They passed the enlisted mess, and Proctor fought the urge to dash towards the controls to open the doors….

The doors which were closed. The enlisted mess's doors were never closed. They must have been closed remotely, either from the bridge or engineering—the only two places on the ship with remote control to any other part of the ship. Which had the renegade marines taken? Both? Unlikely. The bridge was too well guarded.

Which meant that whoever was controlling things remotely was doing it from engineering, and the only one with authority to do that, as far as she knew, was Rayna.

And if she knew Rayna, the other woman had done *something* to sabotage the enemy's plans. She'd designed the ship, after all, and if there was anything Rayna liked, it was adding in extra features to common systems. Gravity deck plates that massaged your feet. Comm speakers that automatically played ocean sounds tuned to your brain's delta waves when you were trying to sleep. Emergency atmospheric force shields that glowed in rainbow colors instead of the customary blue—a completely unnecessary feature, but Rayna did love rainbows, after all.

Which meant that in the next few seconds, before they entered the shuttle bay, *anything* could happen. All she needed was time.

Her ankle twinged as they turned the final corner to the shuttle bay. Her ankle. Hmm ... crude, but effective. With a cry, she collapsed on the ground, reaching down for her foot.

"Really?" said the marine. He looked vaguely disappointed. "That's sloppy, Admiral."

She rubbed her foot. "It just sprained again, asshole." She glared up at him, trying to make it look convincing. It hurt, of course, but a sprain would have hurt far worse.

"Get up." The assault rifle swung towards her.

She got up on her knees, and attempted to put some weight on the foot. With effort, she intentionally made her leg shake, then collapsed on her knee again from the mostly imaginary pain. "I'm ... sorry. I can't. It's bad." She bit her fist, imitating what she might look like if the sprain was as bad as she was pretending it was. It *was* sprained, after all, but the sprain was a few weeks old. All she had to do was remember what it felt like.

And hope that whatever Rayna had cooked up happened soon.

CHAPTER TWENTY-EIGHT

Orbit over Mao Prime
ISS Independence
Bridge

Volz pointed at the two marines. "Is there any chatter on your comm lines?"

One of them shook his head. "I've been monitoring all the channels we usually use. One of them is active, but scrambled. They're using an encryption protocol our comm devices can't decode."

"Qwerty, can you do anything with it?"

The comm officer motioned for the marine, and the soldier rushed over to the comms station, handing the headset off to Lieutenant Qwerty, who inserted one of the earpieces in and started fiddling with the controls.

"Standard quantum encryption. Designed to be unbreakable, unless you have one of the devices encoded with the key."

Volz put his head in a hand. After a few seconds, he looked up. Qwerty was still fiddling with the headset. "Lieutenant? Is it unbreakable, or not?"

"Well, yes and no. Yes, it's designed to be unbreakable."

Volz let out a huff of air. "And the no?"

"*No*, as in, *no one* has ever designed a code I can't break." He looked up with a weak smile. "That is, given enough time…."

"You've got minutes, Lieutenant. Or less."

He nodded and reached down to his station to remotely connect the headset to the console's computer. "I'm locked out of ship comms, but I can use this in tandem with the computer controls I've still got to tap into the signal and, if not decode it then at least figure out how many receivers are tapped into the signal itself."

Volz nodded, and turned back to the marines guarding the doors. "How many soldiers on board? Around forty?" He looked down at the ranking marine's insignia and name patch. Colonel Cooper.

"I've got thirty, sir."

"How many of those do you trust?"

The soldier's eyes narrowed. "I trust all my men, Captain."

"Yes, yes, but how many of these are *your* men? Apparently not all of them."

Colonel Cooper glowered at him. "Apparently."

"Got it," said Qwerty.

"You've cracked the code?"

"No, I've pinpointed how many are tapped into the encoded signal. Looks like there's only six. Two in engineering, two in the shuttle bay, and two are in hallway B deck seven.

Looks like they're en route to the shuttle bay."

"Thirty," said Volz, turning back to Colonel Cooper. "So, counting the two here on the bridge, you've got twenty-two other trustworthy soldiers on board. Where the hell are they all?"

Cooper motioned towards Qwerty. "He should be able to track them all through their comm handsets, assuming they're all carrying them, if he taps into the standard channel."

Qwerty was already on it, and seconds later looked up. "Half are in the enlisted quarters, and the other half looked like they're locked in the ground combat trainin' simulator."

Cooper nodded in confirmation. "Sounds about right, except there should have been more on duty. Whoever's in charge of this op must have sent out orders to the rest without me knowing."

"Looks like we need to review our ship security protocols when this is all over," said Volz, in what he felt was the understatement of the year. "For now, we need to activate the rest of your men. Can we get a signal out to them?"

"Negative, Captain," said Qwerty. "All comms still locked down except for their encoded channel."

"But there's only six of them." He glanced up at Cooper. "You ready to lead a rescue assault?"

The marine looked like he was more than ready to reassert his authority over his men and get control of a situation that had spiraled away from him. "Absolutely, sir." He hefted his assault rifle.

Volz stood up, reaching a hand towards Cooper. "Sidearm. I'm coming with you."

Lieutenant Whitehorse and Commander Mumford both

protested simultaneously. He knew exactly what they would say. And under normal circumstances he'd agree with them—it didn't make sense for a ship's captain to go do the dirty work, especially if it involved live fire.

"Save it. It's the admiral—I'm going. See if you can't get ship controls back while we're gone, and do everything you can to lock down the shuttle bay. Nothing leaves this ship!"

And with a nod, the other marine manually unlocked the doors, and the three of them marched out towards deck seven.

"Captain, wait," called Lieutenant Qwerty.

Volz turned back. "Yeah?"

"They've locked down all the hallways on decks six through nine. The only ones that are open are the ones leading from engineering and sickbay on deck six to the shuttle bay on deck nine."

Volz shrugged, and continued down the hall to the stairwell to deck six. "Good, that narrows it down for us. Let's go save the girl, Cooper."

CHAPTER TWENTY-NINE

Orbit over Mao Prime
ISS Independence
Deck 12, Hallway B

Rayna, where the hell are you?

Proctor rubbed her ankle—only partially acting—and tried to make herself as heavy as possible for the marine who was now reaching down to drag her to her feet.

That's when the other marine yelled. The crack of the assault rifle in close quarters nearly deafened her. Before she knew what was happening, her mind automatically went to Rayna. What had she concocted?

Another crack, and the hand dragging her to her feet went limp. As did the marine the hand was attached to. He collapsed onto Proctor, forcing her to the ground.

Blood spread over her abdomen and legs, and she felt the color drain from her face. So much blood. Where had she been hit? How was she still conscious with that much blood loss?

It took her several confused seconds before she figured out that the blood wasn't hers. It belonged to the dead marine on top of her. It poured from the side of his head. With a grunt she pushed him aside and looked up.

Fiona Liu was there with Ballsy's son, Zivic—they stood over her, a triumphant look on their faces. Liu offered a hand. Proctor used it to heft herself to her feet.

"Nice distraction," said Liu. "And I had some help." A nod towards the pilot.

"I was in sickbay when they attacked," said Zivic. "Followed you out and looked for an opening. Nice job, ma'am."

"Sloppy, but looks like it was enough for you two." She looked down at the two dead marines. "Remind me not to get on your bad side, Liu." The other man's blood was bright on her white uniform, and she fought the urge to wretch. The marine's life was gone, needlessly. He thought he was doing his duty. He probably was—likely under the orders of Mullins or Oppenheimer or … someone. Marines didn't just take matters into their own hands and start shooting shit. Mutiny for a marine was well nigh unthinkable. She grunted back into a kneeling position, and gently closed the dead soldier's eyes.

But there was no time to mourn those lost under her command. Two more. No, three—she'd almost forgotten Doc Patel. Mourn later, Shelby. Mourn later. She got back on her feet and sized Liu up.

"Once an IDF covert agent, always an IDF covert agent," Liu said with a dark grin. She was bleeding from her nose where the marine must have caught her with an elbow, but she sniffed it away. "Come on. There's probably a lot more of them. We're exposed here in the hallway."

"The ship has twenty-eight other marines, I believe," said Zivic.

Liu shook her head. "These weren't marines. I recognize them from my intel days. They're IDF Intel. Or former intel, at least."

"Then how come they didn't recognize you?" said Proctor.

Liu scowled, and indicated her ruined face and hairless scalp.

Zivic shrugged. "They probably would have handcuffed you had they known who you were." He turned to Proctor, thumbing at Liu. "Wait, who is this again?"

As if in answer, a barrage of gunfire erupted down the hall. Liu slammed against Proctor, pushing them both into the wall. She dragged her, still pressed against the wall, down the hallway and around the last corner before the hall that led to the shuttle bay. Zivic brought up the rear, shouldering one of the dead marines' assault rifles.

"They're coming from engineering," said Liu, between a few rounds she squeezed off around the corner.

"How many?"

"No idea. But they've got us hemmed in between them and the shuttle bay, where there's likely more of them."

Another volley of rounds shredded the wall panel nearby, and Proctor hoped it wasn't a wall covering the exterior hull. She'd always advocated for limiting live ammunition aboard IDF cruisers as a precautionary measure against something accidentally going off and puncturing the hull from the inside out. But, given that IDF was a war fleet, and war fleets called for marines and big guns, her generals always outvoted her.

Sensibly, she admitted, but still the thought of assault rifles onboard space ships in the middle of the deadly vacuum never sat well with her.

Liu pointed at the bay doors at the end of the hallway. "Shuttle bay," she shouted over the gunfire.

"That's where they wanted to take us!"

"Exactly. Now it's the last place they expect us to go!" And without waiting for an answer Liu was pushing her down the hallway again, and before she knew it Proctor was facing the door controls. They were locked, but not secured like all the other doors they'd passed. Except ... something was odd about the control panel.

It was configured ... oddly. In addition to the door status and the keypad where she could enter the usual unlock code, there was an additional readout. Pressure and oxygen levels in the shuttle bay. Those shouldn't be there.

More gunfire erupted down the hallway. Zivic crouched behind the corner and answered them with fire of his own. "It's now or never, Admiral!" shouted Liu in her ear.

She was about to enter the door unlock code, but couldn't take her eyes off the environmental readouts on the door panel. Environmental readout ... and controls. *Holy shit, Rayna, you're a godsend.*

With a few quick taps and a confirmation command code, she vented the shuttle bay.

"What are you doing?" shouted Liu again.

"Hold them off for about thirty seconds," said Proctor. She watched the clock readout on the panel. Ten seconds at vacuum. How long before the average person passed out from exposure to vacuum? She couldn't remember. Best to be on the safe side. Forty-five seconds, tops.

The seconds ticked away, almost in response to the regular stutter of assault rifle fire coming from down the hallway. Liu had crouched down behind a door frame opposite Zivic and was returning fire with the fallen marine's weapon she'd grabbed.

Twenty seconds. Twenty-one. Twenty-two.

Rat-a-tat-a-tat. One round struck the wall just inches from her head. These guys were shooting to kill at this point.

Twenty-six. Twenty-seven.

She crouched down on the other side of the hallway, partially behind the frame of another door. It wasn't much cover, but better than nothing.

Even though she couldn't see the clock anymore, the countdown continued in her head unabated. Thirty. Thirty-one.

A round caught her in the arm, knocking her backward. She looked down at it. Red bloomed across her sleeve, mixing with the blood from the dead marine. *Damn. That really should hurt a lot more than it does.*

She was in shock. She recognized the symptoms, almost from a cold, clinical, distant viewpoint, like she was floating above her body. But the sensation of another round whizzing past her ear brought her back to the present.

Liu was shouting something at her, but she couldn't hear. Proctor leapt back across the hallway to the door controls. Forty-six seconds. That should do. With a few taps she sealed the shuttle bay and released the atmospheric valves. The pressure rose quickly. When it was nearly normal she unlocked the doors. They groaned open, and she nearly collapsed through them.

Someone was dragging her. Zivic? Liu? Distantly, she heard the doors close again. Out of the corner of her eye she saw two prone marines nearby, passed out, or dead—their faces were nearly blue and traces of blood tinged their noses and eyes from the decompression. Her handiwork, she supposed. So Rayna's little ploy had worked.

Distantly, she could hear more shooting. Liu must have managed to close the doors, but from the sounds of it, they needed Rayna to come through with another ploy.

No time. Unconsciousness was calling her. And even as she tried to blink herself awake, she started dreaming.

CHAPTER THIRTY

"Will she be ok, dad?"

Her father was a horrible actor, and she knew what it meant when he tried—and failed—to put on a brave face. "I'm sure she'll be fine. Doc Higgins is the best."

His act didn't convince her. "But, I learned in school that cancer was a thing of the past. People used to die of cancer. Used to. Not anymore, not in the goddamn twenty-seventh century!"

Her father rubbed her shoulders reassuringly. A pair of nurses walked past them in the hallway, pausing their conversation as they looked at Shelby, pity in their eyes. "Watch your language," he said, and then sighed. "Shell, people still get cancer. And we treat it, and usually cure it. But we can't cure everything. Bodies are varied, complex things. They're almost like chaotic systems—change one little thing over here, and bam, over there you get catastrophe a few years later…."

Her father the scientist had reverted to his science-speak. Which meant he was trying to cope, which meant the news was bad. "They can operate, right? Just cut it out and kill the cells that get left behind?"

He nodded reassuringly. "That's the plan. Doc Higgins is confident. But, like he said, this tumor was a one in a million shot. It's ... just right in the wrong place, with the wrong type of cells, and at the wrong time—her last routine checkup didn't pick this up, and it should have, so it's had a year to grow unchecked. It's just, everything bad happening all at the same time. One in a million."

The door to Carla's room opened and her mother came out. As she shut the door, Shelby caught a glimpse of her sister in the hospital bed, her head back on the pillows, her face pale, her eyes closed.

"She's calm now. And resting," her mom said.

"Good. She'll need her energy for post-surgery recovery. Doc says the next few weeks are critical."

Her mother turned to Shelby and gathered her up in her arms. "My big girl. This must be so scary for you."

Shelby said nothing, but allowed herself to be smothered with love. She was too angry for tears. Angry at the universe, angry at God for letting this happen. Why Carla? She was just a kid—twelve was still a kid, right? Her mother picked up on the feelings welling up inside her. "Shelby, we need to be strong. For Carla." She glanced down at Shelby's neck, where her rosary would normally be, if it weren't in her pocket. "Are you saying your prayers?"

"Yes," she mumbled.

"Good. With the Lord's help, I know Carla will be just fine. His grace can cover all, my sweet girl. Just put your trust in him."

Ugh. She was preaching again.

But at this point, God was all she had. With a one-in-a-million tumor, the only answer was the one-in-a-million chance that God actually existed and could wave his magic cross-shaped wand and heal Car.

"I do, momma. I'll just ... pray more. I'll pray like my life depended on it."

Because it did. If she lost Car, if she lost her best friend, she didn't know how she'd go on.

CHAPTER THIRTY-ONE

Orbit over Mao Prime
ISS Independence
Deck 11, Hallway A

Colonel Cooper peered around the corner, pointed two fingers towards Volz and then towards the hallway beyond, which Volz interpreted to mean that the path was clear and he should advance.

They were nearly to the locked-off section of the ship, and Volz was still wondering what he was going to do to get through when his handset started vibrating in his pocket. Still advancing down the hallway, he fished it out, glancing down at the screen once he'd found cover behind a door frame.

It was Rayna, in engineering. "I hope you have good news," he said after tapping the comm line open.

"Only the best for you, dearie. Listen. I'm opening the section ahead of you back up, but only from hallway C leading to the shuttle bay. The last two boys with boom sticks are holed up there. Seems Shelby has locked them out of the shuttle bay, but they're trying to punch through."

Volz nodded, and waved Cooper toward the door ahead. Just one more hallway and they'd be in the thick of the action. He heard the pounding of gunfire ahead. "Ok, we'll advance and take them out."

"Wait a sec, dearie." He heard her mutter something under her breath he couldn't quite make out.

They'd advanced to the final door between them and the rogue marines, and Cooper was giving him some hand signals he wasn't quite familiar with. "Rayna, it's now or never. What's up?"

"Just a little something to help you boys out. Hold on...."

The gunfire from beyond the door made Volz's chest pound with every shot. And he knew that with every shot, they were one dice-roll closer to losing Proctor. "NOW, RAYNA!"

He felt the deck shake—or rather, he felt himself waver on his feet. "What the hell...?"

"There. Have fun, boys. Just don't go too far into the hallway or you'll float away."

The gravity deck plates. That would explain why he'd wavered for a moment, almost losing his balance. There was no gravity on the other side of that door. He glanced at Cooper, who was steadying himself and looking down towards the deck plates—he seemed to understand what Rayna had done. Their eyes met, and they nodded. Cooper fingered the door control to open.

They leaned back behind the doors sleeves and peered into the hallway beyond. The gunfire had stopped. Two marines were floating, flailing, through the air. One bounced off the wall, struggling to grasp at any protrusion he could find, and failing, he sailed off, drifting towards the ceiling.

"Release your weapons and push them towards us, or you're dead. NOW!" Cooper shouted through the doorway.

One of the marines twisted around, assault rifle still in hands. Once he caught glimpse of Volz and Cooper, feet planted firmly on the floor and safely sheltered behind the door sleeves, his eyes widened: he knew his situation was hopeless. He pushed the rifle away, and it sailed towards the door. As it approached the threshold it began slowly falling, until it clattered to the floor just shy of Cooper's boots.

"You too, Private," shouted the Colonel.

The soldier, clinging precariously to a lighting panel on the ceiling, reluctantly flung his rifle towards them.

"Sidearms too," said Cooper. They both reached slowly into their vests and pulled their handguns out, which soon joined the rifles beyond the threshold.

Before Volz or Cooper could order him otherwise, one of the soldiers tapped his headset. "Abort. I repeat, abort."

"Another word and you're both dead! Send the headsets over," shouted Cooper, training his rifle on the two floating marines.

They looked at each other, and reluctantly, removed the headsets and flung them towards the door, where they clattered to the floor once they hit gravity.

Volz tapped his handset. "Grannie Rayna, all secure here. Go ahead and turn the gravity back on."

The shuttle bay doors opened. Before the soldiers fell, and before Volz or Cooper could say anything, a figure on the other end of the hallway unloaded her sidearm into the two floating marines with a steady pulse of rounds.

"No! Stand down! Ceasefire!" shouted Volz. But by the time he'd managed to get the words out, it was clear the two marines were dead, as they spun around in the air, blood trailing out of their bodies and splashing out on the walls, floor, and ceiling like a gruesome red pinwheel.

Gravity returned, with further gruesome effect, as the bodies collapsed onto the floor and the floating blood splattered down.

"What the hell are you doing?" roared Volz, his sidearm trained on the woman. He saw Proctor sitting upright on the floor behind her, holding a bloody arm, his son Ethan kneeling next to her with a blood-soaked cloth.

"Those are not marines, Captain Volz," she said.

Cooper spat. "Bullshit. Those were good men you just killed. They had already surrendered and stood down."

She lowered her weapon, set it deliberately on the floor, slowly, but then started walking towards the two dead men. "Wrong. They're IDF Intel, posing as marines. I recognized that one," she said, pointing to the nearest dead man. "And IDF Intel officers never surrender. We were actually all about to die." She reached down and pulled something from the inside the dead marine's vest. She tapped a few buttons, then tossed it over to Cooper, who caught it one-handed.

He examined it, wide-eyed, and showed it to Volz. "Antipersonnel explosive. She stopped the timer." He pointed down at the other soldier. "He have one too?"

She rummaged through his pockets, and pulled out another explosive. A few quick taps deactivated it. "Things were about to get fairly kinetic around here in twenty seconds."

She tossed the explosive over to Volz, who looked down at the timer, which was stopped at nineteen.

"What the hell is going on around here?" Volz yelled, advancing on the woman they'd picked up from the cargo freighter. "Who are you? I want some answers!"

She nodded. "You'll get some. But first, you need to move the ship. Now."

The hairs on his neck tingled—that feeling he always got in his fighter when he knew another bogey was targeting him. "Why?"

"These guys aren't lone wolves. They were going to take the admiral off the *Independence* in a shuttle."

Volz waved out towards the exterior hull in the shuttle bay. "There're no ships out there. We're at high alert and sensor sweeps are constantly tracking everything around us. Besides the Chinese fleet still patrolling Mao Prime's atmosphere, there isn't a ship around for lightyears. Just where do you think they were going to take her?"

She eyed him, questioningly, but it looked like she already knew the answer. "Move the ship. Mullins is out there."

"How? I'm telling you there's no other ship out there."

"There is. Move the ship." Her eyes were cold, her voice insistent. He didn't believe her, but ... he couldn't afford the cost if he was wrong. He looked to Proctor for guidance, but her eyes were glazed over in a daze—she'd probably lost too much blood and was in shock.

Volz grit his teeth, but tapped his handset. "Ensign Riisa, initiate the t-jump to the coordinates we discussed. Immediately."

The momentary pulse washed over him, and he knew

they'd made the jump.

"How far did we go?" the woman asked.

Volz stepped towards her. "You're not the one asking questions around here—"

"Ballsy, just tell her," Proctor ordered weakly from the floor. "And then get me to sickbay."

"A few light-seconds. Close enough to still see what's going on at Mao Prime."

The woman shook her head. "No. Farther. If we can see Mao Prime then he can still see us."

"They were going to take her to Mao Prime?" said Volz.

"Doubtful. No idea what Mullins was planning. But we *need* to be farther away."

"How do you know Mullins is on Mao Prime?"

"I don't."

Volz was about to lose it. "Then what the hell are we running from?"

"Because Mullins is *here*, somewhere, and we can't see him. And yet somehow he managed to get a signal to these Intel assets to execute the big op. Didn't you just detect a tightly-focused meta-space transmission before this all went down? Have you figured out where it came from yet? I doubt it."

He had no response to that, and so Volz grabbed Zivic and helped Proctor to her feet and started walking her back towards the bloody hallway. She leaned heavily on their arms—sickbay seemed so far away. "San Martin," said Proctor. "Admiral Tigre. Miguel. I can trust him."

Volz considered, then nodded. "Ensign Riisa," he said.

"Yes, Captain?" came her voice through his handset.

"Get us to San Martin."

DEFIANCE

CHAPTER THIRTY-TWO

Freighter Angry Betty

Keen woke up with a start. He'd expected to nap for several hours, if not the entire day. To his surprise, the nav computer had sounded the alarm indicating they'd arrived at their final destination.

He brought up the external video feed, hoping against hope that the stranger hadn't sent him to the middle of deep space. That would have put a huge damper on his plans for his dream house.

The image snapped into place. It was Earth.

Earth.

"What the hell? I asked that bastard if we were going to Earth, and he said *farther*. Dipshit."

Oh well. Earth was as good a place as any. He could unload the cargo, land at New Valhalla Station, grab a bite to eat, screw a hooker, down a few bottles, and get a good night's sleep before getting the *Angry Betty* back to Britannia. And then

… cash.
   "Time to get to work," he said to himself.

CHAPTER THIRTY-THREE

Orbit over Earth
Interstellar One

It was a secret he never told anyone. After all, he was the president of United Earth. Over a hundred billion people looked up to him as their fearless leader. Even the ones who didn't vote for him tended to tacitly admit that he was a decent, strong guy. The alpha dog. The head honcho. The unflappable pitbull who never gave up and had balls the size of dinner plates.

But … he hated interstellar travel. Flying in atmosphere? No problem. Even orbital flight was fine. President Quimby could easily look out the window and see the Earth turn slowly below. Or Britannia, or whatever planet he was orbiting. As long as he was orbiting something, he was ok.

But right now, he was not in orbit. Instead, he was en route to Bolivar. The planetary corporate headquarters of Shovik-Orion, and the home base of that traitor, Admiral Mullins, who Quimby still had to play nice with. But before he could get there, he had to surf across an endless ocean of nothingness. Emptiness. A void. An abyss. And it unnerved the hell out of him.

But damned if he was going to let anyone know. "How many more q-jumps left, Kalvin?"

His body man murmured something into the tiny microphone fixed to his lapel, and then replied, "Just ten, sir."

Dammit. He peered out the window again of *Interstellar One*, an aging craft at nearly thirty years old. It was first put into service under the legendary President Avery, after the old one was destroyed by saboteurs among her own staff. That made it ancient, seeing as the old woman herself was nearing one hundred and in a retirement home somewhere warm and tropical.

Oppenheimer promised him the new *Interstellar One* was almost ready. It was equipped with the new ultra-classified t-jump drive that would cut his travel time down to just one or two jumps per trip. That would be glorious. But for now, it was the usual hundred or two hundred plodding q-jumps, a quarter of a lightyear at a time. Plowing their way through the cold, empty deep. He shuddered, and turned away from the window.

Several hours later, and after the welcome distraction of a game of cards with Kalvin Quinkert, Mick Bird, and a few aides, they arrived. Bolivar. The center of all his recent problems—at least, the problems that didn't involve genocidal aliens. *Those* they could handle. They'd had a halfway-decent track record of fending off aliens over the past hundred years. It usually took a few billion people dying to get there, but hey, they got there. Twice.

But rogue admirals in charge of multi-world corporations nearly as powerful as United Earth itself? This was an emergency that could potentially dwarf any Swarm or Russian or Chinese or Caliphate or pirate slaver threat. When the danger came from within, the risk was always highest.

Fortunately, United Earth had elected President Frederick fucking Quimby the Third. He was uniquely suited to negotiating and dealing with assholes, being one himself.

"Is my shuttle ready?"

Kalvin nodded. "Yes, sir. They're waiting for you."

With a heavy sigh, Quimby stood up from the table, regarding with pleasure the pile of chips in front of him. "I'm sorry to bleed you all dry and then run, gentlemen, but I've got work to do. Tyrants to manage, civilizations to save. Yada yada." The other men chuckled obligingly. Quinkert and Bird stood, still chuckling, and followed him out to the hallway and down to the shuttle bay, secret service leading the way and following behind. *Dammit, can't they give me some breathing room even on my own ship?*

The klaxons went off even as the shuttle bay doors opened. At the first sound of the alarms, the closest two agents grabbed him by the arms and pushed him into the small office of the shuttle bay chief and closed the door.

"What the *hell* is going on?"

One of the agents shook his head. "Unknown, sir. This is just protocol. We get you into a vacuum-safe, defendable room when any shipboard emergency alarms sound. Then we reassess and get you to a more secure location."

Quimby waved his arms. "It's fucking *Interstellar One*! What kind of threat do you think is on my own ship?"

Before they could answer, the comm crackled to life in the small office. "Sir, this is the bridge. We're being painted by targeting lasers from an unknown source. We're q-jumping out of here as soon as the calls are finished."

"What do you mean, an unknown source? Can't you just track the path of the targeting laser?" Quimby wanted to pat himself on the back for his technical knowledge. He'd made it a point to study up on weapons technology and tactics in the evenings after the election when everyone thought he was sleeping.

"Usually, sir, yes. But these lasers appear to be coming from … nothing. From empty space."

For the barest moment, his fear of the dead void of space surged within him, before his rational brain reasserted itself. "Set up a broadcast. Tell them President Quimby is here to speak with Admiral Mullins. Tell them I'm—"

"Sir, update … we're receiving an encoded hail for you. It's coming straight from the source of those targeting lasers, which, by the way, have shut off."

Interesting.

"Doesn't matter. We're still getting him out of here," said the lead secret service agent over the line. "The threat is still active. We'll send an advance ship next time and try to sort things out before—"

"Hang on, Mr. Carter, I'm not going anywhere. I'm going to listen to this message first before we decide anything."

"But *sir*—" began Carter.

"No 'buts.' I'm the president. We do what I want. Go win your own election if you disagree. Patch that message through, Captain."

It was a video signal, and the viewscreen in the small office flickered to life. And on the screen appeared his adversary. Admiral Mullins. Smiling. "President Quimby. I'm truly honored that you would pay me a visit here. I'm sorry for the targeting lasers. Automatic response by my tactical folks. I've instructed them to stand down. They're a little jumpy given the new alien threat."

Quimby forced a presidential, authoritative expression onto his face and boomed out, "Where are you transmitting from, Mullins? It looks like you're coming from empty space."

"From my ship. In fact, I'd love to have you aboard and show you around, seeing how you are the commander in chief, after all. This is technically *your* ship." Mullins smiled, but it was a smile eerily devoid of any real warmth. There was a sharpness behind those eyes, and Quimby knew the man was talking out of his ass. Mullins didn't consider Quimby his commander any more than a whore considers the john her faithful husband.

Agent Carter, out of view of the camera, was waving at him, shaking his head *no*, making it quite clear what the secret service detail thought about him going over to Mullins's ship. Which effectively made his decision for him.

"Admiral Mullins, I'd be delighted to meet you aboard your ship. Besides, I think an inspection tour is warranted, seeing how we're spending a shitload on the military budget."

Mullins smiled even more broadly. Quimby had calibrated his words carefully, and mentioning the bloated military budget —the majority of which went to Shovik-Orion—would signal that he knew what power dynamics were at play here, but that he didn't fear the other man enough to refuse the invitation.

He had balls, after all. Gotta demonstrate to the upstart admiral that his presidential balls were bigger. Boulders. Damn Rocky Mountains. In the alpha dog world, there were alphas, and betas. And he would be damned if someone else was going to out-alpha him.

"Excellent, Mr. President. I await your arrival. And I look forward to discussing the new strategic situation of the alien threat. I have some intelligence you should probably see."

Quimby raised an eyebrow. "*You* have intel? I thought IDF Intel was the only—"

"Yes, IDF Intel is the main intelligence gathering organization within IDF, but we have a branch here on Bolivar that I have direct stewardship over. Plus, I'm privy to a few other details and have put the pieces together to form a picture that … is rather unsettling." He seemed to glance around Quimby's office. "Are you alone?"

"Just my body man and secret service." Quimby glanced to his side and with a little nudge of his chin he told them both to leave. "They're gone now."

Mullins started slowly, as if there were a huge burden he were offloading from his shoulders. "Mr. President, I have reason to suspect that the Swarm threat never truly left us. I think they are not only still here, but have agents in place at the highest levels of our government."

"Oh? You think I'm a Swarm agent?" Quimby leaned back in his seat and clasped his hands behind his head. "Or just my veep, like thirty years ago with Vice President Isaacson getting hoodwinked by the Swarm-controlled Russian Ambassador?"

"Oh no, not you or anyone on your staff."

"Then who?"

"Who else in the government or IDF is desperately trying to make contact with the other two Swarm controlled races that we haven't yet encountered? Under the guise of handling a preemptive threat? Who else seems bent on starting a war with the Dolmasi and Skiohra? Who else in the highest levels of the military had extensive contact with the main players from the last Swarm war, and therefore was most open to infection by the Swarm virus?"

Oh shit. Quimby's gut churned at the thought.

"You're not suggesting…?"

"I am. You know it's true."

The enormity of the accusation rested heavy between them. Quimby muttered, shook his head, and stood up. "Oppenheimer under control of the Swarm? It can't be. All my military advisors swear that the Swarm is dead. Gone. Forever."

Mullins smiled and tapped his nose. "Let's talk. In person."

CHAPTER THIRTY-FOUR

Orbit over San Martin
ISS Independence
Captain's Ready Room

Proctor massaged her arm above the bullet's entry point—where a bandage now soaked up the residual bleeding. The nurse had managed to patch her up, give her a few antiseptics and pain meds, but that's all Proctor had time for. She had fish to fry. Plots to uncover. Civilizations to save. *Yada yada,* she thought. Where had she heard that before? She shook her head, and was met with a wave of vertigo. Damn, those pills the nurse had given her sure packed a punch.

"Thank God you're all right, Shelby," said Admiral Tigre, his cheek paunches stretching as his face contorted in concern. The large viewscreens on the bridge tended to magnify every blemish, and she cringed to think of how her haggard old-lady face looked on Tigre's screen.

Dammit, she'd just survived a kidnapping-turned-assassination attempt. What the hell was she doing worrying about her face? Focus, Shelby.

"This is twice now, Miguelito. Let's hope the third time's not the charm," she said.

"IDF Intel did this to you? I just can't believe that Oppenheimer would have signed off on something like this. It's just not like him at all."

"War brings out the best and the worst in people, Miguel. And if someone thinks they're acting in the interest of humanity's survival, then there's no limit to what they're capable of. When you think you're on the good side, you're capable of unthinkable evil." She leaned forward in her ready room chair, eyeing Captain Volz who sat off to the side.

They both knew what people in wartime were capable of. Granger had been capable of sacrificing himself—twice—to save civilization. And he'd been *very* capable of sacrificing others too. He hurled IDF ships into the Swarm carriers like they were bricks rather than vehicles carrying thousands of people. *The Bricklayer*—that was the epithet nickname he'd earned for his ghoulish but necessary tactics. On the other hand, UE's vice president at the time, Isaacson, had been quite capable of betraying them all for a few good hookers and some blow.

Miguel stroked his chin. "So you think Oppenheimer was behind it? I can't think of any other way IDF Intel could be involved…."

"I'm not so sure. You're right: this isn't like Christian at all. I just talked to him, and I've been in regular contact with him since this all started a few weeks ago. Since Sangre. Christian Oppenheimer might be an ass-clenched opportunist, but he's no traitor. I think. But I agree, he must be involved one way or another—how else could all these pieces be pulled together? And as for the mastermind behind the whole op? It's got to be Mullins. Who else could it be?"

Tigre smirked. "*President* slash Admiral Mullins. What a piece of work. Who knew? Who could have guessed old Teddy would want his own little personal empire. He's pulled off a veritable coup, that one. Quimby and Oppenheimer don't dare fire him—they can't risk IDF's Shovik-Orion military contracts. And so here we have a rogue IDF admiral in charge of his own planet, with considerable influence on half a dozen others. Including San Martin. It's crazy."

Proctor snapped her fingers at Ensign Babu, calling for a cup of coffee. He bowed ceremoniously in a mock imitation of a servant, and ducked out the door. "He's quite the demagogue, too. He's hijacking half the GPC. I bet Curiel is furious. He's spent a decade building the GPC up into a legitimate opposition party, talking a good talk and using those movie-star looks of his for what he considers a noble cause, and now a blustery, reckless blowhard comes along, throws some money and starships around, and half of Curiel's people start following him. Including, apparently, some of your people at CENTCOM San Martin, Miguel, and … some of mine."

Her implication was clear. If the late Commander Yarbrough, her previous XO on the *Independence*, could be persuaded to mutiny, if that dead squad of IDF Intel operatives posing as marines were convinced to commit treason, then there could be others. She continued, "I just can't believe there would be anyone else on the *Independence* capable of staging a mutiny."

Both Tigre and Volz looked at her with the same expression, even though they couldn't see each other. The expression was one of skeptical bemusement. "Shelby, that's pretty wishful thinking there," said Volz.

Tigre hadn't known Volz was in the room. "Ballsy? Is that you?"

Volz stood up and came around the table, crouching down next to Proctor to fit into the camera's field of view. "I agree, Miguel. We need to start being a little smarter about this. We can't assume anyone around us is trustworthy. At least where the admiral's safety is concerned."

"Absolutely," said Tigre, nodding. "I've been thinking the same thing."

"We need to get her out of the crosshairs, no matter who is doing the aiming."

Proctor cleared her throat. "Gentlemen, I'm touched at the concern for my safety. But whatever you're thinking, I'm not going to just go hide while civilization faces an existential threat, no matter which mutinous—"

"I've got just the thing, Shelby," said Tigre, interrupting her. "Something that will let you stay on offense, yet out of reach of your enemies, whoever they are."

She leaned back in her chair. "I'm listening."

"A ship. I don't want to say more over this channel, but you should consider it."

"No. I'm not leaving the *Independence*—"

"Hear me out, Shelby. Once you see it, you'll understand—"

"I said I'm not leaving the—"

It was Volz that interrupted this time. "Shelby, we can't

risk it anymore. Either we rotate the entire crew off and replace them with people that you and I can personally vouch for—which, let's face it, is just not feasible—or we get you into an environment where we can guarantee your safety."

"But—"

"Shelby," Volz said, his eyes pleading, "I don't know if you realize it, but, you're kind of a big deal. You're irreplaceable. If we lose you, we lose this damn war before it ever really starts. The Dolmasi. Mullins. Oppenheimer—they're all shooting at you. And, once we're through with those distractions, there's still that Golgothic ship you took out by the skin of your teeth, and who knows if there's more of them." He lowered his voice. "And don't forget, *Shelby, they're coming*," he quoted. "Whoever *they* are, we've got to stall for a little time. Give you space to figure this out."

She could tell they weren't going to give up. She'd humor them. Take a look at whatever Miguel was proposing, then summarily turn him down, get back to the *Independence*, and triple her marine guard. Assuming she could trust that the rest of her marines were actual marines and not intel agents with questionable loyalties….

"Fine," she said to Tigre before turning to Volz. "Ballsy, if you wanted your own ship, there were far easier ways of getting rid of me."

He held his hands up. "Oh no you don't. I'm coming with you."

"Like hell. You're staying here with the *Independence*. We need as many pieces on the board that we control as possible." She turned back to the screen. "Ok, Miguel, where do we go?"

He nodded triumphantly. It was clear he thought he'd have

to fight her far more than he did. *You have no idea*, she thought. "Take a shuttle. Bring an engineer you trust, a *very* small handful of crew, plus no more than six pilots and their fighters. They can escort you in."

"Where?"

Tigre smiled. "Just a hundred kilometers off your port bow."

Just a hundred kilometers? Surely the Independence *would have detected....*

And then she finally understood. Her eyes brightened momentarily as she stood up. "There's another one?"

Tigre smiled. "And this one is all yours."

The door opened, revealing Ensign Babu with a steaming cup of coffee. Proctor blazed right past him out the door, leaving the young man standing there with the cup, not quite knowing what to do. "Coffee's off?"

Volz waved Babu forward, reaching for the cup. "Ensign, never stand between an admiral and a shiny new ship."

CHAPTER THIRTY-FIVE

Orbit over San Martin
ISS Independence
Sickbay

Zivic had gone back to check on Ace and Bucket in sickbay when the call went out from Lieutenant Farrell to his squad. They were to report to the fighter bay in one hour, with their bags packed. This was no patrol—this was a long-term deployment.

Ace's midsection was bandaged from where her restraints had dug in during one of her high-g maneuvers that the inertial compensators could not keep up with. She had suffered some internal bleeding, but was otherwise now fine. The doctor was only keeping her as a formality—for observation, to make sure she hadn't suffered a concussion.

Bucket sat on the bed next to hers, with Zivic in a chair between the two beds. "Farrell wants us down there, *stat*," he said with wry sidelong glance at one of the nearby nurses, who, in the time they'd been there, had already said the word *stat* at least ten times. "We gotta convince her to let you go."

"We could just all three get up at once and run. *Stat*," said Bucket, too low for the nurse to hear.

"Or I could go ask the admiral to just order her to release you. *Stat*." Zivic watched as the nurse struggled with a piece of equipment next to another patient worse off than either Ace or Bucket. She looked flustered as she repeatedly tried to get the monitor to turn on, to no avail.

The nurse jabbed a panel on the wall to turn on the comm, but she was a little too frustrated—the plastic casing cracked. "Nurse Cunningham to maintenance. I need someone down here to fix some electronics, stat."

Zivic and Bucket both held up fists to their mouths to keep from laughing.

A voice came through the comm speaker. "Sorry, we're a little swamped down here since the battle."

The nurse threw down a meta-syringe in frustration. Zivic half expected it to shatter, but it just bounced off the floor and clattered away into a corner. "I've got injured down here. I need someone, *stat*. Or else one of them might not make it. Try explaining yourself to the admiral *then*."

Bucket let a snicker slip out, and Ace shot him with a glare. "Stop being an asshole."

He couldn't help himself. "Stat?" Zivic snorted in an abortive attempt to stifle the laughter.

"Are you blind?" said Ace, watching the nurse rush to the other room, marked *Intensive Care*, to attend to another patient that had started crying out. "She just watched Doc Patel get shot in the chest, and she's the only one here. She's already lost two patients today, not counting Patel. Stop being dicks and give her a break."

Bucket finally recovered from his laughing fit and pointed to the intensive care room. "Look, Ace, I'll give Nurse Stat credit for not cracking under pressure, but we've got to get out of here. Farrell's waiting, and will have our asses on a plate if we're not ready to go for whatever mission this is."

"Don't you mean, *heads on a plate*? Or do you mean *kick our asses*? I really feel like you mixed your metaphors there," Bucket said. He poked at one of his bandages on his shoulder.

"Fuck you."

"Well, that is my call sign, after all." He peeled back half the bandage, revealing the now-dried gash on his shoulder. "At least, until Admiral Proctologist banned it."

"Bucket sounds much better anyway," said Zivic, watching the nurse through the window in intensive care, waiting to make his move. If she could just get distracted for half a minute, they could sneak out, get off the ship and on their mission, and ask forgiveness rather than permission. "And Ace sounds much better than … wait, are you even an Ace? How many bogeys have you shot down, anyway?"

Bucket snorted again, this time pointing a thumb at Ace. "You haven't heard how she got her callsign?"

"Shut your face, Bucket—"

He ignored her. "So we're down at Futwick's, back before we had to change the name, and we'd just finished our first training mission on board the *Independence*—this was about two months ago, before Proctor showed up—and the pilots are down there, starting to get wasted. And Ace here isn't drinking. So I say to her, Ace, why aren't you drinking? And she says, blow it out your hole. So I pour her a shot of whiskey, and one for me, and I say, with pleasure, but I like to do my blowing drunk. So she downs the shot, and I shit you not, two minutes later she passes out. After one drink. Batship, meet Ace."

Zivic saw the nurse duck into the office, and he nearly stood up, but she turned around at the last second as another patient started groaning, calling for her. "Ace, huh? Look, let's just get the hell out of here and get on this mission, and maybe you'll have a chance to be a real Ace. Farrell says this mission might involve a bit of shooting...."

Ace cocked her head and asked, almost absentmindedly, "do you think Qwerty's going on this mission?" She fingered a handmade pink thread bracelet on her wrist.

Zivic started to wonder what in the world would make her ask that, and wondered if the bracelet was from her mysterious *girlfriend* when he saw what he was waiting for. Finally. The nurse went into the office and shut the door. Bucket jumped off his bed and grabbed his pants, which lay folded on a nearby chair. "Ok, let's get out. Stat."

The distant look disappeared from her face as Ace pulled out her IV and ripped the blanket off, and the three of them rushed the door. They were gone long before the nurse emerged from the office, but they were only halfway to the pilots' locker room when Farrell's voice came over the comm. "Ace, Bucket, Batship, where the hell are you? We're leaving in twenty."

Bucket tapped a wall monitor that they passed, turning on the comm receiver. "Would you say you want us there, *stat*?"

Zivic batted his hand away from the monitor. "We're almost there, Lieutenant. Batship out," he added, cutting off

Farrell's response. "Come on."

The rest of the squad was waiting for them in the locker room, already suited up. Thomas "Barbie" Adams, the Australian, greeted them with a nod. Vo "Spectrum" Pham was sitting off to the side, fiddling with a game on his datapad. And Farrell himself was seated at the command desk, talking on the comm with the bridge. He watched them come in and pointed to their lockers, indicating that they should suit up. He himself was still in his regular uniform.

"What, is he not coming?" said Zivic.

Spectrum, still playing his game, shook his head. "Negative."

"Negative? You mean, *no*?" said Bucket. He sat on the bench and pulled on his flight suit pant legs.

"That's what I said."

Barbie stood leaning against the bulkhead with his arms folded, patiently waiting for them. "Seems you're going to be the squad leader, Batship. Hold'em's staying here."

That caught Zivic by surprise. "What?"

"Orders from the admiral herself. Wants a small squad accompanying her on some secret mission. Wants you heading it up. Guess she wants one Volz here and one Volz with her."

Zivic scowled. "Name's Zivic, not Volz."

"He's your pops, ain't he?"

"In name only," he said, without thinking. The others laughed.

"You mean, in sperm only," said Bucket.

"Look," he said, exasperated, struggling with his flight suit's collar air seal, "He left when I was five. Mom married my real dad, the one who raised me and took care of me, Mr. Jesús

Zivic, a year later."

"Jesus?" Bucket thumbed towards him, grinning at Barbie. "Guess that's where he gets his messiah complex from."

Zivic frowned. "What the hell is *that* supposed to mean?"

"Nothin'. Just that, you *do* love riding in to the rescue. And making a big show of it."

Ace, finished with her flight suit, punched Bucket in the shoulder. "Lay off. If Batshit didn't have his *messiah complex*, as you put it, I'd be dead. So shut up, get your suit on, and let's go kill some Dolmasi bastards."

Spectrum chimed in, still not looking up from his game. "You mean GPC bastards."

"GPC?" said Zivic and Ace at once.

"Think it's a coincidence that someone managed to get sympathizers on the *Independence* to take a shot at the admiral, and then we're here at the epicenter of GPC activity?" He finally tapped his datapad screen off and tossed it aside. "All signs point to GPC. I think we're about to go mop up the scum, so to speak."

The door opened, and in walked Ensign Babu, Admiral Proctor's personal assistant. "You all ready?" he said.

"Coffee's in the other room, Babu," said Zivic.

He scowled. "Not why I'm here. Finally," he added. "I'm coming too. I've got basic flight training, so I'm grabbing a suit, just in case. Any spares?" He looked questioningly at Farrell.

"In the locker." Farrell paused his muttered conversation with whoever he was talking to on the bridge and nodded towards the corner. "You're not getting in one of my birds unless it's an emergency though, Ensign."

"When is it *not* an emergency these days?" Babu opened the locker and grabbed an extra suit, stuffing it into his bag. "Don't worry, I'm not planning heroics. It's just, with the admiral, I've learned it pays to be prepared. You never know what she's got up her sleeve or what she'll order you to do."

Bucket smirked. "Like, for example, if she wants tea or coffee. One sugar packet or two. Stevia or sucrose. Almond or vanilla. I tell you, it's a wild ride you're on, brother."

Babu scowled. "Up yours, Bucket. I'm gonna be a starship captain someday, and you'll be calling me *sir*, sir."

Bucket's eyebrows shot up an inch. "From personal lapdog slash assistant coffee-getter to starship captain? You're either under the influence or delusional."

Farrell finally terminated his call and pointed to the door. "Ok. Out. Proctor's shuttle's leaving in five. Don't embarrass me, people. The admiral asked for the best. Unfortunately, the best is currently on swing shift in their bunks, so you'll have to do. Get out of here."

They all rushed out the door, Bucket still fiddling with his air seals. Zivic caught Babu by the elbow as they left. "Hey, ignore him. You'll make it. Trust me, Proctor only does this to people she sees potential in."

Babu brightened slightly. "Really?"

"Really. I mean, hey, she asked a fuck-up like me to lead this mission, didn't she?"

Babu looked less-than-convinced as he went out the door, leaving Zivic to wonder if maybe Proctor wasn't a little delusional herself for asking him to head the mission. And then wondering if shooting down one hundred and one GPC fighters would count the same as Ballsy's one hundred Swarm fighters.

"I guess we'll find out," he whispered to himself, and followed the others out the door.

CHAPTER THIRTY-SIX

Orbit over San Martin
Shuttle

Proctor leaned forward in the shuttle's copilot seat, peering through the port, searching for the ship that Admiral Tigre swore was there.

"Still nothing?" she asked. Lieutenant Whitehorse, piloting the shuttle, shook her head no.

"I'm just following the course the admiral gave us. We *should* be nearly there. Just three klicks away. But ... judging from these sensor scans, if I didn't know it was Admiral Tigre giving us these coordinates, I'd say we'd been had."

Proctor leaned back and craned her head to talk to Rayna Scott, who was sitting across from Fiona Liu. Proctor wondered if she would regret bringing Liu along. Who knew what kind of intel she would absorb on this trip. But leaving Liu behind for Volz to deal with had seemed less than desirable. Besides, she wasn't bringing any marines along—

Tigre had assured her his very best were waiting for her on the new ship—and she already knew Liu was good in a fight.

Rayna was also good in a fight, in her own way, Proctor acknowledged wryly. Though the engineer was currently fidgeting with her seatbelt buckle. Proctor leaned in a bit more. "Rayna? Do you know anything about the new stealth tech IDF was researching? I authorized the initial spending fifteen years ago, but the early efforts were ... not promising. I'd assumed they'd never amount to anything...."

Rayna spoke to her seatbelt buckle—as long as Proctor had known her, the brilliant engineer had always addressed whatever mechanical device was nearby rather than the person talking. Even in a meeting with top IDF brass, Proctor would notice Rayna subtly glancing over to the light switch and talking towards it rather than the generals and admirals. A quirk, but having her brain on their side was more than worth it.

"If you're talking about actually bending light around an object, you're right, on a large scale it's not feasible. Bending a single wavelength around a small object? Sure. Bending all wavelengths around a large object? You'd have better luck using a hydrowrench for a circuit diagnostic."

Proctor waved a hand towards the front viewport. "Then what do you think? Is it possible? Did IDF Research actually come up with a way to do it?"

Rayna shrugged, and actually glanced up to meet Proctor's eyes. "Could be. They may have come up with another mechanism. Rather than bending light maybe they just painted the hull really, really black and prayed they didn't occult any starlight."

If their shuttle was moving at all, there'd be no way to tell, since to Proctor's eyes the distant stars were fixed points. Except for the five fighters trailing them, there were no objects nearby to judge their speed. No point of reference. And so the subtly shifting stars directly ahead of them took her by surprise. The shift was so small she almost missed it.

The nav computer saw it too. "Coming to a full emergency stop!" called Whitehorse. She worked furiously at her controls, trying to figure out what had caused them to stop. The nav computer claimed there was an obstruction, but nothing showed up on the main sensors.

Lieutenant Qwerty at the shuttle's tiny comm console sat up a little straighter. "Ma'am, Admiral Tigre is callin'."

She nodded for him to patch it through, and Tigre's voice boomed over the cramped compartment's speakers. "Shelby, do you see it?"

She looked out the viewport again. Nothing but black emptiness and distant points of light. The stars that had seemed to be shifting earlier had disappeared. "No. Miguelito, what the hell is going on?"

"It's right in front of you. Watch—they'll open the shuttle bay for you to land."

And then, as if the darkness itself was peeling back, a section of the view ahead of them lit up with an almost piercing brightness. When her eyes adjusted she recognized the interior of a small shuttle bay, just a few hundred meters ahead. "What the hell…."

"IDF Research has made some progress since you left command, Shelby. We've nearly perfected stealth, though as far as I know there are only two ships in existence. Luckily, IDF

Research has a major laboratory and production facility here on San Martin. So I nabbed one for in-field testing. And now it's yours until we figure this shit out."

Qwerty tapped a few buttons, and nodded. "Yeah, looks like the approach vectors and landing coordinates are coming in now. Just room enough for six of us in there." He glanced over at Proctor. "Small ship, Admiral."

She murmured her reply, still transfixed on the blotch of light floating before them—the interior of a shuttle bay, surrounded by stars. "Doesn't need to be big. Just needs to be fast and run silent. This could be just what we need to get to the bottom of everything. Without a target on our backs."

Ensign Babu deadpanned, "Fantastic. This will make my job a *whole* lot easier."

"Fewer bullets to jump in front of for me?" asked Proctor.

"Screw that—that's the marines' job, ma'am. No, I mean, it's a small ship. Easier to keep track of you and supplied with coffee. Do you have any idea how hard it is to keep up with you on a ship the size of the *Independence*?" Babu was talking absentmindedly, still staring at the light from the open shuttle bay with blackness and stars surrounding it.

"I'm sure this has all been very hard on you, Ensign."

"You have no idea, ma'am," he murmured, which made Proctor smile. In the few weeks he'd served as her personal aide, she'd come to rely on his dry humor and sarcastic asides. And the coffee.

The shuttle glided past the shuttle bay doors and settled into a cramped parking space off to the side as the five fighters behind them soared in one by one.

"Miguel, what tech does this stealth rely on? Rayna here

tells me that multi-spectral light-bending just isn't possible."

"Not over an open channel, Shelby," his voice boomed over the comm. "I'll be joining you shortly and we can talk aboard the *Defiance* before you head out. See you in a few."

CHAPTER THIRTY-SEVEN

Orbit over San Martin
ISS Defiance
Conference Room

The conference room was small. Everything was small on the *Defiance*. The deck officer, whose name Proctor still did not know, had briefly shown her to her quarters, which were little more than a bed within a closet.

Proctor and her small, trusted group of crew members had been sitting at the ship's conference room table for under two minutes when the door opened again and Admiral Tigre stepped through, his uniform sleeves a little too short and a few stains from the day's lunch dotting his pant leg, but wearing that broad smile she had grown to love over the years.

"Shelby," he said, "so good to see you again. I wish the circumstances were better."

"As do I," she replied, standing up to give him a hug.

"We need to be brief," he said. "We don't have much

DEFIANCE

time."

"Time?" said Proctor. "What's going on?" She sat down, uneasily. Tigre pulled a chair away from the wall and sat down.

"It's IDF Intel," he said leaning an elbow onto the table. "They've been running regular sensor sweeps in the system, outside the purview of CENTCOM San Martin."

"That's ... odd," said Proctor. "Isn't the local office of IDF Intel supposed to report directly to you?"

"It should." Tigre ran a hand over his thin white hair. "It's disturbing to say the least."

Lieutenant Whitehorse raised a finger. "I'm sure IDF is on high alert in every system due to the recent Dolmasi incursion."

Tigre nodded. "Yes, it is, but I've never lost control over the day-to-day operations of Intel activities within my command area," he said. "CENTCOM San Martin covers half a dozen star systems. It seems like Oppenheimer is consolidating operational authority across all military divisions."

Proctor shrugged. "We did that thirty years ago during the war," she said. "It allowed us, or rather, allowed the top brass at the time, to consolidate and coordinate intelligence-gathering activities with the war fighting efforts."

"Yes," said Tigre. "But the funny thing is, CENTCOM Bolivar has no such restrictions. Only CENTCOM San Martin, CENTCOM Britannia, CENTCOM Veracruz, and CENTCOM Indira have lost direct control over their local branch of IDF Intel. It's almost as if—"

Proctor finished his sentence for him. "As if any Central Command, or any other IDF command center not affiliated with Shovik-Orion is being stripped of all operational authority, no?"

Tigre looked glum. "Yes, yes—that is my concern. Which means that the Central Command on Earth is not only tolerating Mullins, but supporting him. Endorsing him. They either subscribe to his views, or they're being held hostage by Shovik-Orion's lucrative defense contracts. Or rather, what would happen to our ships and combat systems if Shovik-Orion decided to bail on UE all at once."

Proctor shook her head slowly, rubbing her temples to resist the looming headache. "I can't believe we're even talking about this in the middle of another alien invasion. It's the same bullshit political drama that played out last time this all happened thirty years ago. Let's just hope that this time we can expose the traitors before the real enemy strikes too hard, too deep."

"Real enemy?" Admiral Tigre, scratching at the sides of his mustache. "The real enemy is always the one you trusted the most. The one that can hurt you the most. Let's face it, Shelby, if Mullins is working against us, if he's working against IDF, and working against Earth, *he* is the real enemy, not the Dolmasi. Not even the Swarm."

The conference room, already quiet, turned morgue-level quiet at the mention of their old enemy. Proctor calmly folded her hands in front of her on the table.

"You ... don't suppose the Swarm is back, do you?" said Lieutenant Whitehorse. "I mean, if admirals are acting strangely, issuing rogue orders you guys don't understand ... what I mean to say is, if the left hand doesn't know what the right hand is doing, isn't that kind of how things were during the Second Swarm War? Everyone suspecting everyone else of treachery? Since the Swarm was able to infect people with their virus and control them? No one knew who was Swarm-corrupted and working for the enemy and who was still themselves. Hell, the entire Russian high command was corrupted at one point."

Proctor wanted it not to be true, and so far the evidence had pointed elsewhere. The recent attack of the Golgothic ship and now the new offensive by the Dolmasi bore no relation to how things played out during the Second Swarm War. This was odd. This was different. This was something new. Yet it was still something able to make humanity fight each other. That was the hallmark of an effective … no, a *brilliant* enemy. One who could divide its foes, make them fight amongst themselves, and then move in for the kill when everyone is distracted, pointing fingers and guns at each other.

"I highly doubt this is the Swarm," said Admiral Tigre. "But I'm hoping, Shelby, that with the *Defiance*, you'll be able to get to the bottom of everything."

Proctor wished that were the case. She wished the answer to their problems were as simple as taking command of the new ship. Granted, the *Defiance*'s new technology was impressive. But technology was next to useless if you were lost in the fog of war, flailing at shadows and held at the mercy of unseen enemies.

But during the inspection of the *Defiance*, and during the most recent battle, especially during the aborted kidnapping attempt, she had come to the conclusion that it was time to take the offensive position. The best kind of defense she knew. "Okay, here's the plan. We're going to attempt communication with the Dolmasi."

Every head in the conference room turned towards her. Every eye widened. Proctor held out a hand towards Lieutenant Qwerty and continued, "Mr. Qwerty here is our secret weapon for this particular battle. If we could just communicate with the Dolmasi, and *through* them unravel the conspiracy, that would empower us—enable us—to get our own house in order so we can finally face the external threat undivided."

"You heard that moon in the Jakarta sector disappeared, right? Tal Rishi?" Admiral Tigre, his expression already grave, looked almost scared. Or, at least, he'd look scared if Proctor didn't know any better. She knew Miguelito was made of solid tungsten, despite his tendency to wear his emotions on his sleeve.

She nodded. "Yes, I did."

"Just imagine, Shelby. The power to make a world disappear. An entire world. Or, worse yet, the power to *move* it. What if whatever we are dealing with has the power to make that moon reappear right in the orbital path of New Jakarta itself? Or, worse, what if they have the power to transport that moon lightyears away, and put it in the path of Earth? Or Britannia? If our enemy has that power...."

"We are pretty much screwed," said Lieutenant Zivic, who had been uncharacteristically quiet until then. The other four pilots were down in their ready room, presumably playing cards and bantering. She was sure he'd be there too if she hadn't requested his presence in the meeting.

"Words right out of my mouth," said Proctor.

"Ma'am," began Fiona Liu, "there's also the issue of the

possibility that Mullins has a stealth ship of his own. It all adds up—that meta-space signal at Mao Prime that came out of nowhere, pointed straight at us. That was probably him, and he was almost certainly pulling the trigger on that botched kidnap op."

"That certainly is a possibility," said Tigre, nodding. "And I can equip you with some specs, some data, that might help you detect him when he is running silent—or *if* he is running silent—but I'm afraid that if you're flying one of these stealth ships, and you don't want to be seen, no one is going to see you."

The implications of that were terrifying, almost as terrifying as the aliens' alleged ability to move entire planets. Or at least make them disappear. Proctor wondered if perhaps the two technologies were related: what if the disappearance of Bolivar's moon was not a coincidence, but rather the next stage in Admiral Mullins's schemes. But what his endgame would be in such a scenario she couldn't fathom.

Tigre was watching her. "I know what you're thinking, Shelby, but at least there is some good news—the two technologies couldn't be more different. The stealth technology is actually quite basic at the fundamental level. Sure, we've got some special EM-absorbing coatings, radar-absorbing coatings, that kind of stuff. But the workhorse of the stealth system has more of a … theatrical bent, if you catch my meaning."

Proctor chewed on this information for several moments before Rayna Scott broke her silence. "Oh, my God. You're just putting on a light show, a trick, to fool their sensors, aren't you?" she said.

Tigre held up his hands. "You caught us. The game's up."

Proctor couldn't suppress the look of horror that she knew was spreading over her face. She wasn't sure whether she should feel horrified or gleeful. On one hand, essentially relying on a magic trick to keep her safe was foolhardy indeed. On the other hand, it might help them detect Admiral Mullins when, and if, he decided to come after her himself. "You can't be serious," she said.

"It's actually quite sophisticated software," he said with a grin and Proctor swore she saw a wink in there too. "The hull, in addition to being painted with the special EM-absorbing coating, has also essentially been converted into a computer monitor. Or rather, a highly-sophisticated holographic computer monitor. It automatically detects the location of the sensors and cameras that are attempting to track it, performs a little computational wizardry, and makes the hull look like the appropriate star field from the point of view of the observer. Mimics the spectral output of each individual star it's supposed to be impersonating. It's actually quite impressive."

Commander Scott was nodding her head approvingly, looking back and forth as if performing the computations herself, and even looked both Proctor and Tigre in the eye she was so excited. "That's not just sophisticated, that's bloody brilliant. Not even multi-phase, multi-source, multi-spectral analysis could ferret out the signal if it were done properly with a small enough lag-time. Hell, even if you ran multiplexed inverse Fourier transformed…."

"There she goes again," said Ensign Babu. Rayna flashed him a mock glare—the two had actually taken to each other quite well in the short time Babu had been aboard the *Independence*.

"So," said Proctor, "we are undetectable. We're running silent. We've got, as I see it, three missions. Number one, figure out how to communicate with the Dolmasi and end their attacks. Number two, gather intel from the Dolmasi, and any other source we can, to figure out who the hell is behind this conspiracy to kidnap me, or to kill me—I'm not yet convinced it was Mullins. And, even more importantly, figure out what their goal is. What their endgame is. And number three, the usual." She glanced around the table, meeting them all in the eye one by one. "Save civilization. Again."

Ensign Babu raised an eyebrow. "I used to watch an old show when I was a teenager, and it reminds me of you, Admiral."

"Oh?"

"Yeah, every week the heroine beat some new danger—monsters, vampires, demons. And when she died, on her tombstone they inscribed: *She saved the world. A lot.*" He allowed that to sink in for a moment before he dryly held up a finger, then raised an eyebrow, and added, "For the record, I don't think you're going to die on this mission, Admiral."

Proctor was speechless. And after a moment she decided that it was quite funny and laughed, which gave tacit permission for everyone else to laugh. And, in reality, it was a little funny. Granger was sure he was going to die on any number of occasions when he saved civilization back in the day, and seemed to pull through every single time.

Except for that final time. And his tombstone would forever be the event horizon of a black hole.

Unless….

Shelby, they're coming.

Dammit Tim, what were you trying to tell me?

CHAPTER THIRTY-EIGHT

Orbit over Bolivar
ISS Vanguard

It took his secret service chief far longer than he would have liked to coordinate with security on the *ISS Vanguard*, Mullins's ship, but after another hour President Quimby finally took the short shuttle ride over and met Mullins in the shuttle bay.

"So exactly how long have we had stealth, and why the hell wasn't I told about it yet?" Quimby extended a hand to the admiral, who met him in the bay, alone. He interpreted that move as the other man trying to send the signal that he considered himself such an alpha dog that he didn't even need sycophants and aides hanging on his every word and ready to answer his beck and call.

Either that or he didn't want anyone listening in.

"Just a few months, actually. I've only had the *Vanguard* since August, and to my knowledge she's only one of two prototypes. Still working out some kinks before Shovik-Orion's Bolivaran shipyard goes into full production." His grip was firm. Not too tight, and lingering just long enough to let Quimby know that he wasn't afraid of him. Good. He could work with that. There were other motivations than fear, and the president was a man who would use whatever tool he needed to get his way. And by the end, he'd make the admiral fear him all the same.

"Assuming Shovik-Orion still has funding in the next budget." Quimby said. "Believe me, my friend, you don't have a bigger ally than myself in the budget process coming up with congress, and I've got a fair amount of political capital to spend. But as you know, politics is nasty business. Some days I'd rather be making actual sausage than the shitfest we have to do in New York."

Mullins's eyes narrowed at the mention of money. Good. That was his one weakness. Even as he made a big show of throwing his weight around and letting his balls hang out, his real nut-sack was in the wallet, and if Quimby threatened to kick it, even subliminally, Mullins would bend.

"I'm surprised that congress would even hesitate funding our contracts given how central we are to nearly every military system. And given the fact that we're currently in a three-front war." The admiral smiled. "But let's save the budget negotiations for another day, as riveting as they are. Even though my detractors tell you otherwise, my loyalties lie first with IDF, and the survival and prosperity of United Earth. Come, Mr. President, we have much to discuss."

Quimby's secret service detail went ahead of them, led by Agent Carter, greeting their IDF counterparts on the ship and coordinating the details of the president's stay with Kalvin Quinkert and Mick Bird. Quimby followed Mullins into the lift, then onto the bridge itself for a brief inspection tour, before they finally settled into the captain's ready room.

Quimby dove right in. "So, talk to me. I just can't believe that Oppenheimer could be controlled by the Swarm. He's the leader of IDF. How could their influence have escaped our notice all this time, and how can you be so sure that they are not, in fact, all dead, just like the top brass swears they are? We haven't seen hide nor hair of them in thirty years."

Mullins brought over two cups of coffee. Both black, without cream or sugar, as if he expected them both to take it the same way—strong and unsoftened. And he was right. Black coffee was like blunt talk—in-your-face refreshing. "I assume you want it strong?" Quimby nodded. Another little detail he filed away—his adversary was perceptive, even in his dick-wagging. He wondered how much of it was bluster and show, meant to distract from what his true intentions were, and how much was true character.

Probably all show. True character was rare.

"Thank you."

Mullins sat down across from him. "Of course Oppenheimer would claim the Swarm is dead. The worst enemy is the one you don't think exists. And yet here we are in the midst of an invasion by an unknown alien race. The so-called Golgothics. They've only sent one ship, but when's the next one showing up? And what are they doing to Ido? What did they do to El Amin? Where did Tal Rishi go? What are they doing to Titan, and half a dozen other moons across our space that are somehow, against all the laws of physics, *growing in mass*? Believe me, Mr. President, this is just the tip of the invasion, and if we don't have firm, solid, unwavering leadership, we could fail."

Was that a veiled threat? Of course it was. But, like the most skilled of diplomats, he'd couched it in terms of doubting Oppenheimer's leadership, not Quimby's, keeping the doubt of Quimby's leadership implicit. Quimby replied in kind: "I've seen no indication he's under any kind of alien influence." He thought it prudent not to mention that Oppenheimer suspected Proctor of being under Swarm control, which would have implied that Oppenheimer didn't, in fact, believe the Swarm was truly gone, as Mullins claimed he believed. But Quimby was willing to follow Mullins down this rabbit hole, just to see where it would lead.

Mullins chuckled. "Nor would you. When the Swarm was controlling half the Russian high command back during the Second Swarm War, no one knew, except for Russian Confederation President Malakov himself, who managed to set things up such that he alone was left untouched by the Swarm. They're good. Very good. You simply can't tell someone is under Swarm influence just by talking to them."

"So what's your proof, Admiral? You do realize that over half the members of my senior military staff don't trust you? Ever since your harebrained assumption of power on Bolivar and acceptance of the executive chair at Shovik-Orion, in direct violation of half a dozen conflict of interest laws and regulations, no one trusts you. In fact, they're all scared shitless by you. Scared you'll pull the plug on all our military systems if they speak out too firmly against your brazen conflicts of interest."

The admiral waved his hand as if batting aside a pesky fly. "My proof is simple reason. Logic. Look at the pieces of the puzzle. Start at the beginning. Granger flies into the black hole with a shitload of President Avery's anti-matter bombs, supposedly closing the Swarm's link to our universe. Now stop right there. Stop … right … there. Good lord, have you thought about how idiotic that assumption is? From *our* perspective, he finally crossed the event horizon only a few *weeks* ago. And yet, *somehow*, the anti-matter closed the meta-space link thirty years ago? Clearly, there's a breakdown in logic there. We wanted to win that war so badly that we believed what we *wanted* to believe. After ten billion dead, we were desperate to think that the war was over, and that we'd won."

Quimby had to admit the man was right. The explanation of the Swarm's defeat—the *public* explanation, at least—never sat well with him. It was too easy. Too convenient. "So you're suggesting that Granger didn't, in fact, close the Swarm's link to our universe?"

"I'm suggesting that maybe it was in the Swarm's best interest to let us *believe* we'd closed it. So that we'd let our guard down. Think about it, Mr. President. In the closing days of the war we were actually doing quite well. The Dolmasi and Skiohra were both on our side. President Avery had retooled society such that we were churning out starships by the hundreds and conscripts by the millions. We were the sleeping dragon, and once the Swarm woke us up, there was no stopping us, Swarm technology and viral influence be damned. It was in their best interest to let us think we'd won. In the meantime they'd regroup, and then come at us … smarter."

"What, by leaving sleeper agents among us? Then coming

at us with a new ship design that pokes holes in random moons?"

Mullins smirked. "Random?" He waved a hand toward the viewscreen on the wall, which picked up on his movements and automatically displayed a predetermined chart and map. "Take a look."

Quimby examined the star chart and accompanying lists of data, but couldn't decipher it. "Help me out here. What the hell is this?"

Mullins stood and pointed at certain spots on the map. "Earth, Britannia, Bolivar, San Martin, Mao Prime, and New Jakarta. Six of the largest worlds of United Earth. And each of them has, or in San Martin's case *had*, a moon somewhere in their solar systems or in a solar system within five lightyears that was attacked by that alien ship."

"So you think the Swarm is targeting moons near our major population centers? To destroy them and rain debris down on us? El Amin exploded, sure, but have you heard that Tal Rishi just flat out disappeared?"

Mullins nodded. "Yes. And the rest of the moons' masses are slowly increasing."

"So what does it mean?"

"It means what I'm telling you. The Swarm is *here*. They never left. And in the thirty years they've been hiding, they've been developing new technology to end us once and for all. Think about it. Tal Rishi disappeared. Exactly where do you think it's going to reappear? What if it reappears just a few thousand kilometers from Earth, and slams into it? Would be quite the fireworks show. Same goes for Britannia. Bolivar. All of them."

Quimby stood up and began to pace. "So what you're telling me is that you think the Swarm essentially faked their own deaths, laid low for thirty years, developed moon-flinging technology, maintained a few sleeper agents among our top ranks so that when they decide to fling some moons at us we'll be busy fighting among ourselves because of all the chaos caused by the sleepers?"

Mullins shrugged. "More or less. It's so simple, it's actually quite brilliant. And Oppenheimer is *very* busy keeping us looking the other way with this pet Dolmasi war of his and his strange insistence on seeking out the Quiassi and Findiri."

"I still can't believe he's just trying to start a war to distract us from a Swarm invasion."

"You don't have to believe it. You can see it. Come with me aboard the *Vanguard* to San Martin, and you can eavesdrop on a conversation I'll have with Miguel Tigre. Just to see. See if his conclusions are the same as mine. And see what he says to me when he doesn't know you're listening. Determine if he's in bed with Oppenheimer. Christian says he wants to find the Quiassi and the Findiri. Why? To truly end all *known unknown* threats against us, as the saying goes? Or is it something else? Watch Tigre's reaction when I tell him the latest news that I found out just moments ago before we walked in here."

Quimby stopped pacing the ready room. "And what is that?"

"Ido just disappeared too."

CHAPTER THIRTY-NINE

The dreams always came when events felt out of her control. And even within the dream, Proctor marveled that she was able to recognize something like that rationally, even as the dream proceeded against her will.

"You're going to be in so much trouble, Shell," said Carla. She didn't even bother wearing the wig anymore. She flaunted her shiny scalp like a trophy. Generals and fleet admirals decorated their chests with bars and insignia. Cancer survivors wore their scars like well-earned medals.

Except it was premature to use the word 'survivor'.

"You just worry about keeping lookout and let me worry about the mission."

The mission. That's what they called their pranks. It gave the hijinks a sense of gravitas that otherwise would be absent by just calling them what they were. Stupid, childish pranks. In this case, using a miniature plasma welder Shelby had "borrowed" from the school's shop to fuse the lock on the door on the principal's office.

The plasma torch was acting finicky, refusing to ignite. "Shell, come on. Hurry! The secretary will be back any second!" Carla whispered furiously from the doorway that faced the sitting area outside the principal's office where his assistant usually worked.

"It's fine. She'll be occupied for another five minutes at least with those doughnuts. That was brilliant, by the way, Car—giving her your 'scan-day doughnuts'."

"Scan-day doughnuts." *It had become a monthly ritual. Every time Carla was due for a neutrino-enhanced magnetic scan to check the progress of treatment, their father would take a quick shuttle up to New York City to buy a dozen of the best doughnuts in the world from a little shop on Ninth, and they were always still warm by the time she was finished with the scan.*

But this time, they were secretary-bait.

"Screw that, I miss my 'scan-day doughnuts' already," *Carla said, still peering around the corner.*

Shelby took a deep breath, thumbed a few of her rosary beads under her shirt, and lifted the torch up to the lock, whispering a silent prayer. "This will totally be worth it. Best mission yet. Just imagine Principal Calderon's face tomorrow on morning announcements when he says," *she dropped her voice to a mock version of the man's,* "the culprits will be found and dealt with swiftly and—"

A deep throat-clearing interrupted her. "Fairly? Or were you going to say 'mercifully'? Because I assure you, mercy is the last thing on my mind this time...." *Principal Calderon, arms crossed, stood over Shelby, who was still kneeling down with her arms raised, miniature plasma-welder in hand.*

"Uh...." *Shelby glanced back at Carla in the doorway, who had frozen like a deer in the headlights.* "Amicably? Congenially?"

"Miss Proctor, I thought the last time I had you in my office we agreed that the next juvenile prank would be your last. You agreed to be on your best behavior. You swore it would never happen again. That you would start acting like an adult."

Shelby racked her brain for a pithy response. Even in the dream, adult Proctor came up with half a dozen good ones, but teenage-Proctor never got the chance. Before she could even open her mouth, the secretary had appeared, her face urgent. Her hand waving a phone.

"Josh, it's Doctor Proctor. He says these two need to get to the hospital right away."

Principal Calderon looked like a kid who had had his candy sack taken away from him on Halloween. Shelby could almost hear the swears under his breath. He turned to her. "Miss Proctor, the time will come when you can't use your sister's illness as an excuse for bad behavior."

Shelby stood up, making a show of dusting off her knees. "I'm so terribly *sorry*, Mr. Calderon, I—"

Carla interrupted her. "I think what my sister is going to say, is that we're going to milk this cockamamie tumor for all it's worth, sir. Lord knows we've earned it."

Shelby wanted to kiss her. She didn't even look back to see the look on the principal's face as she left the office, her arm around her sister's shoulder, the other hand rubbing her scalp for continued good luck. "Sis, you never cease to amaze me."

Carla scowled. "Hey, we got off that time. But the next time we won't be so lucky."

"The next 'mission', you mean? And I love that you automatically assume there will be a next mission. Because you're right, there will be. And this time I've got the perfect Calderon mission. It'll involve a diving board, the local media, and possibly a goat. Come on, let's get to the hospital and hear the good news. It's probably just the doc with the results of your scan."

CHAPTER FORTY

Orbit over San Martin
ISS Defiance
Bridge

"We're all ready down here, Admiral." It was oddly comforting to hear Rayna's old voice coming out of the comm on this new ship. "These engines are a real beaut. Purring like warm kittens—I think I just might adopt them. Smother them with motherly love. Buy them awkward presents. Embarrass them in front of their girlfriend. I've got a real mom vibe going on here."

"Thank you Rayna," said Proctor. "Lieutenant Zivic, are your pilots ready?"

Zivic's voice answered through the speakers. "Yes, ma'am. Ace and Bucket's injuries are still smarting, but they keep insisting, and I quote, *it's only a flesh-wound.*"

Another voice interrupted him. "I *said* I'm fine." That must be Ace, thought Proctor. "Admiral, is Lieutenant Qwerty up there?"

"Yes," she said, puzzled.

"I talked with him earlier about a way we—the pilots—can maintain contact with the *Defiance* while she's stealthed. I think I've got a solution. Can you spare him later? I'd like to discuss it with him."

Proctor nodded. "By all means, Lieutenant Broadside. After we've made the q-jump and determined the lay of the land once we've arrived."

She turned her head to the comm station where Lieutenant Qwerty was finalizing his preparations. "Everything ready on your end?"

"Yes, ma'am," he replied in his drawn-out drawl. "Except for this damn shoelace that broke. I swear, if Shovik-Orion's boot suppliers were half as good as their tactical—"

"I meant, is the stealth system ready, Mr. Qwerty."

"Oh. Right. I've tapped into the stealth programmin' and I can manipulate the apparent spectral pattern of one specific star that appears on our hull from the *Independence*'s point of view, and encode messages in the spectrum so we can stay in contact with Captain Volz."

"Excellent work," she said. "Let's test it out. Send a message to old Ballsy that we're ready to head out. Engage the stealth, and see if they can make out the message."

"Also ma'am, I've already discussed the use of the emergency long wave radios with Ace. I didn't think we'd need to go over it again. Maybe those pain meds are messing with her noggin, if you know what I mean."

Proctor frowned. He had a point—this mission required a high state of readiness. Of course, didn't all their missions?

She made a note to talk to Zivic about it later. "I'll keep that in mind. Now, engage stealth."

Qwerty tapped a few buttons. Proctor wasn't sure what to expect when the stealth device engaged. She supposed there would be no discernible change from their point of view, so she was surprised when the viewscreen blanked out, where before they had a full view of the blue planet of San Martin below them and the star field beyond. "What happened?" The screen stayed blank. *Oh, for the love....* "Don't tell me we're blind with this thing on!"

"The viewscreen cameras don't have anything to pick up, no ma'am. But we still have passive sensor capabilities."

"Passive sensors. I suppose active scanning sensors would be a dead giveaway for our location."

"I'd assume so, ma'am," Qwerty said with a tip of an imaginary hat. "But passive's are still pretty thorough. We're not blind down in the microwaves, radio, and of course neutron, gamma, and neutrino detectors."

Proctor grit her teeth. This would be ... quite an experience, to say the least. "Begin message to Captain Volz. You read me, Ballsy? If you do, tell me what you really think of this mission." She glanced over at Lieutenant Qwerty again.

After a moment of studying his console, he nodded. "There it is, ma'am. Thar she blows. Detecting a passive phase modulation in their magnetic engine containment envelope. Running it through my handy-dandy translator...." He nodded approvingly at his console. "They call my son Batshit, Shelby. But he's got nothing on you. Stay safe, and we'll be looking over your shoulder. Assuming ... we can see where your shoulder is." He looked up. "End of message."

Proctor smiled. "Loud and clear, Ballsy. All right, people, let's get this show on the road. Set a course to Sangre de Cristo. I think it's time we had another chat with Secretary-General Curiel. Maybe we can untangle his relationship with Admiral Mullins and start to get to the bottom of this."

Lieutenant Qwerty nodded. "Message sent, ma'am." He continued nodding. "Ready when you are, Shelby." A nervous expression passed over his face and he looked up suddenly. "That was Captain Volz, ma'am."

"Yes, thank you, Lieutenant. I assumed so." She turned to the navigation station, which was only three feet in front of her and to the left. The bridge was almost as tight and cramped as her quarters. "Miss Liu? Have you familiarized yourself with the controls?" She had asked the former IDF Intel officer to take the helm, since space was cramped and they needed everyone on the bridge to actually serve a purpose.

And recent events had shown her she could trust the young woman. With her life.

"Yes, Admiral. I had basic navigation training as part of my intelligence operative training at the Academy, and these controls are as straightforward as they come."

Proctor nodded. "All right. Set a t-jump course to Sangre de Cristo. Let's go get some answers."

Usually she would be able to tell when the jump had occurred by the shifting star field on the viewscreen. But as the viewscreen was blank, she had to rely on the telltale shift in her inner ear's sense of equilibrium. The very brief moment of vertigo passed quickly, and Liu announced, "Arrived at Sangre de Cristo, Admiral. High orbit."

"Thank you Ms. Liu."

"Stealth is holding steady, Admiral," said Qwerty.

"Thank you," said Proctor, standing up out of her chair, and peering at the empty screen. "I'm afraid I'm not going to get used to this. I hate flying blind."

"Hang on, ma'am, let me see if I can work some magic," said Qwerty. He tapped a few buttons, shaking his head, mumbling to himself. After about a minute of silence across the tiny bridge he looked up, a look of triumph on his face. "Here we go, let's see if this don't work." The viewscreen shifted to reveal what Proctor would have called an infrared view of the planet, and the fixed star field behind it. It wavered and flickered slightly almost as if heat currents were passing in front of it, but at least now she could see what was going on. Or rather, confirm with her own eyes that they were indeed orbiting Sangre de Cristo. She could just make out the ruined habitation dome that was destroyed by the nuclear weapon.

The nuke inadvertently delivered by her own nephew. The same nuke that someone had killed her Danny for.

Focus, Shelby.

Proctor shook her head in delighted amazement. "Mr. Qwerty, you have outdone yourself this time. You're a polyglot, and the now you apparently can do rapid signal analysis at the drop of a hat. If they don't give you a pay raise I'm sending a sternly-worded letter to your supervisor."

"Aw shucks, ma'am, writin' a letter to yourself would be awfully kind." He tipped his invisible hat again. "Honestly, signal analysis isn't all that much different than figurin' out a language. I mean, sure, it's nouns and verbs and morphology and all that malarkey versus carrier waves and Fourier analysis, but there are actually a lot of similarities. All you have to do is look for the patterns."

Proctor's inner voice repeated the phrase. *Just look for the patterns. But what if there was no pattern? What if it was one-in-a-million?*

Fiona Liu swiveled her chair to look at him, interrupting Proctor's thoughts. "Why do they call you Qwerty, anyway?"

"Well ma'am, seeing how it's my name and all, makes sense, don't it?"

Liu raised a single eyebrow. "Really? Your last name is Qwerty? As in, Q-W-E-R-T-Y?"

Qwerty grinned. "Yes ma'am," he drawled, but hesitated. "Or rather, it is now. Funny story behind that. You see, I applied to the Academy on a dare and—"

Proctor cleared her throat. "Mr. Qwerty, I am confident this is a good story, but … it can wait. Civilizations to save, remember? Right now we need to find Curiel, and while I'm interrogating him I need you to decipher an entire alien language. Possibly two, if the info that Krull gave us about the Ligature is off in any way. Please run a passive comm scan on all bands, both civilian and military, and see if we can't track him down. Last I heard, Sangre was his center of operations."

"Yes ma'am," said Qwerty. He swiveled his chair back around and began scanning, looking up at Lieutenant Whitehorse, who nodded, and the two, as if by prior agreement, began to split the work between them.

"How is the *Independence* doing," she said. Her old ship had just t-jumped in moments ago. It struck her how she already thought of the sleek cruiser as her *old ship,* even though she'd only been on it for two weeks. "Let's send Captain Volz a message that says—"

Qwerty hesitated, "Uh, Adm'ril, I don't exactly have the comms crew with me. Just a mom and pop operation we have going on here," he shot a wink over at Lieutenant Whitehorse, "No offense, ma'am, I didn't mean to marry us off so fast."

He was right, of course. Proctor was used to barking out orders, and having a bridge full of officers at her beck and call to carry out her instructions. This would take some getting used to.

Ensign Babu cleared his throat from the corner of the bridge. "If you need an extra bridge hand, ma'am, I, well, I do have two of them."

"Ensign Babu, pardon me, you are entirely correct. Please, if you would, go get me a cup of fresh coffee."

Babu actually looked crestfallen. Maybe he couldn't take it as well as he dished it out. He ducked out of the door to the bridge and returned a few minutes later with the steaming cup. "Thank you, Ensign," she said. He perked up at that, and she made a mental note that he'd probably benefit from an actual mission sometime, just to give the man a break from his coffee-duty. But nothing too dangerous—good assistants were hard to come by, and after her last assistant, the late Ensign Flay.... She brushed the line of thought aside.

Lieutenant Qwerty looked up from his console with a look of mild surprise. "Ma'am? Speak of the devil. The *Independence* is receiving a hail from a compound in Maria de Lujan—one of the domed cities. It's Curiel, asking for you."

CHAPTER FORTY-ONE

High Orbit over Earth
Freighter Angry Betty

The cargo bay on the *Angry Betty* was a cramped, awkward space. For all the advances over the years in spaceship design, and even in things like materials science and manufacturing processes, nothing could ever replace the need for duct tape, and Chris Keen saw that it had been put to liberal good use in the bay. Hole in the plasma cargo pallet jack? Duct tape. Light panel coming loose from the ceiling? Duct tape. Smuggling compartment doors not closing properly? Duct tape. Graviton emitters coming unscrewed from the q-jump drive? Duct tape.

But in the center of the bay, resting on an array of wooden pallets, was the massive steel shipping container full of gallium. He imagined it sloshing around as the orbital thrusters maneuvered them into a very particular inclination around the planet below, though now that he thought about it, he wasn't sure if it was still all liquid. He'd kept the cargo bay at a chilly ten degrees C, well below the point the liquid gallium would solidify into a massive, solid chunk of metal. Now that it was frozen, the whole steel shipping container, combined with the solid chunk of gallium within it, basically formed a metal block the size of a small house.

Weirdest shipment ever. But the customer had specified that the temperature in the cargo bay be ten degrees, so ten degrees was what he set it at, no questions asked. All he had to do was repeat his mantra.

Three million dollars. Three millions dollars. Three million dollars. Country estate. Women. Parties. Cars. Hell yeah.

He went through the checklist the customer had given him. All the miniature orbital thrusters were retracted into the cargo container, as well as the dispersal nozzle and pump equipment. He checked that the gallium was, in fact, solidified. A multi-tool analysis sensor confirmed it had solidified to the core. Check, check, check.

When the final item was checked off his list, he got ready to send the signal to the recipient. The customer had assured him another ship would take the cargo off his hands once he'd arrived and gone through his delivery checklist.

Time for pay-day, bitches.

He thumbed the comm switch on his data pad, and keyed in the channel the customer had given him to signal the other ship. At least, he assumed there was another ship he'd deliver the gallium to.

Static.

Nothing happened.

He keyed it in the comm channel again.

Nothing.

Nothing that is, until his ship exploded.

But Chris Keen wasn't around to appreciate the expanding cloud of glowing slag—the remains of the *Angry Betty*, a fiery maelstrom surrounding the still-intact, now red-hot steel shipping container full of gallium.

And as the cloud cooled several minutes later, the thrusters poked out of their pockets in the steel walls, ignited, and pushed the battered, glowing-hot container along a very particular orbit high over planet Earth.

CHAPTER FORTY-TWO

Orbit over Sangre de Cristo
ISS Defiance
Bridge

"Lieutenant, send a message to Captain Volz. Tell him to take the call for me. Have him tell Curiel I'm ... washing my hair or some shit."

Qwerty nodded, and typed. "...or ... some ... shit. Got it."

"And then patch us into the conversation. This should be good."

Moments later, the link was live. The viewscreen, which had shown the wavering infrared image of San Martin, was replaced by a split screen of Volz and Secretary General Curiel, as telegenic and youthful as the last time she saw him a few weeks ago, when they were both being shot at by unknown assailants.

"Captain Volz," began Curiel, "I had hoped to talk to

Admiral Proctor. When will she be available?"

"She's indisposed at the moment, Mr. Secretary General. But I speak for her. How can I help you?"

Even though he was obviously well-trained for work in front of a camera, with a face to match, he struggled to contain his displeasure. "Well ... first off, please relay my appreciation for her assistance over Earth a few weeks ago. I regret that we didn't have the time in the immediate aftermath of ... the incident, to have a proper conversation."

Volz smiled. "Oh, you mean the incident where a GPC sympathizer destroyed our shuttle bay, killed half a dozen flight deck staff members, and then launched a stolen nuclear weapon out the back door, nearly incinerating Northern Europe? *That* incident?"

Proctor chuckled to herself. *Ballsy, you're good.*

Curiel almost blanched. "Yes. That incident. Our investigation is still ongoing as to how that bomb was stolen and how it was smuggled aboard your ship. Please relay my assurances to the admiral that I'll get to the bottom of it. Eventually."

"Eventually?" Volz leaned in towards the camera. "I'd hope that you get to the bottom of it faster than *eventually*. Losing a nuclear weapon is *kind of a big deal*, Curiel."

The Secretary General's face clouded over with annoyance. "Just tell Admiral Proctor that we're working on it, but we've got bigger fish to fry. The bigger threat right now is the Dolmasi. My people in the Veracruz sector are telling me that they're detecting massive fleet movements. They're not going to stop at Mao Prime. And you can't just count on the Skiohra to bail you out like last time."

Proctor snapped her head back to Whitehorse. "How did he know about that? That's classified."

Through the comm, Volz seemed to read her mind. "I see the GPC's intelligence service is second to none."

Curiel waved a hand. "Please. Everyone in the system could see what happened, even if we weren't privy to the conversation that took place between the Matriarch and Proctor. The Skiohra show up in their big-ass ship and all of the sudden the Dolmasi pull up and leave? Of course the Skiohra made them stand down."

Volz shrugged.

"And the reason I'm calling, besides to warn you about the fleet movements … I need to pass a message to her."

A smirk crossed Volz's lips. "A message? Who in the world is using the Secretary General of the GPC as a messenger boy?"

"Oh Ballsy, you sure know how to press people's buttons," murmured Proctor as she saw the anger flash on Curiel's face.

"I only agreed to it because of the importance. Because of how the events are tied to each other." He took a breath, as if trying to suppress his anger. "Patriarch Huntsman asked me to request a meeting with Admiral Proctor, as he believes he has something that she wants. Or rather, knows someone that has what she wants."

Volz stroked his beard stubble. "Very well. I'll let her know. What, does Huntsman want to set up a meeting with Proctor and Huntsman? Isn't that something our secretaries could have done? Or are you taking on secretarial duties in addition to being a messenger boy? Huh, well, I guess you are the *secretary* general…."

Proctor couldn't help laughing out loud.

Curiel's face grew redder. Before he could explode, Volz held up his hands. "Sorry, Mr. Secretary General, it's been a rough few days. Repelling the Dolmasi attack—we sustained casualties. You'll forgive us for being a bit, uh, lacking in patience at the moment. Now, what does this information actually mean? And who's this oh-so-secret source of Huntsman's?"

"Huntsman is on Britannia right now. And he's with his source, who apparently is very eager to pass on the critical information to the admiral, but didn't think it prudent to go through the usual channels as she is under constant watch. You see, the source has very ... particular knowledge about the Dolmasi, and doesn't feel comfortable sharing it with the ... powers that be. There's too much at stake."

"The source?" Volz leaned even further in.

"Not over an open channel."

Volz turned to his side to say something to the officer filling in at comm. Moments later he turned back to the camera. "We've encrypted. As long as your side is secure, we're fine." He leaned in farther, his lined face filling the entire half of the screen. "Source?"

Curiel hesitated, but relented. "Former President Barbara Avery. He's with her now, and asks that Proctor get there immediately, before ... well, let's just say I'm sure there are people who don't want the information she has getting out. You know what I mean. I understand you've had recent ... difficulties ... on board your ship? People you've trusted that perhaps you shouldn't have?"

Proctor gripped her armrests. Curiel knew about the

mutiny—the kidnapping attempt on Proctor. That either meant he was behind it—unlikely—or that his intelligence people had contacts on board the ship, or contacts within the organization that was behind the attack, whether IDF Intel or Mullins or ... someone.

But more importunely, she finally had a lead. From a source she never would have expected.

From ninety-nine-year-old former United Earth President Barbara Avery.

CHAPTER FORTY-THREE

At the hospital in downtown Boston their father met them in the reception area of the oncology clinic.

His face was grave.

"Girls, sit down. Carla? You feeling ok?"

Her face flashed with nervousness. "Yeah. Why?" They both sat down. Their father sat next to them. His eyes were squinting a little, his brow furrowed.

Oh no. Dad never could hide his emotions. The news was bad. Real bad.

"I'm afraid I have good news ... and ... bad news," he said, opening the envelope in his hands. The results from the scan. Shelby wanted to cover her ears. Even though adult Proctor, dreaming, knew what he was going to say, she wanted to run away. Escape the injustice of it all.

"Yeah...?" Carla's voice had started quivering.

"The bad news is, you're in big trouble. Principal Calderon told me everything. Girls, this behavior is inexcusable."

The bad news? Principal Calderon was the bad news? Shelby felt her face bloom into a wide smile.

"And the good news is, the scan came back completely clean. Not a single malignant cell left. It's actually quite miraculous. You're cured, honey."

It took a moment for the news to sink in, and when it did, Carla exploded with squeals and shrieks and laughter. Shelby joined her. She'd been imagining this day for six long, grueling months. It was like a godsend. The doctors had said that just like the tumor being one-in-a-million, the cure would be just as elusive. This type of cancer was breathtakingly aggressive and resistant to treatment.

And so, at her mother's urging, Shelby had prayed, and prayed, and prayed.

And great jumping Jehosephat, it worked. It actually worked. There was a God, and he liked children and puppies and scan-day doughnuts....

Speaking of which ... but her father was one step ahead of them. "Do you know what I think we should do to celebrate? We should have some 'scan-day doughnuts'!"

Carla's face was pained, embarrassed. "Uh, dad, I kind of used those as secretary-bait. Sorry."

He grinned. "I know that. No, I'm saying we should skip the rest of school today, all fly down to New York, and get the doughnuts in person, hot out of the fryer. It'll be fun—you deserve it, sweetie, after ... everything."

Carla squealed again. It was the best day ever, and Shelby pulled her rosary out and kissed it. I believe, she thought. Dammit, mom, you were right. And I believe.

CHAPTER FORTY-FOUR

Orbit over Sangre de Cristo
ISS Defiance
Bridge

They had orbited Sangre de Cristo for almost twenty-four hours, giving Admiral Proctor some much-needed time to recuperate from the wound in her arm and giving the *Independence* time to continue repairing the damage sustained during the engagement with the Dolmasi at Mao Prime. And giving them all some time to figure out what to do next. Avery had summoned Proctor, through the GPC's Secretary General Curiel, no less. But she didn't have time for meetings with people in retirement homes. With open war between United Earth and the Dolmasi, and Titan—along with several other moons in the UE—continuing to swell with mysterious added mass, her time to make on social calls with former presidents was down to zero.

Proctor rubbed her forehead—a headache had settled in

and the recent revelations were only contributing to the pain. "What the hell is former President Avery doing in the middle of this? She's retired."

Fiona Liu, scrunched behind the tiny navigation station, swiveled back to face her. "Actually, during my stint at IDF Intel, I heard that she keeps her fingers in a few pots. No actual power, but enough people owe her favors that she's managed to at least stay in the game as a spectator."

"The game?"

Liu shrugged. "You know. The game. That's what we called it in the service. The behind-the-scenes maneuverings, the backstabbing, the blackmail, the extortion, the backroom deals, the above-board diplomacy, and the secret threats. The fog of war. All of it. And from everything I've heard, Avery lived for it back in her day, and she could never quite give it up once she left office."

Proctor nodded. "She *did* love it. She had so many secret programs going on that I don't think the top brass ever uncovered half of it. In fact, it was her secret anti-matter bomb project that ended up winning us the Second Swarm War, in a way that not even she foresaw—if those warheads hadn't have been on the *Victory* when Granger piloted it into the Penumbran black hole…."

"Makes sense, in a twisted way."

Proctor raised an eyebrow. "How so?"

"In complicated situations like that, like in the Second Swarm War, there was no way to know exactly what was going to work, or through which path victory would be achieved. And so Avery—at least, this is my theory—basically had a scattershot approach. Her goal was to throw as much shit against the wall as she could and wait to see what stuck."

Sometimes it seemed that way. The fog of war could be so thick at times that Proctor often wondered if it might not be a wiser course of action just to strike out in random directions to keep her many enemies off guard and unbalanced. Throw as much shit against the wall and see what stuck. Eventually, one of the one-in-a-million chances would stick, and they could all go home and take a long vacation.

Life doesn't work that way, Shelby.

"No. We don't have time for that." She turned to Qwerty. "Send word to Captain Volz. I want to go confront Mullins. Make him see some reason. See if he's behind this attempt to get us into a war with the Dolmasi," she added, with a knowing glance at Liu. "Oppenheimer doesn't seem to have the balls to do it, so I guess *someone* has to."

Qwerty nodded, but before he could acknowledge, Lieutenant Whitehorse caught her attention. "Ma'am, I'm getting odd sensor returns from the debris field of El Amin."

She leaned forward. "Odd? How so?"

"Nothing terribly urgent, it's just that ... well, I'm doing a passive optical scan of the debris field—which is getting wider by the second, but the size distribution is off. And it doesn't match the scan from when we first showed up in the system."

Proctor stood up and approached the tactical station. "Show me."

Whitehorse brought up a graph of the size distribution of the debris field, and overlaid it on the one taken several hours previously. Sure enough, there was an odd bump on the new graph that was not there on the old. "There. See it? I can't explain it. A bump, centered on ... one hundred and twelve point five square meters."

"What's the uncertainty? Does the data have error bars? Could this just be an artifact of ... I don't know ... our angular position with respect to the debris field and Sangre de Cristo, or something like that?"

"Uncertainty is less than point one percent on any given data point. This is ten times that. Could be a fluke...."

Proctor rubbed her forehead again. "Or it could be something else. One hundred and twelve square meters cross section ... tell me, Ms. Whitehorse, do you think it's coincidental that the bump in the data just happens to occur at the same size as your average light cruiser?"

Fiona Liu cocked her head. "Are you thinking there could be a fleet hiding out there? Curiel? As far as I know he doesn't have more than a few ships loyal to the GPC."

"Perhaps Mullins has something else up his sleeve."

Lieutenant Qwerty glanced up. "Or, ma'am, could be Dolmasi."

The look on his face told Proctor that he wasn't guessing. "Meta-space activity?"

"Yes, ma'am."

She walked over and gripped the edge of the comm station. "Mr. Qwerty, are you ready? You've had two days to learn their language and the Ligature's protocol from Krull's notes. Was that enough?"

He grunted, then grunted some more, then coughed violently, before screeching something vulgar-sounding. "Excuse me, ma'am. That was Dolmasi for, *you can bet your cheesy grits I'm ready.*"

Proctor raised another eyebrow. "You suppose the

Dolmasi have cheesy grits?"

"Be a shame if they didn't, ma'am."

It was enough, in spite of the urgency and dread of the situation, to make her chuckle. To take the edge off. "All right. Set q-jump coordinates. Take us out there, Ms. Liu. And please inform Ballsy where we're going—I imagine we'll need some backup."

CHAPTER FORTY-FIVE

Wreckage of Moon El Amin
ISS Defiance
Bridge

"Fighters on standby. Just in case." The orders went out, and Proctor imagined Volz was doing the same thing on the bridge of the *Independence*. As much as she liked the silent, invisible, and incredibly deadly *Defiance*, she missed her ship.

"Ready, Admiral," said Liu.

"Initiate."

The screen shifted, and the wavering infrared image of Sangre de Cristo was replaced by a cloud of rock and dust and glowing debris as the remnants of El Amin collapsed back in on itself, initiating new explosive collisions that ejected massive bands of material out into space.

And, right there on the screen, sidled up to an assortment of giant rocks, hung a Dolmasi fleet.

"Gotcha," she murmured.

"Reading eighteen Dolmasi cruisers, with an assortment of fighter craft. All mostly powered down to avoid detection." Whitehorse looked up. "Looks like they were hiding here, probably massing their forces for an attack on Sangre or San Martin."

"And now?"

Whitehorse examined the sensor readout. "Looks like they're powering up."

"Weapons?"

"Not yet." Whitehorse shook her head. "I think, maybe, that the fact they can only see the *Independence* might suggest to them that we're not looking for a fight."

Proctor stroked her chin. "Send word to Captain Volz. Have him tell Admiral Tigre back at San Martin what's going on, and to send backup."

Qwerty got to work on the message, and when he was done, he looked inquisitively at Proctor.

"What is it, Lieutenant?"

"I think we should open a channel to the Dolmasi, ma'am."

"Why? When we open our channel to talk them, they'll see there's two ships. Might spook them, and they could just start shooting."

Qwerty shrugged. "Don't see any way around it, ma'am. If we wanna test out my Dolmasi chops, I gotta shoot the shit with an actual Dolmasi." He pointed at the screen, "And that there is an actual Dolmasi fleet. The more I talk to them, the more I'll understand them."

She grit her teeth. There wasn't time. Tigre hadn't shown up with the San Martin defense fleet yet. And yet Qwerty was right. The best way through this emergency would be through simple communication. Talking to their enemy. Understanding them, rather than fighting them.

"Open a channel."

CHAPTER FORTY-SIX

Wreckage of Moon El Amin
ISS Defiance
Bridge

On the viewscreen, Proctor watched as the eighteen cruisers slowly turned to face the *Independence*. Even in infrared, she could see the running lights powering on all up and down the sides, and before long, the group split into a formation of nine ships each.

"That's a Dolmasi attack formation," said Proctor. She spun towards the comm station. "Mr. Qwerty, it's now or never."

He gulped, nodded, and took a deep breath before tapping his channel open.

"Sssssss ... ssstok valek kirsak? Ssssss ... sssskirsak kasavska ssss...."

He continued on, making a series of seemingly random hisses and grunts. The formation of nine ships on the left swung wide around a large asteroid and momentarily disappeared before coming around the other side.

"Admiral, they're powering up weapons!" yelled Whitehorse.

"Huh. Well they didn't like that one bit," said Qwerty. "Mighta come on too strong there."

Proctor grimaced as the formation on the right followed suit and swung several dozen kilometers out before circling around to flank the *Independence*. "Too strong? Let's make our best effort to not start another war here, Mr. Qwerty."

"Yes'm. From what I can tell from Dolmasi culture and its affect on their language, you need to start a conversation from a position of … bullheadedness and strength. Almost overblown. Otherwise, they'll think we're too weak to even bother responding. You can tell from their emphasis on morphological structure that their language has been heavily influenced by—"

"Mr. Qwerty, as a former university professor, I appreciate the lecture. But for now please focus on helping us to *not die*."

"Loud 'n clear, ma'am." He cleared his throat again. "Ssssss … kirsakus ankelifalakus kirsak!"

Whitehorse shook her head. "Ma'am, it's not working. Their targeting systems are coming online. An attack on the *Independence* is imminent."

Proctor stood up. "All right, that's enough. Rayna, how close can we get to one of their ships before they can detect the stealth effect on our hull?"

"Right on top of them, basically. Just got to stay far enough away so their cameras can't resolve the refresh rate on the projectors—basically stay a diffraction limit length away.

Fifty meters?"

"Ok. Ms. Liu," she turned to navigation, "half thrust, and take us right on top of the lead ship there on the right."

"Ma'am? At that range, if they fire at us, we're goners."

"We're not going to let them. Do it."

A deadly silence fell over the tiny bridge as they watched the lead Dolmasi ship grow larger and larger on the screen. Before long, it was so close that Proctor knew if she went and looked out a port she could essentially reach out and touch it.

And they knew that one blast from the Dolmasi antimatter beam would be enough to end them all.

"Holding at fifty meters, Admiral. Matching their course and speed."

"Good. Now target the other formation. Fire a few low-velocity gun rounds. Enough to hurt them, but not bad."

Everyone turned toward her. "Ma'am?" said Whitehorse.

"But also enough so that the other formation knows they've been fired upon from this direction. Look—*Independence* is over there at three o'clock. It'll confuse the hell out of them."

Whitehorse shrugged, but did as ordered. "Direct hits on the cruiser at point."

"*Now*, Liu. Get us the hell out."

Liu scowled in confusion but directed the *Defiance* to arc above the plane of the engagement. "Clear of the enemy formation, Admiral. Holding at z plus five klicks." She turned towards Proctor. "Might I ask what that was all about?"

Proctor watched the screen intensely. "If my suspicions are correct…." She trailed off, gazing at the two formations still angling towards the *Independence*, which itself had started to turn to bring its main guns to bear. "That the Dolmasi are here is not a random occurrence." She turned to face her small crew. "Three things. First, Oppenheimer has been getting after me for weeks to use the meta-space pulse technology against the Dolmasi. He claimed it would disrupt the Ligature, which it clearly does—that much was obvious at Mao Prime—and that disruption aligned with his long-stated goal of finding and neutralizing the latent Quiassi and Findiri threat. Second, I suspect it also summons them. A giant sign that says *here I am, come get me*. It's why the Dolmasi showed up at Earth after that nuke exploded with the meta-space shunt attached. *And* the Golgothic ship, for that matter."

She paused, long enough for Liu to lean in expectantly. "And the third, Admiral?"

"I believe the meta-space pulse also disrupts their higher reasoning functions. Like language. Reasoning. Exaggerates their natural tendency toward violence. Incites anger and uninhibited fighting. What they do next could not only confirm that hypothesis, but also point to why they're here in the first place, and also confirm the motive behind Oppenheimer's insistence upon using this stupid weapon."

And, as if the Dolmasi were waiting for the cue from Proctor, the formation that had been fired upon unleashed a barrage upon the ships nearest the *Defiance*, raining a shower of green beam pulses with destructive force against the hulls, which shattered and broke and exploded outward into space. The nearby formation returned fire, and soon, the *Independence* forgotten, the two groups pounded into each other with bloodthirsty ferocity.

"And that motive?" said Whitehorse, though her face

suggested she knew the answer as she watched the scene unfold. Dolmasi on Dolmasi violence and utter destruction.

"To start an interstellar war. And to assure that we come out on top…" Proctor finally sat back down with a sigh, "by making all our enemies go insane."

CHAPTER FORTY-SEVEN

Wreckage of Moon El Amin
ISS Defiance
Bridge

"Admiral, two of the Dolmasi ships are disabled, and a third is losing power." Whitehorse looked up. "What are your orders?"

Proctor was still deep in thought. That the Dolmasi were this affected, this unstable, meant that someone nearby had recently deployed a powerful meta-space pulse. Hell, that the Dolmasi were even here at all suggested as much. "Nothing. We do nothing. We can't afford to do otherwise, as appalling as this is to watch."

Qwerty motioned towards her. "Ma'am, getting a message from Captain Volz."

"Read it."

Qwerty jumped right in. "Shelby, are you sending out meta-space messages? I wonder if that's not … affecting the

Dolmasi somehow. Like how we talked before. I'd suggest shutting it down, whatever it is."

Proctor glanced at Qwerty questioningly. "Wasn't me, ma'am." He double checked his console status board. "But it could very well be an echo from the pulse that clearly lured the Dolmasi here, and wigged them all out somethin' fierce. If they get strong enough, meta-space echoes can last for hours...."

"Mr. Qwerty, you're up. Do something. Pull out all the stops. If you can't put an end to this, no one can."

Qwerty swallowed hard. "I ... I'll try, ma'am. But nothing I was sayin' earlier seemed to be making an impression. I was confrontational, vulgar, blasting—everything I could think of that they would respond to."

"Well try something else!" Proctor watched as the infrared screen lit up with anti-matter beams as the Dolmasi ships pounded into each other.

Qwerty was shaking his head, and muttering strings of Dolmasi words into his receiver.

"Wait," she said. "You're talking to them through the Ligature, right?"

On the viewscreen, a nearby Dolmasi ship exploded. "Yes, ma'am."

"The Ligature is a Skiohra invention. And it was imposed upon the Dolmasi by the Swarm. Maybe we need to talk like one of them. Less confrontational. More...." Her mind raced. How did the Swarm always talk? At least, through the beings that they controlled?

Manipulative. Confident. Almost ... smarmy and overly familiar. *Friend.* They continually called beings they targeted for incorporation into their family, *friend*.

"Be ... kinder, Qwerty. More agreeable. The Swarm was never insulting to us, even as they annihilated billions."

"Roger that," he said, and leaned back into his receiver. A different string of sounds came out of his mouth and throat. Less guttural. Softer. More agreeable.

Lieutenant Whitehorse watched the screen, and whistled. "Well I'll be damned."

Proctor turned to watch it too. The anti-matter beams ceased. She couldn't be sure, but it almost looked like each Dolmasi ship actually *turned* to look at the *Defiance*. "We're still stealthed, Lieutenant?"

Whitehorse slowly nodded, and triple checked her instruments. "Yes, ma'am."

The silence was almost eery. The Dolmasi ships, some of them half-destroyed, simply hung there in space, pointed towards the *Defiance* as if they could see it.

"Ma'am, they're ... hailing us."

"*Us?*" She spun around to Whitehorse. "Is that stealth working or not, Lieutenant?"

Whitehorse furiously worked her console, checking and rechecking, but Qwerty answered for her. "Sorry ma'am, they're not so much hailing *us* as hailing *you*. On a broad channel. I ... don't think they know exactly where we are, otherwise they'd use a tighter beam."

"*Me?*"

"Yes, ma'am. They clearly want to talk to ... ahem ... *The Consort of the Invincible of Earth*." His face took on a pained expression. "Sorry, ma'am. I think by *consort* they mean *companion*."

"So it's English now?"

"Broken English, but yes."

Proctor gripped her armrests, almost unsure of what to do. But this was clearly the breakthrough they'd been waiting for. Been working for. "Can you re-route our response through the *Independence*? Make it look like we're transmitting from there?"

Qwerty nodded. "I think so. Tight beam to *Independence* through laser, and then they broadcast through regular comms."

"Do it."

Half a minute later, the viewscreen shifted. "Well I'll be damned," Proctor muttered under her breath. The screen was filled by the image of a Dolmasi. After all these years, she'd almost forgotten what they looked like. Vaguely reptilian, skin scaly with a somewhat greenish hue. Eyes like fire and a stare like flint.

And this one looked familiar.

CHAPTER FORTY-EIGHT

Wreckage of Moon El Amin
ISS Vanguard
Bridge

Admiral Mullins turned towards President Quimby, who was staring at the screen with his mouth half open. "See, Mr. President?"

"Is that ... is that a Dolmasi?"

Mullins nodded.

Quimby couldn't seem to peel his eyes away from the screen. "Ugly sons of bitches, aren't they?"

Next to the alien's image, another appeared.

Her. Admiral Shelby Proctor.

"Just as I suspected, Mr. President." He gave a surreptitious nod to his tactical officer. "Shall I give the order?"

Quimby waved him off. "Hold on, Ted. Let's see where she's going with this."

Mullins drummed his fingers on his armrest impatiently.

Very well. If the bastard needed more proof before the order was given, all the better.

More plausible deniability for himself.

CHAPTER FORTY-NINE

Wreckage of Moon El Amin
ISS Defiance
Bridge

"It's Kharsa. Vishgane Kharsa," said Proctor, almost under her breath.

Qwerty's eyes narrowed. "Ma'am?"

"The same one Tim and I talked to thirty years ago. During the Second Swarm War." She watched the alien's face, looking for signs of familiarity, any sign that the alien also recognized her.

But in place of recognition, Kharsa looked … agitated. His eyes flitted back and forth, his hands squeezed and clenched the air restlessly.

"Well, regardless ma'am, you're live. He can hear you."

She cleared her throat and slowly stood up. "Vishgane Kharsa? Is it really you?"

He hissed.

"I'm Proctor. Do you remember me?"

More hissing. The alien looked like he was only barely holding it together.

"We fought together. Side by side, thirty years ago, you and I. We beat them. We destroyed our enemies. The enemy that kept your people as slaves for thousands of years. And now ... it's good to see you. Friend."

The hissing turned to something a little more ... mellow. Kharsa opened his mouth and tried to speak.

"Consort. Vishtak sustaka ... shtsh ... stalsh.... Why? Why? We'll ... destroy you. Kirsak. We'll destroy you, if ... kirsak. If we must. If we need. We'll destroy ... back. KIRSAK!"

Proctor held her hands up and outward. A universal sign of peace. Submission. "I swear to you. We are not your enemy. We do not want to fight you. Our enemy is...." She trailed off. It occurred to her that she still had no idea who their enemy was. The truth was, the enemy was ... themselves. Mullins? Curiel? Whatever was changing Titan and destroyed El Amin? "Our enemy is ... not you. We want only peace. Only friendship."

"Kirsak. Same with Valarisi. Swarm. They want make friend. Make *us* friends. Slaves. Kirsak. Kirsak."

She turned to Qwerty, questioningly. She mouthed the word Kharsa kept repeating. *Kirsak*.

In as low a voice as possible, Qwerty replied. "I think it's an insult. Like a cross between dog, son of a bitch, and, I think, *slave*."

Slave. It made sense. The Swarm made the Dolmasi their slaves for thousands of years. Made them their enforcers—

their mindless, will-less warriors.

"We destroyed them, Vishgane. You and I. Made them *less* than ... kirsak."

His eyes flared wide. Pupils like embers.

"There ... is ... no worse. Than kirsak."

The meaning was clear. Kharsa considered death better than slavery. "I agree, Vishgane. But they're gone. And we are not your enemy."

He seemed to consider this. After a moment, he spoke. "No. No enemy."

"We are friends. Allies. Let us ... let us fight together. Join our forces against that which assails you."

Kharsa's eyes defocused and flitted somewhat, like he was trying to remember something he'd forgotten. Something he knew long ago and was struggling to remember. And then he seemed to find it.

He nodded.

Proctor remembered, thirty years ago, Kharsa had been particularly diligent in learning human mannerisms. The nod was significant.

"Our enemy is ... human. You know that, Consort."

She really wished he'd stop calling her that. To the Grangerites, she was *The Companion of the Hero of Earth*. To the Skiohra, she was *Motherkiller*. And now ... *Consort*? Good grief.

But his enemy was *human*? He stared at her. He seemed so sure of it. And, maybe he had a point—perhaps something Mullins was doing was targeting the Dolmasi. Or perhaps Curiel was doing it. Or maybe even Oppenheimer.

"It is, Vishgane. And we'll track them down. And make them pay. Bring them to justice. No matter who it is. We'll get to the bottom of it. I'll defend you from whoever among my people is assailing you. Allies, you and me. Friends."

Kharsa seemed to force himself to manipulate his facial muscles in a way that seemed grotesquely unfamiliar with him. Slowly, his mouth spread into an awkward smile—or at least the best impression of a smile that the Dolmasi was capable of.

"Friends. Again."

CHAPTER FIFTY

Wreckage of Moon El Amin
ISS Vanguard
Bridge

Mullins smiled too. Finally. There was the proof. At least, proof that Quimby would believe, the stupid bastard. "You see?"

"See what?" The president still stared at the screen, watching the two talk—the Dolmasi leader and Proctor.

"Mr. President, have you not studied the briefing on the Swarm that Oppenheimer has surely supplied you with? You do recognize this language, do you not? This very particular wording?"

Quimby swiveled his seat toward Mullins. "I see Proctor defusing the situation, Mullins. In a fashion that, while admittedly a little unnerving, is effective. You'll note that nobody is firing at each other. Seems like a win to me."

Oh for god's sake....

"Mr. President. If you've read your briefings—which I'm sure you have—you'll undoubtedly know that this particular terminology was what the Swarm used. They wielded considerable influence over individuals infected with the Valarisi virus, a process that they called *making friends*. And once someone was ... converted, if you will, or fallen under Swarm control, they became *friends*."

Quimby's eyes narrowed, and he glanced back up at the screen. Good—Mullins could see the little wheels turning in the asshole's head.

"And now, she's not only using the same *friendship* language that was so particular to the Swarm, she's claiming she's allies with the Dolmasi, and that she will help them hunt down the humans who are the Dolmasi's enemies."

And now for the clincher. "Furthermore, Mr. President, we've detected a steady stream of meta-space communications between the ships out there, *including* the *Independence*. Is it not clear to you what is happening?"

Quimby stared at the screen, watching the two continue to talk. He nodded slowly. "You were right. I don't know how, but you were. She's under Swarm control. So are they. The Dolmasi. Holy *shit*. I ... I can't believe it."

"Believe it, Mr. President."

Quimby turned back to him. "Oppenheimer too?"

"I'm almost sure of it. She's acting on his orders, after all. And did you see his reluctance to use the meta-space pulse to finally put a stop to this? To end the threat once and for all? He's complicit. I'm one hundred percent sure he is Swarm-controlled."

The little wheels churned. Mullins could almost see steam

coming from the president's ears. Good god, people voted for this ignoramus?

"Ok. Do what you have to do."

Mullins nodded solemnly. "Yes, Mr. President." He paused. "By the way, Mr. President, we have on board several ... warheads. Banned warheads. Anti-matter bombs. Some of the original produced under President Avery during the war. I'd go to prison if I used them and it was discovered, but ... *you* could authorize it. It's a pretty damn big decision though. Something that none of your predecessors since Avery ever ... dared to do."

At the word *dared*, Quimby's nostrils flared. He could play this man like a fiddle.

Quimby's eyes opened as wide as his nostrils. "*I* dare, Admiral Mullins. *I* decide. *I* make the decisions. And this one's mine. I authorize the use of anti-matter warheads against the Dolmasi. Do any have meta-space shunts attached?"

Mullins smiled. "Of course."

"Then you have my authorization. Fire."

CHAPTER FIFTY-ONE

Wreckage of Moon El Amin
ISS Independence
Bridge

Captain Volz watched and listened to the negotiations, sitting on the edge of his seat. He didn't even realize he was holding his breath as several points in the conversation until his vision swam a little bit.

It was working. Shelby had done it. She'd actually done it. Qwerty had figured out the Dolmasi language enough to grab their attention, and force them to talk. And now Shelby was actually getting them to stand down.

They might actually win this thing. Win without even firing another shot.

Lieutenant Cobb, the tactical officer, shouted. "Sir! Detecting ... oh my god."

"What?" Volz spun around to face the officer.

"It's an ... anti-matter warhead. It just fired from ...

somewhere."

"An *anti-matter warhead*? Are you sure?"

"Yes, sir. The gamma signature coming off it is unmistakable."

Oh my god, indeed. "Those are banned! What the actual hell? Where did it come from? Where is it going?"

Cobb shook his head. "Unknown. And it's trajectory is … not towards any single ship. It's just … going in the general direction of the Dolmasi fleet."

"Guided?"

"I think so."

"Take it down. PDCs. Weapons clear. Fire."

The viewscreen changed to show the exterior of the ship, and Volz watched streams of shells leap off the *Independence*'s hull, racing towards the warhead. But the missile looped and swerved. It was indeed guided, and had a sophisticated ordnance evasion package to boot.

"Increase rate of fire. Take that thing down!"

CHAPTER FIFTY-TWO

Wreckage of Moon El Amin
ISS Defiance
Bridge

"Admiral! Someone just fired an anti-matter missile!" yelled Whitehorse, interrupting her conversation with Kharsa.

She spun around. "Where did it come from?"

Whitehorse shook her head. "Unknown."

Proctor drilled her eyes into Liu. "He's here. Isn't he? *Mullins*."

Liu nodded. "It would seem so."

On half the viewscreen the camera tracked the progress of the missile, which raced out towards the middle of the space occupied by the Dolmasi fleet. Streams of fire from the *Independence* leapt out, attempting to take it down.

"Lieutenant, fire. All PDCs we have."

"Admiral? That will give away our position."

"Do it."

The viewscreen erupted in even more weapons fire as their own PDC cannons tracked the missile.

But it was hopeless. It swerved and dodged, and when it was in the middle of the Dolmasi fleet, it exploded.

The viewscreen blinked momentarily at the explosion. When it came back on, everything looked the same except for the quickly dimming fireball that had been the missile.

Whitehorse shrugged. "Huh. Whoever shot that wasn't even aiming at anything. All Dolmasi ships intact and accounted for. Guess we got lucky."

Something was wrong. They did not just *get lucky*.

She turned to resume her conversation with Kharsa, but paused when she saw his face.

It was frozen. His eyes open as wide as she'd seen them.

"Vishgane? We're investigating that missile. Are all your ships ok? I didn't see it damage any of your vessels but…."

She trailed off. Something was wrong. He wasn't responding. Just staring at her.

Whitehorse flagged her attention. "Ma'am. I think I know what happened. There was something attached to that warhead."

Proctor finished her sentence. "A shunt. A meta-space shunt. Like the ones that were on the nuclear warhead that…." She couldn't even finish her own sentence. *The nuclear warhead that Danny's ship fired at Sangre de Cristo.*

"Except … well, ma'am, this was an anti-matter warhead. Fifty gigatons. This completely dwarfs the bomb over Sangre de Cristo, and the one that came out of our own hanger deck and detonated over Earth. And subsequently, the energy released into meta-space was … immense."

The viewscreen image of Kharsa disappeared.

"Where did he go? Get him back."

Qwerty shook his head. "Sorry ma'am. They terminated the transmission."

"Admiral, they're coming about. Kharsa's ship and the ones in his formation. They're advancing on our position."

"Move us. Keep our heading random. They shouldn't be able to track us. Buy us some time to untangle this mess. Qwerty, keep trying to get them back."

And on the viewscreen, something else appeared beyond the Dolmasi fleet. Something big.

Something huge.

The *Magnanimity*. Polrum Krull's ship.

"Incoming transmission from the Skiohra, Admiral," said Qwerty, glancing up nervously up at the giant Skiohra generation ship that had just appeared. "It's a broad-range signal designed to blanket this entire area. Text only."

"Read it."

Qwerty's eyes grew wide. "We have terminated the Ligature. It is gone. You can abuse it no more. Go in peace, Motherkiller." Qwerty looked up. "That's all, ma'am."

And, as quickly as they'd arrived, the Skiohra q-jumped away.

Proctor couldn't believe it. "They destroyed their own meta-space link. They destroyed the Ligature." After thousands —tens of thousands?—of years, they'd destroyed their own method of communicating with each other over long distances. Even short distances. From what she knew of Skiohra physiology, the mothers on board their generation ships even used it to communicate simultaneously with the thousands of children living within them, in addition to their thousands of children already born.

The Swarm had used the Ligature for their own corrupt purposes, but at its core, it was still a fundamental part of Skiohra society, despite the fact that it had been used for thousands of years to control the Dolmasi, and presumably the Findiri and Quiassi—though nobody could be sure of that.

Proctor could not keep an involuntary shudder from running the length of her spine. Even at the height of the war against the Swarm, the Skiohra had not destroyed the Ligature. But now, in reaction to humanity's actions, they had done so. There would be consequences. Of that, Proctor was sure.

Liu glanced sidelong at her. "But what does that mean?"

Proctor stared at the screen, at the assembling Dolmasi cruisers. "It means … that the only moderating influence on the Dolmasi … the only thing that ever kept their warlike tendencies in check… is now gone."

CHAPTER FIFTY-THREE

Wreckage of Moon El Amin
ISS Vanguard
Bridge

"Sir, the shunt worked as designed. Nearly forty percent energy conversion," reported one of the tactical officers near Mullins. He'd let the president sit in the captain's chair, relegating the real person in charge—himself—to a seat at the tactical station. "Conversion completed within two point five nano-seconds. Resulting meta-space power spike ... about fifteen million exawatts."

"That ought to grab their attention," said Mullins.

"Sir," the tactical officer continued, "before the warhead detonated, there was a second source of PDC cannon fire aiming at the missile."

"Source?"

The officer shrugged. "Unknown. It's like it came from empty space, near a point here...." He tapped at a spot on the holographic schematic of the local volume of space displayed above the tactical board.

Proctor.

"It's another stealth ship. Proctor is on it. Only thing that make sense."

"Good Lord, how many of these things did we build?" said Quimby.

"Officially? Two. The *Vanguard*, built at Shovik-Orion's Aegis shipyards at Bolivar, and the *Defiance*, which should have been in the safe keeping of Admiral Tigre out of San Martin, but it looks like the old softie has turned it over to Proctor." Mullins looked at the viewscreen at the front of the bridge. "Ah. There's our cue to leave. The Dolmasi are coming around and forming up into attack wings. Navigation, get us the hell out of here. We can't have the president in a war zone, after all."

Quimby looked like he might actually protest. Mullins could see the conflict in the man's face—on the one hand he didn't want to look weak, like he was running from danger. On the other hand, people died in battle, and powerful men tended to gain and keep power because they were good at not dying. "Unless, you'd prefer to stay, Mr. President? Watch how the chips fall here?"

A pause, then a forced laugh. "Nothing else to see here, in my opinion. Get me to Britannia. I think it's time to get the joint chiefs of staff together and have a discussion about how much longer we want Admiral Proctor running around. And Oppenheimer—he should be at Britannia right now anyway."

Mullins smiled, and gave the signal to the navigation officer. "Most wise, Mr. President. Most wise."

CHAPTER FIFTY-FOUR

Wreckage of Moon El Amin
ISS Defiance
Bridge

"Admiral, the Skiohra q-jumped away, but there's something else. Right as they q-jumped into the vicinity a minute ago, there was another q-jump signature from somewhere nearby. Something left just as the Skiohra showed up." Whitehorse glanced at another flashing indicator on the tactical board, and smiled. "Also, Admiral Tigre just showed up with the San Martin defense fleet."

Proctor sat back down and watched as the Dolmasi fleet ordered itself into several attack wings. It seemed their mental instability was gone. Gone with the Ligature. And in it's place, a cold, clear-minded general leading his warriors into battle.

"It was the source of that missile. That other q-jump signature." She motioned to Qwerty. "Get me Tigre."

A moment later, Admiral Tigre's lined face appeared on

the screen. "Miguel, how many stealth ships are there?"

"Two."

"You're sure?"

"Pretty damn sure. These beauties aren't cheap, or easy to build. I had one—the *Defiance*. And, if I'm not mistaken, I believe the other one went to Mullins. The *Vanguard*."

Shit. The old bastard was behind it all. Setting up a war between them and the Dolmasi. As a screen and a front, to keep them all distracted while he seized power. It was the only explanation.

"Regardless. We've got a situation here. Is your fleet prepped for battle? These Dolmasi look like they mean business, and I don't think we can talk our way out of it this time."

"We're ready. I've got seven heavy cruisers and ten frigates. Add in the *Independence* and the *Defiance* and we're about evenly matched."

Proctor sighed. "That's what I was afraid of. I'd rather be in a position to kick their ass. But you go to war with the army you have, Admiral."

"Indeed," grumbled Tigre.

The first Dolmasi attack wing swung by, unleashing a storm of green anti-matter beams on Tigre's fleet even as the *Independence* swung up and around to flank them.

"Zivic, get your ass out there," she said into her comm.

"Yes, ma'am!" came the reply. And she could have sworn that he added, just as the link cut out, "*Finally*."

CHAPTER FIFTY-FIVE

Wreckage of Moon El Amin
Lieutenant Zivic's Cockpit

"All right people, look alive. There's five of us and five hundred of them, but keep your heads and we might stay alive," said Zivic as the five birds lifted off from the tiny hangar deck and blasted out into the void. There were far more than five of them, given that the *Independence* and the San Martin defense fleet had shown up, and there didn't appear to be anything close to five hundred Dolmasi fighters, but the true number—the HUD claimed two hundred and thirteen—was enough to pose a problem all the same.

An indicator on the HUD told him that his bird's extremely long wave radio was receiving a signal. He flipped it on with a blink of his eye.

"Whitehorse to squad," came Jerusha's voice through the heavy static. The ELW radio was only used in extraordinary circumstances, and it was Ace's idea to use it now since it would be difficult to get a spatial lock on the stealthed *Defiance* using the ELW radio instead of the usual comm signals. But it made for nearly incomprehensible communications. "Orders are to assist ... defense of the San Martin flee—. *Defiance* is stealthed so we'll ... fine. *Independence* ... plenty of fighters, ... Dolmasi seem to be focusing ... San Martin fleet anyway."

"Roger that," said Zivic. "On me, people. Ace and Bucket take my three, Barbie and Spectrum on my nine. Let's go show these bastards what real flying looks like."

They shot out towards the unfolding battle engulfing the San Martin defense fleet. A dozen Dolmasi light cruisers were descending on the *Farragut* and the *Enterprise*, green beams lancing out with terrible destructive power, viciously slicing into the hulls. Zivic winced when he saw a body fly out from one of the gashes in the *Farragut*.

"Break. Delta formation. Wrap around and take the bogeys out at Z plus one."

The five ships broke out of formation and looped around and up from the plane of approach, catching a group of Dolmasi fighters by surprise that had been harassing one of the San Martin light cruisers. Three puffed into debris and shrapnel before the others had even noticed the fighters.

"Ace, careful there. Bucket, help her out." He fired off another few shots at a hapless bogey even as he watched Bucket loop around Ace and blast the tail she'd picked up.

Barbie whooped over the comm. "Take that you flying two-faced dolphins!"

That was a new one. Playing off the word *Dolmasi*, Zivic supposed. No time to speculate. "Watch Spectrum's six, Barbie, he's got a tail."

"On it, mate."

Barbie swung wide and up, as if leaving the plane of battle, before he pulled a hard six and pointed "down" as Spectrum shot by with his Dolmasi tail, which quickly exploded in a muted fireball as Barbie peppered it with slugs. "Oh boy, put another shrimp on the barbie," Spectrum called over the comm.

"Wait … I thought we called you Barbie because your voice sounds girly, Barbie," said Zivic.

"Nah," Bucket said, "It's because of that idiotic catch phrase. What the hell does that even mean?"

"Exactly what it sounds like, mate." Barbie said, seemingly confident that was an adequate explanation, and returned to formation with Spectrum, and the pair darted off to intercept an incoming squadron of Dolmasi fighters.

"Bucket and Ace, help them out. Looks like they're going for the *Farragut*—she doesn't look to be in good shape…."

He squeezed off another few shots and felt the satisfying rush of euphoria as another bogey blew apart into glowing slag. A glance at a counter on his HUD told him that he'd reached twenty. "Eighty-one more to go," he muttered.

"These are apples to oranges, Batship. One of these counts for two Swarm fighters, at least," said Ace.

"Tell that to Ballsy. If I say something like that, I'd never hear the end of it. Watch your ten!" He pushed his controls to swing up and wide over her wing as she dropped down, exposing the approaching pair of bogeys to his sights.

"Thanks," she breathed into her headset.

"Let's go help them out." He pointed his fighter towards the *Farragut*, which was spouting huge gouts of flame as propellant mixed with oxidizer near the port engine. The five fighters zipped around the broken vessel, picking off any Dolmasi fighter that strayed too close. Before long, the fires gushing out from the tears in the hull went out, and the rush of Dolmasi fighters had slowed to just a trickle.

"I think they're good. Let's go help the *Libertador* with those other bastards. That's Admiral Tigre's ship—Proctor will flay me alive if we let something happen to—"

A green flash nearly blinded Zivic and he yelled out. "Batship, PULL UP!"

Ace's voice in his headset was loud enough to ring in his ears, but he managed to pull his bird away at the last second. Right where he was headed, a pair of Dolmasi anti-matter beams were boring into the *Farragut*'s hull. Right near where the reactor room would be….

"Get away! Now!" Zivic ordered his squad, and they peeled off towards the *Enterprise*.

And just in time. An explosion ripped through the main body of the *Farragut*, and the rest of the ship convulsed, breaking apart in a thrashing cloud of debris and fire.

He swore out loud.

Dozens of voices were yelling out over his comm-line as other squads rushed to intercept a wing of Dolmasi fighters veering towards the other ships in the San Martin fleet. Ace's voice broke through the confusion. "Come on, Batship, *Enterprise* is taking it on the nose. If we don't help relieve the —"

She didn't even finish her sentence before it too exploded. His viewscreen dimmed to block out the glare.

"I sure hope she's got a plan," Bucket muttered over the

comm.

"It's Admiral Proctor. She's *always* got a plan," replied Zivic.

But as he watched the tragedy unfold, he started to doubt it.

CHAPTER FIFTY-SIX

Wreckage of Moon El Amin
ISS Defiance
Bridge

They'd lost the *Farragut*. And the *Enterprise*. And three frigates. Proctor surveyed the layout of the battle—the remaining ships flitted in and out of the expansive debris field left by the destruction of El Amin, and the fighters swarmed among them. Sixteen fully-armed relentless Dolmasi cruisers among them.

They were losing. If she didn't do something, quickly, all would be lost. The Dolmasi were fighting in a way that she hadn't seen before.

It was like they were unleashed. Whatever the Ligature had done to them through the centuries, whatever moderating, calming influence the Skiohra had had on them through the meta-space link was now gone, and it manifested in the very feel of the battle.

They were ferocious. They were fast.

They were lethal.

"Captain Rojas, pull to starboard and relieve pressure on the *Libertador*, and we'll cover you."

Whitehorse was concentrating intently on her tactical board—the designers of the *Defiance* had streamlined and simplified the ship's design such that just about all the ship's military functions could be controlled by a single officer, if necessary, to be able to run light with a small bridge crew. But it didn't mean it was easy. "I ... I don't think Tigre's going to make it, Admiral. The *Libertador* is listing—its port dorsal thrusters are stuck on, and there's no power to the other thrusters." She looked up at Proctor with a pained look. "She's starting to spin out. And in this debris field...."

She didn't need to finish the sentence. Proctor watched in horror as the *Libertador* arced slowly, surely, towards one of the larger asteroids—a giant chunk of rock that was slowly orbiting the gradually-coalescing fiery ball that would some day be the new El Amin.

"Miguel, you've got to cut that dorsal thruster," she yelled into her comm. "Miguel!"

Tigre's voice cut through the din of the bridge. "It's ok, Shelby. Remember Tim's old moves? Here, hold my beer."

Whitehorse, Babu, and Liu all looked up, brows all furrowed, not understanding him. But the meaning was quite clear for Shelby. Tim Granger's old moves often involved launching starships at enemies like they were common bricks. He used ships like a brute force projectiles, earning him his nickname, *Bricklayer*. "Miguel ... no!"

But it was too late. On the screen, the pair of active

thrusters on the *Libertador* flared with a sudden rush of increased power, and the massive ship accelerated into its arc. Except now, with all its power dumped into those two thrusters, the path changed slightly.

Right into the path of a Dolmasi cruiser.

"Miguel…."

The *Libertador* rammed straight into the Dolmasi ship, puncturing it on its stern like a skewer. And the pair of them rammed right into a second Dolmasi ship, nudging it into a new course.

Straight into the giant chunk of rock. The three ships crashed into the surface of the asteroid, triggering explosions that ripped through all three….

Culminating in the triggering of the *Libertador*'s reactor. Tigre must have removed the safeties, allowing the anti-matter to be liberated from its control matrix during the secondary explosions that ripped thorough the hull. And in a blinding flash, all three ships disappeared, taking a significant chunk of the asteroid with them.

When the glowing slag dissipated, half the asteroid was gone. Including the *Libertador*, and the two Dolmasi ships.

Whitehorse had been yelling at her, but she hadn't even heard. "What?"

"I said, Admiral, we were hit by a few stray mag-rail slugs. We're venting something. Which means—"

Proctor finished her sentence. "They can see us."

As if on cue, the nearest Dolmasi cruiser unleashed its anti-matter beam straight at them. The ship jolted so hard that Proctor almost thought they had hit an asteroid themselves.

"Hull breach! Down in the fighter bay," said Whitehorse.

"Babu, you're on damage control. Go coordinate the marines—they're on patch duty." Proctor gave Babu a slight nod as he ran off the bridge, then turned her attention back to the battle. "Get us into that debris field."

"That won't hide us, ma'am."

"No, but whatever we're venting may just blend into the clouds of dust and debris from the remains of that explosion, and might throw them off for long enough for us to get a few well-placed kicks in."

The *Defiance* veered towards the tumbling asteroid and the glowing remains of the three destroyed ships. A pair of Dolmasi cruisers followed them, pelting them with blast after blast of the green anti-matter beam.

"Shelby, get the hell out of here!" Volz's voice shouted out of the comm.

"The commander doesn't just turn tail and run from the battle, Ballsy, you know that—"

"Shelby," he interrupted, "look around. The battle's over. They're just mopping up now. We've got half our strength left, while they've only lost a few ships. It's over. Let's get the hell out of here before we lose everything."

Dammit, he was right.

She'd lost. She had been on the verge of victory, nearly defusing the Dolmasi threat once and for all.

And now Admiral Tigre was dead, she was about to die, and lose the entire San Martin defense fleet, all within a few minutes.

"You're right. We need to protect San Martin. Regroup there. Their orbital defense platforms should give us cover if we're pursued. Odds will be better."

But not much better.

She flipped another comm switch. "All fighters, come home, combat landings. Now!"

It took an agonizing full minute before the last fighter screeched to a landing on the fighter deck. "Now, Liu!"

Moments later, the q-jump drive engaged, and San Martin appeared on the viewscreen, replacing the dull, glowing slag cloud left by the *ISS Libertador* and the other ships. While Proctor was grateful to not be flying blind, the inverted colors on the infrared screen made everything feel eerily unfamiliar, as if she were living in some sort of alternate universe. *Focus, Shelby.*

Liu let out the breath she had apparently been holding. "We made it."

Proctor stared at the screen as the other ships in the San Martin defense fleet q-jumped in around them: too few. Finally, the *Independence* snapped into existence, and she allowed herself to breathe as well.

"Not all of us. Not by a long shot." She stared at the screen, waiting for the inevitable. "And those bastards are going to show up any minute."

CHAPTER FIFTY-SEVEN

The shuttle from Boston to New York was quick, not even making it to sub-orbital space before beginning its descent through the atmosphere. Twenty minutes after blasting off the launch pad, the four of them were already waiting at a crosswalk on eighth avenue with a crowd of people. Traffic was heavy—there was a UE Congress session starting that week, and all the diplomats from fifty different worlds were streaming into the city.

"Carla, dear, stop prancing," said their mother, who was grinning ear to ear.

"Sorry, mama, I just can't help it." Carla looked like she was on cloud nine, even though their father had hinted on the shuttle that there might be some punishment at school for their "missions." But right then, in that perfect moment, nothing could bring her down.

The crossing signal changed and the crowd of people waiting on the sidewalk began to cross the street. Shelby and Carla followed their parents in the last group that moved out onto the street before the warning signals began to flash indicating another light change.

"Come along, girls." Shelby watched her father eye the traffic nervously. These off-world folks brought lots of people with them. Aides, attachés, personal assistants, family members, drinking buddies, corporate cronies—lower Manhattan became an unruly madhouse during the General Session of the UE Congress.

As always, the dream proceeded relentlessly. There was no stopping it.

In the dreams, Proctor, or at least the adult version of Proctor hanging over the child version of Proctor like a ghost, would always scream out at this point. And sometimes, in her ghost mind's eye, she thought she saw teenage Proctor cry out too. Could almost hear her screams.

A ground car raced around the corner. It was an ungodly bright green, complete with air spoiler and what she assumed were racing stripes —some unimaginably expensive toy of the son of some inter-solar corporate oligarch or senator, the plaything of a scion son of a rich family, which scion held other human life in such low regard that when, after Carla's limp body landed in a broken heap across the street, the monster kept right on driving as if he'd only hit a speed bump.

She flew like an angel. Like one of her mother's imaginary angels.

She tumbled like a rag doll. Soaring through the air, until it collided with a red brick wall on the other side of the street and collapsed into a heap.

Proctor had learned, years later, that the police had indeed apprehended the driver, though through his rich father's string-pulling, he got off with only a year in a UE prison.

One year. One year in exchange for Carla's life.

As it always did, even in the dreams, time slowed down. Adult Proctor simultaneously watched her sister fly through the air, and watched teenage Proctor kneel over her, screaming, weeping hysterically.

"Car! Carla! Carla! Oh God, Carla! Oh God, Carla!"

Distantly, she knew she was hearing sirens, her father's shouts, her mother's screams, and somehow teenage Proctor managed to calm her nerves enough to search her sister's neck for a pulse. The broken, twisted neck.

She felt it. It was weak. It was slow. But it was there.

Carla's eyes were open, skewed up and to the right, wide open. Her mouth formed words. Shelby leaned in close to hear them.

"Shell. Shell. Listen. That brick wall jumped out of nowhere ... saved me. It's a miracle ... would have died. Would have flown into ... the pit ... the hole ... the pot. Boiling oil. Where they fry the donuts. The oil is black. A hole. A hole. But not empty. But the brick wall. It's a miracle, Shell. Shell. The elf bird. Follow it to Mars. Look, it's there...."

Shelby looked to where Carla was staring. A crow, perched in a branch above them—Carla, in her delirium, must have thought she was back in the shooting range simulator, seeing the crow as the elf bird. She was talking gibberish. And now her eyes closed, and Shelby felt her pulse. It was still there. Weak, but there.

One in a million, she whispered, as with her other hand she reached for the necklace under her shirt. She thumbed a few beads and repeated the prayer.

"Please God, don't take her now." She repeated it like a mantra, even as she was pulled away by the emergency crew, even as the emergency shuttle took off for the hospital three blocks away. Right up to the point where the emergency room doctor stepped into the waiting room, his head bowed low, his eyes pained. And when he looked up to deliver the news and met her eyes, she knew.

Her one in a million God was a false idol.

She did not believe.

The doctor spoke incomprehensible words, and left. Her father was an inconsolable, blubbery mess. And her mother sank onto her knees pleading to an imaginary vending machine deity for her daughter back. She would do anything. Give anything. A transaction. Put a coin in, out comes a blessing from the vending machine god. One thing in exchange for another. Everybody wins.

But all Shelby could do was serenely stand up, rip the necklace free—a handful of beads scattered onto the floor—and throw the remaining bits at her mother's feet. She left before she said something she would regret for the rest of her life.

CHAPTER FIFTY-EIGHT

Orbit over San Martin
ISS Defiance
Bridge

They waited several hours, enough time for Proctor to rest, but the Dolmasi fleet never pursued them in all the way to San Martin. Perhaps they thought there was a larger defense fleet held in reserve. Or perhaps they were more damaged than it appeared during the battle. Either way, the *Independence* and the *Defiance* orbited San Martin, along with the remnants of the San Martin defense fleet.

Eight ships. Eight, out of the original eighteen that Admiral Tigre had brought with him.

She couldn't even bring herself to do the math. How many people per ship? She tried to think about something else.

Damage control and repair was enough of a distraction. "Liu, what's the status of the stealth? Are we back up yet?"

"No, ma'am." Liu seemed to work tirelessly. She didn't

even look up, and hadn't had a break in hours. She just hunched over her console on the bridge, struggling to get their stealth system back up and running, studying the manuals, occasionally consulting with Lieutenant Qwerty who would lend a hand with the various systems checks and diagnostics.

At least, that's what she assumed they were working on. Proctor had bigger fish to fry. She'd been talking on and off for the past hour with Captain Volz, debating whether to request a fleet transfer from the nearest UE system in case the Dolmasi showed up again and the planetary defenses were inadequate. But then that would leave the other world with their ass hanging out if the Dolmasi decided to strike there instead.

Technically, it should be Oppenheimer's call, but her trust in the Fleet Admiral of IDF had waned to a point where she wondered if he wasn't even on their side—at the very least he was displaying a frightening level of incompetence.

"What do you think, Ballsy? Are they going to show up again?"

She could almost hear him shrug over the comm. "Doubt it, if they haven't by now. Nothing's stopping them from waltzing in here and razing the surface after snuffing us out. Poof. One billion dead. Biggest loss since the war."

"It could be that they know nothing about what orbital defenses we have. They're good, but not *that* good: just a few dozen ion beam cannons on the surface and orbital mag-rail platforms. If the Dolmasi come in just right, out of reach of the platforms and the cannons, then we're goners."

"I guess we'll have to stay in range of the platforms. At least until the *Independence* has finished repairs—Admiral, we got hit pretty bad over here. We'll need to dock at Wellington Shipyards at Calais for at least three months. Hang on, I've got news…." His voice cut out as he listened to a report from one of his bridge crewmembers. "Ok, we've got a report from the scout ship that CENTCOM San Martin sent back out to El Amin. The Dolmasi fleet's gone. No sign of them. And q-jump signatures indicate they got the hell out of dodge."

She shook her head in relief. Good, at least *that* disaster was averted. For now. "Who's the new commander here? Who was Miguel's second in command?"

"Vice Admiral Tillis. Good guy. I knew him on the *Farragut* back in the day after you left for IDF HQ."

"Good."

Volz's voice changed. "Why? What are you thinking?"

"Ballsy, something's going down. That anti-matter torpedo that just *appeared out of nowhere*? First of all, there shouldn't be any left. They're banned. Second, it had a meta-space shunt attached to it. Third, and I repeat, *it came out of nowhere*. That can mean only one thing. Mullins has a stealth ship. And he's provoking a war with the Dolmasi. Something about those meta-space spikes seems to draw them in. Provoke them. Today his target was San Martin. Tomorrow? The only question in my mind is, where does he arrange for the next attack? That's my priority right now. We need to stay one step ahead of him, and prevent him from starting a war we can't win."

He chuckled. "And knowing you, from the sound of your voice, your mind is made up about where you're going next. Earth? To stop him just in case he goes to the center of civilization? I'd bet you anything he tries to unleash that meta-space shunt there. That's where our force is strongest. That would provoke one hell of a battle."

She nodded, and suddenly it hit her.

Polrum Krull. The Ligature. "She destroyed it. Why would she do that to themselves unless she thought…."

"Shelby?"

"Just a hypothesis. Less than that. A thought. Krull destroyed—at least she claims she destroyed, or perhaps she just temporarily shut it off—the Ligature. The meta-space communication system they've had for millennia that allows them to instantly interact with every being connected to it. But the meta-space shunts interact with it in a way that dumps astronomical amounts of energy into meta-space, and subsequently into … every being attached to it, including the Dolmasi."

"You think its absence presents us an advantage? From what we saw at El Amin, once the Ligature was gone, the Dolmasi went off the rails. It was like the Ligature was a calming influence for them all these years."

"Right. I think it was. And with the Ligature gone, Mullins's meta-space shunt may still work, may still summon the Dolmasi and make them even crazier. We can't just count on it *not* working. And given what the Skiohra did to the Ligature, we have no idea what effect that shunt will have— you'd think they wouldn't just destroy it on a whim, and if destroying it now *doesn't* prevent Mullins from pulling meta-space shenanigans then one must wonder why Krull pulled the trigger. Perhaps it was just to prevent the shunted meta-space energy from bleeding over into the Skiohra's mental link with one another."

Volz grunted. "Basically leave all the other races using the Ligature high and dry. Save the Skiohra, but screw the Dolmasi, the Quiassi, the Findiri, and whatever random Russian still on that thing."

She nodded, but she she hadn't gotten to the point yet. "But, and here's the key, from my Swarm research thirty years ago, I learned that the Ligature also acted like a one-way channel. Like a meta-space diode. And like a regular electronic diode, it's a one-way street. You have a call going in one direction, and a response going in the other. But always one thing at a time. One direction at a time. Now that it's gone…." Her face scrunched up, trying to remember all the technical work she did with meta-space signals and the Ligature when she was Tim Granger's XO during the Second Swarm War.

"You think we can counter it?"

She nodded. "I think so. With the diode gone, it's no longer a one-way street. And anytime you have a two-way street, in terms of wave properties, you can have one of two things. Constructive interference, or destructive interference. And since meta-space signals are indeed waves…." She turned around to Whitehorse at tactical. "Lieutenant, you've got a new job. Adjust our meta-space transmitter, building on the specs that Oppenheimer passed to us to recreate a meta-space pulse, but this time, invert the phase to what would typically be found in a pulse produced by a meta-space shunt."

Whitehorse slowly nodded. "Yeah, ok. It'll take me awhile, but I think I can do that. Can I test it?"

"No, you may not. This has to be kept absolutely secret. Come up with your best simulations, and that will have to do." She turned back to the comm. "In the meantime, I've got an appointment to keep."

"To Earth? Head off Mullins, in case he's going there?" said Volz through the comm.

"No. I'm going to Britannia."

He sounded genuinely surprised. "Britannia?"

"I've got a … social call to make. Former president Avery wanted to talk to me. I ignored her, and then … El Amin happened. Mullins launched that torpedo. And who started the anti-matter weapons program in the first place? Avery. Could it be that, after all these years, there are still a few that she squirreled away, and Mullins knew just where to find them? Whatever it is she's got to tell me, I figure it's time I heard her out."

"Got it. What have you got to lose?" Volz replied.

"That's exactly what I'm hoping to find out."

CHAPTER FIFTY-NINE

Orbit of Britannia
Shuttle

Proctor wondered what someone might see—if anyone was watching—when the shuttle left the bay. Would it appear to emerge from the black emptiness of space? Would they catch a glimpse of the shuttle bay's interior, like she had when she arrived onboard? Britannia's orbital space was teeming with ships—IDF cruisers and frigates, industrial transports, merchant freighters, leisure yachts and corvettes for the ultrarich, and smaller colonial transports for everyone else. Out the window she saw one such colonial transport, probably packed to the brim with settlers from Britannia's overcrowded cities bound for one of the newly established settlements on Rivadavia. Inflated real estate prices tended to drive off the sane and keep the speculators, the heirs to large fortunes, and those willing to cram themselves into apartments scarcely fifty square meters. She watched a particularly bulging colonial transport escape from the upper atmosphere full of the sane, the hopeful, and the young, and wished them well.

Would they make it? Would they be waylaid by pirates or slavers, or Dolmasi, or another Golgothic ship? So many dangers in the universe. Maybe Oppenheimer was right. Maybe humanity needed to focus on finding the Quiassi and Findiri before they found humanity. Maybe nothing could be left to chance. The two unknown alien races could be benevolent, but she supposed that chance was one-in-a-million, given what she knew about intelligent races—humanity being exhibit A of just how shitty intelligent beings could be to each other.

"Hold on, ma'am," said Lieutenant Zivic, who she'd asked to pilot the shuttle. She tightened her restraints, and nodded at the small squad of marines accompanying her. They were traveling light—just her, Zivic, and five discreetly armed marines. They were only going to a retirement community at the outskirts of Whitehaven on the seashore, after all, no need to draw undue attention. And it was Britannia, the center of human civilization after Earth, so barging in with a platoon of armed-to-the-teeth marines would probably not be well-received in the sea-side resort where Barbara Avery had retired.

A short time later, after a few minutes of choppy atmospheric reentry and Zivic having a small argument with port control, who insisted on knowing the exact identity of everyone on board—everyone save Proctor—they were there.

The secret service met them in the driveway of the compound, along with a middle-aged gentleman Proctor recognized as Avery's long-time body-man-turned secretary. He'd started as the late Vice President Isaacson's body man, but after his untimely death at the hands of Swarm-corrupted

Ambassador Volodin, Avery decided the kid knew too much, and rather than ship him off to one of the remote new colonies at the edge of explored space, she brought him onboard, and then decided she actually liked him. What was his name? Connelly? Connor? Yes, Connor.

"Ms. Avery is expecting you, ma'am. Welcome." He held his hand out in greeting and muttered something into his earpiece.

Proctor shook the outstretched hand. "Are we alone?"

"No. Huntsman is here." His face betrayed what he really thought about the idea of a wacko upstart prophet having the ear of his boss, one of the most significant and powerful presidents UE had ever seen, and one who had a remarkable ability to stay relevant this long past her tenure. Without another word, he waved her along, not to the front door of the sprawling residence, but around a side path to the rear, where, in the middle of a garden veranda, surrounded by fountains and hanging grape vines, sat a shriveled former President Barbara Avery in a wheelchair, like an old, wizened elf.

The old woman cackled and smiled, the deep lines and wrinkles bunching up around her face. "Shelby, how the fuck are you?" Her arms quivered as she pressed herself to a stooped standing position, and waved Proctor in for a surprisingly solid hug. "Fucking doc says I have to stand up and walk around at least twice a day. This counts." She collapsed back into the wheelchair with a grunt.

"As foul-mouthed as ever, I see," said Proctor, sitting across from her, a smile spreading over her face. She'd only met the former president a handful of times during the Second Swarm War, and just twice afterwards, but she was still as feisty and vulgar as ever.

"You know what they say about shriveled old cunts like us, Shelby." She trailed off and picked up her cup, taking a sip.

"What's that, Barb?"

Avery shook her head. "Fuck if I know. Fuckers talk about us behind our backs. They can fuck off—I'm rich and have my own beach resort, and they're eating shit."

Proctor couldn't help but smile at the over-the-top vulgarity. She took a deep breath, relishing the scent of the ocean breeze coming off the water just a hundred meters down the rocky slope from the veranda. She remembered her own beach property she'd bought just the week before Admiral Oppenheimer showed up in her classroom at Oxford Novum University. A month ago. What the hell had they done about her class? Had the students kept showing up? Had the administration replaced her? Someday, preferably soon, she could go back both to her new house and her classroom, assuming she still had a classroom to go back to.

"Barb, why am I here?"

Avery cackled. "What, don't want to see me? We're old friends, Shelby."

"Barb, we hardly know each other." She turned to Conner, who'd returned with a steaming hot Irish coffee—how he'd known what she wanted was beyond her. Damn, the man *was* good—she saw why Avery kept him.

The former president waved a dismissive shriveled hand. "Nonsense. When you're ninety-nine fucking years old, you hold on to any friend you've got. All my friends, all my family, are dead, Shelby. All I've got left are the old shrews down the street I play backgammon with, you, Connor—though between you and me I think he works for IDF Intel," she paused to eye the man who stood not ten feet away, who shrugged at her in return with a slight smirk on his face, "and maybe Quimby. But now that he's president he don't come around so much, the fucker."

Shelby nearly spit her drink out. "You're buddies with President Quimby?"

"Buddies? No." Avery tipped back her drink, which, from the smell wafting over, Proctor could tell was a dark bourbon, possibly infused with chocolate. "But I was mortal enemies with his pops when I was president and he was president of the senate, and so I did what the old adage says. Keep your friends close," she took the last swallow of her drink, "and your enemy's children supplied with loud toys. Naturally, I gave my enemy's child the loudest, most obnoxious toy of all. The presidency."

Proctor snorted. That was one of her favorite things to do a few decades ago—giving her brother's kids annoyingly loud toys as payback for all the ways he'd tortured her as a little kid when she was nearly twenty and still grieving Carla.

The thought brought back memories of Danny. And the awful, mysterious circumstances of his death. "I used to do that with my brother's kid."

Avery nodded. "That's why I brought it up. That's why you're here, Shelby. That's why I've got that cunt Huntsman here. He's got some information for you. Or at least, he thinks he does. I want to make sure he thinks he's giving it to you."

"What information? What could a fanatic so-called prophet have to tell me? I'm trying to fight a war here, Barb."

"He knows what happened to your Danny."

Danny? She remembered the grainy video Admiral Tigre had produced for her, with the unidentified ship docked with the *Magdalena Issachar*.

Avery nodded at Connor, who ducked out of the veranda.

"Danny died. Falling through Sangre de Cristo's atmosphere in nothing but a vacuum suit."

"So he did. And I'm sorry." The former president finished her drink and set the cup aside. "But do you know who tossed him out there? I'm guessing you don't. Huntsman is here to tell you."

She thought about Avery's words, and how she had phrased things. "And what do you mean, *make sure he thinks he's giving it to me?*"

Avery laughed. "How long have you known me?"

"They always said you were ten steps ahead of everyone else."

"Ten? Fuck. Make that ten fucking thousand." She pulled a flask from her hip pocket and tipped it into her empty cup. "Pay attention. You surely know I'm being watched, right? They'd never let me sit here and hold court with admirals and upstart prophets without listening to every word. Just keep that in mind dearie, and you just might learn a thing or two."

What the hell was that supposed to mean? She was about to press further, but a sound behind them cut her off.

Patriarch Huntsman appeared behind the wheelchair, holding a bottle of beer and a data pad. "Admiral Proctor! What a surprise," he said. "The prophecies are true, after all, and here you are. The Companion to the Hero of Earth," he pointed to Proctor, "the Facilitator of the Ascension," he indicated Avery, "and the Prophet of the Next Generation," he said, thumbing towards himself. "Just as the prophecy foretold, gathering just weeks after the ascension itself."

Proctor resisted the urge to roll her eyes. "And whose prophecy was that, Mr. Huntsman?"

A small smile. Almost humble. "Mine, of course."

CHAPTER SIXTY

High Orbit over Earth

The steel shipping container had cooled somewhat. It no longer glowed red-hot, but it was still scalding. Hot enough for the heat to penetrate to the core of the house-sized chunk of gallium, liquifying the entire fifty tons of metal.

The gallium didn't slosh, didn't churn, as one might think it would moving so fast around the Earth. It was, of course, in free-fall, and orbiting at an altitude where normal freighters and cruise-liners never ascended. But soon, something changed. A vibration rippled through the gallium. Something was disturbing it.

A nozzle extended from the rear of the container, just above the thrusters. With a clank, the pump's engine engaged, the aerosol device sucked gallium from the compartment, injected helium, and the nozzle dispersed the pressurized mixture out behind the make-shift craft. It dissipated like a faint, silver cloud. A glittering trail left behind by the accelerating cargo container.

Now the sun rose above the horizon, now it fell.

When it rose, the glittering microscopic particles of gallium melted, forming an ever-expanding gallium haze left in the wake of the container.

When the sun fell behind Earth's limb, the cloud froze as the gallium solidified.

And still the steel container accelerated, spreading the trail of silvery metallic cloud in an undetectable band around the Earth.

Undetectable to anyone not looking for it.

CHAPTER SIXTY-ONE

Britannia
Whitehaven Oceanside Estates

Proctor eyed the self-proclaimed prophet warily. "And? This better be good. I don't have time for your delusional Grangerite bullshit."

Huntsman chuckled softly and sat down on the couch across from her, to Avery's right. "It's good. If you care about your nephew, it's good."

"What the blazes do you mean, *if I care about my nephew*? My nephew is dead. And if I find out you have anything to do with it, Huntsman, you'll find yourself flying out of one of my airlocks before any UE criminal court can get to you."

He scowled. "Of course I don't have anything to do with it. It wasn't even GPC."

"Are you sure?" said Proctor. "And if you are sure, how would you know that? Are you in bed with Curiel?"

Avery cackled. "She means figuratively, dear. No need to

tell us about your raucously gay sex life. I know all about your values."

Huntsman scowled again. "I might not be a Mormon bishop anymore, Madam President, but I do have my standards."

Avery waved another dismissive hand. "You missed the point. I was hoping for a nice racy story to get me all bothered. Whatever. Go on, then."

Huntsman glared at her, but held up the data pad. "My sources tell me that it wasn't GPC at all, in spite of what certain parties would want you to believe. It started with the GPC, but it ended with none other than … well, see for yourself." He handed the data pad over to Proctor.

It was the same video feed Tigre had showed her. The grainy image of the *Magdalena Issachar*, and the unidentified ship docked with it.

"That's it?"

Huntsman's face fell. "What do you mean, that's it?"

"*That's it*, as in, I've seen this. You think I don't have access to all the orbital video feeds from the military satellites over Sangre de Cristo?"

"But they were tampered with. This is the original video feed."

Proctor smiled. "Interesting. How did you know they were tampered with?"

Huntsman actually went red. "Because one of my tech guys analyzed the video and it showed all the hallmarks of tampering. Said something about sample rates and interlacing pixels and … stuff."

Why in the hell had Avery summoned her here to get

information she already had? How had she phrased it? *He's got some information for you. Or at least, he thinks he does. I want to make sure he thinks he's giving it to you.* And then she hinted that someone was listening in on them. Which meant, what? That Avery was going to try and tell her something … in code? She studied the older woman's facial expression and demeanor.

Nothing. Just stone. Staring at Proctor intently.

Proctor stood up. "Barb, I'm sorry, I've got a war to fight. Civilizations to save. I'm sure you're familiar with the routine. If you'll excuse me—"

"Sit down, Shelby." Avery's ragged voice took a sterner note. "I turn one hundred next week. Doc says I've got ten more years, tops, assuming I don't take the new stem cell-based hormone shit. Which I won't. Shit's unnatural." She reached out a hand and waved two fingers, which summoned Connor from wherever he was waiting. "This is the real reason why you're here, Shelby." Connor handed Avery a data pad, which she held out to Proctor.

"What?" said Proctor.

"What?" said Huntsman.

"What, you didn't think I'd summon the admiral here just because you thought you had some information, that she ended up already having anyway? Of course she'd already have that video, dipshit."

"But then—" Huntsman had gone even more red, understanding that he'd been played. He looked around himself, probably half expecting to see military MPs move in.

Avery cackled. "Calm down, jackass. It wasn't you that asked *me* to come here. It was *me* that summoned *you* here. You might think you're ten steps ahead of everyone, but in reality,

I'm fucking ten miles ahead of you all. Now listen. I've brought you here for one simple reason. You have the ear of Curiel, and the information I'm about to give the admiral could have a significant bearing on the events of the days ahead. I want you to go to Curiel, and give him a message. But first, take a look, Shelby."

Proctor accepted the data pad from Connor, and brought the information up on the screen.

It couldn't be.

"How did you...."

She scrolled through. It seemed remarkably complete. And impossible.

"When I was still president, I initiated several top secret programs. Weapons and intel programs of course—the antimatter program being the most ... *visible example*," she paused, and seemed to wink at her. "But one of the lesser known programs was of a more analytical and academic bent. Didn't have the interest of the top generals, so I was able to sneak it through under some lesser-noticed programs. And when I left office, I took the results with me because I deemed it necessary. And now I'm giving it to you."

"You managed to infiltrate the Dolmasi merchant fleet, and interpret their language?"

"Not all of it, just a modest vocabulary and list of rudimentary grammar rules, but yes."

Qwerty was going to have a field day with this. "How did you...."

"Not important. Suffice it to say I had friends in high places back then. And coming off saving not just one civilization but three, I had a lot of fucking favors to call in. I trust your multi-lingual show off of a lieutenant can use this?"

Interesting. She apparently knew about Qwerty. Proctor nodded silently, still poring over the data.

Avery swiveled in her wheelchair to stare Huntsman down. "Now, dear, go back to your friend Curiel, and tell him he's got bigger fish to fry than arguing with Quimby or Mullins or Proctor or Tigre or whatever political enemy-du-jour he's fighting against. Tell him no one cares about his show-boating. It's time to face the real threat."

"And that is, Madam President?" He looked skeptical.

"The real enemy is coming. They may already be here." Avery held up a finger and waved it towards Connor, indicating she was ready to go. "If we don't all start fighting it together rather than fighting amongst ourselves, I fear the worst."

CHAPTER SIXTY-TWO

Orbit over Britannia
Shuttle

Proctor was so lost in her thoughts during the shuttle ride back up to orbit that she didn't even notice Babu calling her until he waved a hand in front of her face.

"Ma'am? Ma'am? We're nearly there."

"What? Oh, yes, thank you, Ensign." A quick glance out the viewport told her that they'd cleared the atmosphere and were angling towards an apparently-empty direction of space above Britannia, which she knew was occupied by the stealthed *Defiance*. Liu had finally managed to get the damned thing online again—the young woman was resourceful, she'd give her that. When she put her mind to something, she worked doggedly, single-mindedly, and achieved it.

She had been lost in thought about former President Avery. While the Dolmasi language research would certainly be very helpful to Lieutenant Qwerty, it just didn't make sense why Avery didn't just transmit the blasted file to her instead of going through some round-about scheme to get Patriarch Huntsman passing her a note through Secretary General Curiel to meet him at Avery's retirement compound, only to show her a video she'd already seen. It didn't add up.

"Hold on," she said, looking up at Ensign Babu. "Send word to the *Independence*. I need to talk to Ballsy. One on one. In my ready room on *Defiance*."

Babu passed the message forward to the pilot, and Proctor slid back deep into her own thoughts. Before she knew it, she was sitting in her ready room, hands cupped around a hot cup of coffee courtesy Ensign Babu, and facing Captain Volz. His face looked grim.

"I've got the final numbers from the El Amin engagement with the Dolmasi. You ready for them?"

"No."

He looked taken aback, but she waved him on.

"Ten ships lost, five with heavy damage. Eleven thousand five hundred and two dead, over a thousand still in critical condition. Overall, nearly ten thousand wounded."

She set her cup down and held her head in her hands. "Dear God." Even one was too many. Eleven *thousand*? "We can't afford this war. Either in lives, or ships. However you want to measure it. Mullins is going to pay."

"There's more," said Volz. "You took a pounding here on the *Defiance*. There's a chance that another ship, if they know just how to look, might see you even when you're stealthed."

"And you can bet that Mullins knows just how to look. If we're ever in the same orbit as him again, we'll need to have our finger on the q-jump button." She picked up her cup again and drained it. "Ballsy, how do you fight a man who's determined to plunge our civilization into an apocalyptic war? Just think what Mullins could do if he, for example, went to Earth and unleashed his meta-space pulse and baited a Dolmasi fleet there?"

"You think he'd do that?"

"Well he's certainly shown he's capable of it. He did it at El Amin. I'm certain he and Shovik-Orion are responsible for the development of the meta-space shunt. That pulse at El Amin was generated with a small anti-matter bomb. The smallest version that came from Avery's secret weapons program. And even with the smallest version, Mullins was able to generate a meta-space pulse larger than any we've seen so far, and it wreaked such havoc with the Ligature—or at least with the mental state of the Skiohra that Polrum Krull decided it was better to destroy it rather than leave theselves vulnerable. Just imagine what Mullins could do with one of the full-size versions of that bomb."

"You think there are any more still around?"

She chuckled darkly. "Funny you should ask. Avery even mentioned them a few times during our conversation." She paused. "In fact, it almost seemed like she was emphasizing them. Hinting at something. The tone in her voice. The way she said it…."

Volz leaned in. "What did she say?"

"It was in the context of the Dolmasi language data she gave me. She mentioned she had a handful of secret programs running, and that the anti-matter bomb development program was just one of them, the language program being another. And … well, it's silly, but … she *winked* at me."

"Excuse me? She winked at you?"

"Yes."

Volz seemed to be waiting for something more. "And?"

"Ballsy, you didn't know Avery like I did. I only met her a handful of times, but she never, ever, *winked*. She was always direct. Always in your face. A vulgar trash-talking no-bullshit straight-shooter. Wink? Barbara Avery would have sooner curtsied and offered to make me tea and crumpets."

"So? What does it mean? Was she trying to tell you something? Something between the lines?"

Proctor thought for several moments, trying to piece it together. "It's been bothering me: it's odd that she summoned me there just to give me the Dolmasi language information. It's something she could just as readily transmitted to us."

"And risk all of UE knowing that she's still an active player and helping you?"

"Oh, they already know that. Having me as a guest did nothing to hide that. Better to transmit a coded message if secrecy and discretion were her goals ... *oh*."

"Oh, what?"

"Code. I remember thinking it at the time, but dismissed it. Maybe she brought me there to give me the data in person because what she wanted to tell me was coded?"

"Coded how?"

"Maybe in the data itself. The language data. I mean, let's face it, the language data is valuable, but in retrospect, it wasn't *that* valuable. Nothing Qwerty couldn't have figured out on his own in a couple more sessions with the Dolmasi." She tapped the comm button on her desk. "Mr. Qwerty, please come to my ready room. Bring the datapad I gave you."

Moments later, Qwerty sauntered through the door. "Summoned to a top secret meeting? Wow. I'm gettin' popular."

"Like I told you before, Mr. Qwerty, you are the most valuable officer in IDF at the moment. Please have a seat." When he'd settled, she reached out for the datapad, which he handed over. "Tell me about the language data. Has it been helpful?"

He shrugged. "Well, yes and no. Yes, there are a bunch of words there I didn't know yet. And a few grammar rules I'd gone back and forth on, but honestly, those particular rules weren't *that* important. I would have gotten the meaning across either way. There were a few morphological issues it helped me out with, but again, nothing groundbreaking."

She flipped through the various data files. "So, nothing you couldn't have figured out yourself given a few more days?"

He smirked. "Honestly? A few hours."

"Notice anything ... strange? About the data? Or the datapad?"

"Ma'am?"

"You know. Odd. Files that shouldn't be there. Encoding algorithms that seem out of place or ... just things that might pique your curiosity as to why they're there?"

"Honestly, ma'am, I wasn't looking for anything like that."

She tossed the datapad back to him. "Well look now."

He fiddled with it, swiping back and forth between files and indices and folders. He shook his head every now and then. Finally, he looked up. "Sorry ma'am. Nothing out of the ordinary."

Proctor stroked her chin. "Damn."

Volz pulled the datapad toward him and examined it. "Well, back up. Maybe it was in something she said. Not in the datapad, but in her words. Was there anything else odd about that conversation?"

Proctor shook her head. "Now that I think about it Ballsy, the whole thing was just weird. Surreal. Why the hell have me there with Huntsman, when she knows he's a complete moronic snake-oil salesman? He's a total fraud. Inventing an entire religion and making off with who knows how much cash and power and influence. Plus, he's in bed with Curiel. Surely Avery knows that. Why have both of us there? And then acting like we were old friends, when in fact we'd only met a few times. And then why give me data that, in the end, isn't all that helpful?"

"Would she have known it wouldn't be helpful?"

"Avery rarely did things on a whim. No, this meeting had a purpose, and the more I think about it, the more I realize we have no idea what that purpose was."

The three fell silent. Qwerty looked almost uncomfortable to be there, but had nothing else to add. Proctor looked up at Volz, momentarily forgetting her polyglot lieutenant was there. "Ballsy, I've been having dreams. Well, a dream. The same dream. Over and over."

"Oh?" Volz leaned in, very interested. "Are you a believer in dreams? Subconscious trying to tell you something?"

She made a face. "No. I most certainly do not believe anything of the sort. But…." She hesitated. It sounded so foolish. "But, well, it's not exactly a dream. It's a moment from my childhood that I'm reliving over and over again. When my sister died. She told me, talking about a bird we used to hunt in a simulator, *follow the elf bird to Mars*. I ... just couldn't help thinking about it as we were talking about the Mars Project. Avery's anti-matter bomb program."

Qwerty nodded. "Well, that makes perfect sense."

They both turned to him. "What?" she asked, incredulously.

"Elf bird," he said. "Avery." He glanced from one to the other, and back again. "Get it?"

Proctor slowly nodded. "What, you think *Avery*, in my subconscious mind, gets turned into something like ... *aviary*, and from there to *bird*? And that I should follow the bird?" She shook her head. "Stupid. Just plain stupid. We're wasting our time."

Qwerty shook his head. "No, ma'am, that's not it at all. The surname *Avery* comes from the old English name *Alfred*. Alf, or rather, aelf. Means elf. And red, is like ... counsel, or advice. So Avery literally means *elf's counsel*."

A strange feeling washed over her. Such an ... oddly specific meaning—how could the death ramblings of a little girl sixty years ago have any bearing on what was going on?

Qwerty continued. "So maybe in your dream your subconscious is telling you to take Avery's advice."

"Yes, but what *is* her advice? She's told us nothing we don't know."

Qwerty perked up. "What about in the words themselves?"

Proctor shook her head again. "No, nothing she said is ringing a bell or sticking out to me—"

"No ma'am, I mean in the vocabulary words." He reached for the datapad, which Volz relinquished. "Maybe something about their order, or just which ones she included and which

DEFIANCE

she excluded...." He paged through the lists of words and their supposed meanings, muttering occasionally to himself.

Proctor was skeptical. "I don't know. It sounds too simple. Too obvious. Why would she risk so much on just a simple—"

"Bingo," Qwerty announced.

Both Proctor and Volz stared at him.

"It was in the vocab words. The second word of each definition lays it out for us. It's like an acrostic—a poem where the first letter of each word spells something out. This one is only slightly more sophisticated, easy to miss, but easy to catch if you know you're looking for ... something."

Proctor waved him along. "And? What does it say?"

He picked the datapad back up and cleared his throat in an overly theatrical way. "Ahem. Dear Admiral. Hard times coming. I saved several bombs for occasions like this. Use them wisely."

"Oh my God. She did stockpile some. I mean, Mullins had to get his from *somewhere*, right? There's got to be others she's hidden away somehow. Qwerty? Any indication of where?"

Qwerty swiped back and forth between different files, muttering and shaking his head. Finally, "Aha."

"And?"

He looked up. "Had to switch to the vocab files titled *numbering system*. Same deal, an acrostic method using the second term, this time with letters and numbers. C-A-L-A-I-S, I-C-C-1-7-0-1-5-2-D."

Proctor nodded, understanding immediately. "Calais. Wellington Shipyards in the Britannia system. Ballsy, check the registry for a ship with registry number ICC 170152D."

Volz accessed the computer terminal at the desk, and

moments later came up with a nod. "A missile frigate. Mothballed. Cold and dark, in deep storage."

"That's our bird. Probably filled to the brim with anti-matter bombs." She paused for a moment. "What's ... what's the ship's name?"

Volz almost looked like he went white. "The ... *ISS Elf Owl.*" He set the datapad down. "Well. Holy shit."

Qwerty eyed her. "Well if that don't fry the grits I don't know what does."

Follow the elf bird to Mars, she'd said. To Mars. The Mars project. The anti-matter bombs. Somehow, they were necessary. She'd need them in the days ahead.

Proctor paused. She *knew* the linguistic connections here had to be coincidental. It was absolutely impossible that a dying Carla had somehow foreseen this moment. Less than even a one-in-a-million chance. Still, she couldn't ignore Avery's message, unnerving, inexplicable coincidences be damned.

"Fine. Set course for Calais. And then we're on to Earth, just in case that's where Mullins decides to lure the Dolmasi next. And send in Ensign Babu. I've finally got a job for him."

CHAPTER SIXTY-THREE

Orbit over San Martin
ISS Defiance
Pilot's Ready Room

"And then, just like that, in less than five seconds, I told her, 'Bingo.'"

Zivic sipped his terrible coffee, rolled his eyes, and glanced at Whitehorse, who was looking similarly annoyed. The brilliant Lieutenant Qwerty, while personable, had turned out to be quite the self-promoter. "You actually interrupted the admiral with *bingo*?"

"You can bet your cheesy gr—"

"Please stop saying *cheesy grits* in regular conversation. Normal people don't do that." Whitehorse stood up from the table in the pilots' ready room and began rustling around in one of the cupboards for something to eat. "It makes you sound like…." She glanced over at Zivic for help.

"An idiot?" he offered.

"Now wait just a minute," Qwerty began, apparently only just beginning to sense that he'd lost his audience. "I was only saying that I thought it was rather brilliant of me, if I say so myself—and I do—to come up with the solution to the code within five seconds of the admr'l asking me to look into it. That's all. All humility here. Like my grans always said, *he who toots his own horn should—*"

He was interrupted by the doors opening and in walked Ace. She stopped in mid-step when she looked up into the room. "Oh. Hi!" She may have blushed—Zivic couldn't quite tell since she'd suffered light burns on parts of her body, including her cheeks. Wait ... was she ... *into* him? After all? What about that girlfriend that Jerusha had mentioned? That meant that ... just maybe ... if he said *just* the right thing ... maybe a smooth move later when they were talking fighter jock shop....

"Hey Jamie. Looking for someone?" Whitehorse smiled at her, and finally found what she was looking for in the cupboard. She tore open the wrapper and started grazing on the apple strudel kibble meant to be a high-energy snack for pilots in a cockpit.

"Yeah. Qwerty, actually."

He waved a palm in front of himself. "Well, here I am. What's the problem?"

"Oh, no problem. I just ... well, I was thinking about the ELW radios, and how hard it is to understand each other through all the static. I was thinking, couldn't we just ... tap those things into the regular antenna we use on the normal commline? Basically boost the signal?"

Qwerty looked like he was about to start a patronizing

speech about communications transmitters and antennae when Whitehorse interrupted him. "Good idea, Jamie. Unfortunately, it really wouldn't do anything. The regular comm channels are at such a wildly different frequency that the lengths and geometries of the antennae really aren't suitable for use in each other's system."

Qwerty nodded, only adding awkwardly, "Impedance matching issue."

Ace looked crestfallen. "Oh. Ok, well, it was just a thought." She turned back to Qwerty. "Well, goodbye, Billy." She left in a hurry.

Zivic glanced back at Qwerty. "*Billy?* I thought it was Billy-Bob?"

Qwerty looked annoyed. "It is. But I keep telling her to call me Qwerty."

Whitehorse chomped down another handful of kibble, and piled another package of it in front of Zivic. "Wait a minute. You never finished your story on the bridge. About your name. I find it hard to believe that anyone's name, first or last, is actually *Qwerty*. Like the keyboard layout."

"Oh, it's not. Like I was telling you, I applied to the Academy on a dare. My brother Tom, you see, he was a rascal, and we dared each other to do all kinds of shenanigans. Back in the country on Bolivar, there wasn't much opportunity for *real* shenanigans, I mean, no show-stoppers you can pull out there. So he says, *I dare you to just show up at the Academy on the first day, and see how long you can go before someone calls you out.* And, well, I did."

"Wait, you just … showed up? No plan? No … nothing?" said Zivic.

"I showed up. Hadn't ... properly thought things through. And when they asked me my name, I got flustered and said *Billy-Bob Qwerty*. And I thought, man, what a stupid, stupid name. I couldn't come up with something better than that? And they stared—my Lord, how they stared. Then they couldn't find the name on the list, so I got sent back home, and was so embarrassed, that that night I hacked into the Academy's database and inserted myself right there into the class of '72. Got a thing for languages, you see. And that extends to all patterns. Codes. Programming. Data transfer protocols. You name it, I can crack it."

Whitehorse was shaking her head in disbelief. "Wait. No, just wait. You're trying to tell us that you somehow hacked into the computers at the Academy overnight, inserted your name, and then you somehow flew through the four years and never once did someone discover what you'd done and called you out?"

Qwerty shook his head, and helped himself to some of Whitehorse's kibble. "Oh, I was found out, all right. Nearly a month later. But by then I'd already tested out of all the comms classes, all the programming classes, and most of the first and second year technology classes. Was my roommate that ratted on me. But by that point, I was, to put it mildly, the star of the show, and the commandant swept the whole thing under the rug." He chewed another handful of strudel. "Of course, as punishment, he made me keep the name."

Zivic and Whitehorse were both shaking their heads. "I'm ... so sorry," Zivic said.

"What was your last name before ... all that?" said Whitehorse.

"Bill Kwerdie."

Zivic could have sworn Whitehorse's jaw dropped a full inch. "Say again?" she said.

"Bill Kwerdie. K-W-E-R-D-I-E. Kwerdie." Zivic thought, for just a moment, that maybe he was playing a joke on them, but his face was so entirely innocent and serious, his usual manner so without guile, that he dismissed the thought. But still....

"Anyway, I suppose I should be off and figure out how to patch through to your fighters before Lieutenant Broadside tracks me down again. Fifth time today."

The change of subject was welcoming. "Wait, did you say *fifth*?" said Whitehorse, incredulously. "Ace has tracked you down *five times* today? Just to talk about that radio?"

"Well, twice about the radio, once about what we ate last night—the food stores on this ship leave a little to be desired, if you know what I mean—once to ask me about Bolivar, and another time to tell me that she'd been studying up on German, I think. Apparently her great-great grandpa was German. Asked me about a few words. Conjugations. Frankly, I was trying to figure out inflected Dolmasi noun declensions and she was distracting me, so I think—"

Whitehorse was shaking both hands in the air at him. "Wait, wait, back up, back up. She's tracked you down five times today to talk about ... radios, what you ate last night, where you're from, and to make small talk about *German*." She paused, and a hand came up to her mouth. "Oh my god. She's into you. Hard."

"What?" said Qwerty.

"What?" said Zivic.

"Don't you see?" Whitehorse heaved a sigh, and took a patronizing tone, as if explaining something to a kindergartener. "When a girl likes a boy, she'll try to talk to him and catch his attention. Sometimes she'll try to be extra helpful." She looked from one to the other and switched to her normal voice. "Guys, isn't this obvious to you both?"

Zivic grumbled. "Well ... yeah. I guess."

Qwerty shrugged. "I had no idea." He bent down to fiddle with one of his boots. Apparently his shoelace had come loose again. "Ain't never had a girlfriend, and frankly, ain't planning on it now, so—"

Zivic pointed down at his boot. "What the hell is that?"

On one of his boots, the top was tied together with a pink piece of string that, upon closer inspection looked like several pieces of pink string. Like a bracelet that had been untied and used as a shoelace.

"Oh. Ace offered this to me when she saw me trying to tie it this morning."

Zivic glared at it, like it was an affront to his own manliness. "She gave *that* to you? She wears that on her wrist all the time. I thought…." He struggled for words, not wanting to admit to them that he was holding out hope that she'd be into him and not, in fact, already in a relationship with another woman like Whitehorse had suggested. "I thought ... *someone* gave that to her, is all."

"Well she gave it to me, and it helped with one boot, but now this other one is acting up, so—" He looked up suddenly. "You really think she ... likes me?"

Whitehorse rolled her eyes. "Oh, for the love…."

Zivic shook his head. "Qwerty, how is it that you can learn

a language in a matter of hours, you can basically decipher any pattern, any code, in a matter of minutes, but you can't pick up on the basic human signals that a girl drops when she likes you?"

Whitehorse answered for him. "He's an idiot."

Qwerty looked genuinely embarrassed as he stood up. "If you good folks'll excuse me." He gave a tip of an imaginary hat. "Got some radio work to do…."

He left in a hurry.

Zivic choked down the poor excuse that passed for coffee in the *Defiance*'s galley and ignored the package of apple strudel kibble that Whitehorse had opened and piled in front of them. Then he started laughing.

"What?" said Whitehorse.

"Qwerty. Oh, and what about the whole *she's got a girlfriend so don't even think about trying anything on her*?"

She shrugged. "Ok. I made it up."

"You *lied* to me?"

"Uh huh. And I'd do it again if it meant I could get your head out of the clouds and out of her pants and back down here on this mission."

"You lied to me."

"If you don't eat, you'll never have the energy to save the girl, Batsnip." She popped of few of them in her mouth.

Batsnip?

"You lied to me," he repeated again.

"Oh stop with the hurt puppy routine. Besides. Qwerty needs a head start. Needs all the help he can get, that one. Now eat."

"Not hungry." He took another painful gulp of the black

sludge. No sugar anywhere in the galley. The *Defiance* had not even technically been christened yet, much less been fully stocked. "And stop it with the saving the girl shit, all right?"

Whitehorse shrugged. "Sorry. Just thought you could use a laugh." She munched on a few of the strudel pieces. "You know, I was thinking the other day about Sara Batak."

"You never even met her, did you?"

"Of course I did." She scowled. "I had to interview her—make sure she was good enough for my former fiancé." The scowl gave way to a small smile. "You know I still care about you, right? I mean, not like *I want to get drunk and do something I might regret* care about you, but we had something really, really good, Ethan. And I don't want to see you get hurt. So I sat down with her while she was in sickbay and you were … I can't remember where you were honestly. Anyway, we talked."

He felt his eyes burn. He wasn't ready for this. "Look, Jerusha, I don't want to rehash—"

She continued on, ignoring him. "She was good, Ethan. Really. I could tell. I mean, I know you only knew her for a few weeks, and I give you shit about having the complex of swooping in and saving the girl. But she was some girl. You could have done a lot worse."

Why was she doing this now? Why was she torturing him? He set his mug down and started to push away from the table. She caught his arm before he could stand up. "Ethan. I know it hurts. She's gone. She's dead." She stared him straight in the eye. "Don't let it kill you too."

"Thanks for the concern." He tried to smile, but failed.

"I'm serious. I'm watching you out there, when I'm at tactical. I see some of the stunts you're pulling. I mean, I know you're batshit crazy, but you don't have to *literally* be crazy."

"I'm not. But in case you hadn't noticed, there's a war on. Lots of people shooting at me. And when bullets fly, you do what you have to do."

He was trying to make it sound tough. Like he was a stalwart warrior who set his jaw against the rising tide of war and destruction, and buckled down to save the day. Be the hero. Be better than his dad and his lousy hundred kills during the battle of ... whatever battle that was, and ... dammit. She was looking right at him. Through him. It's like she knew he was putting on a show.

"Ethan," she began. But stopped, and stood up. "You're already a hero. What more do you have to prove?"

She left. He didn't even hear the door close behind her.

Because it hadn't. Someone else was standing over him, and he nearly jumped when they spoke.

"Lieutenant Zivic?" said Ensign Babu.

He was wearing the spare flight suit he'd borrowed earlier.

"What the hell are you doing, Ensign?" Zivic said, eyeing the suit warily. The other man was not fighter pilot.

"We've got a mission. Straight from the admiral herself. Top secret."

"She's letting *you* into the cockpit of a fighter?"

Babu waved that aside. "Of course not. But I *will* be piloting a small missile frigate. Those things basically fly themselves anyway. And you'll be my escort. You and another pilot you trust. Who is it?"

Zivic was about to protest, but the mention of a secret mission straight from the admiral herself snapped him into the moment, Sara Batak forgotten. "Bucket. He's an ass, but he's good."

Why hadn't he chosen Ace? Was he trying to protect her? *Dammit, Jerusha Whitehorse, get out of my head.*

"Ok. Go grab him. Don't tell a soul where we're going."

"Where *are* we going?"

Babu smiled. "We're staying right here. Britannia system. Calais. One of its little moons, near the shipyards. We're going to bring in the cavalry—right up your alley."

He looked askance at the ensign. "*You're* the cavalry?"

"The coffee cavalry, at least," he replied. A self-deprecating joke. Zivic was starting to really like this guy. Probably meant he was going to die.

Shit, my humor's gotten a bit dark.

Zivic stood up. "Do I get a chance to shower first?"

Babu actually grabbed him by the elbow, rank protocol right out the window, and led him to the door.

"No. We're already late."

CHAPTER SIXTY-FOUR

Orbit over Britannia
ISS Vanguard
Bridge

"Look, there it is again," said the tactical officer. He pointed to his monitor, and Admiral Mullins leaned in to peer at the signal on the screen.

"Maybe. Then again, wouldn't they detect this themselves? Surely if we can, then they can. And if *they* can't, then why? And what about the *Independence*? Wouldn't they see it?"

The officer shook his head. "No idea, sir. But the only thing that can explain this reading is if there were a very, very minor misalignment of the phase in a ship's stealth system. But not just that: it has to be somehow coupled into the phase of the ship's power reactor, such that anyone detecting it will just assume it's just a noisy echo of the signal from their own reactor, and not think twice about it. That's probably why the

Independence isn't picking it up."

"But why would they do that?"

The officer shrugged. "They took some damage at El Amin, probably. Then, after a hack repair job, they might have crossed a few wires."

Mullins nodded slowly. Behind him, President Quimby barked across the bridge. "Ted. Why aren't we going yet? I need to get back to Earth."

He ignored him. *Let the old bastard stew for another minute.* "Very well. What's it doing?"

"It's just orbiting Britannia, near the *Independence*."

"And nothing has happened with the *Independence* in the past hour? That shuttle that left? It never returned?"

"No, sir."

"What was it's course?"

"Calais, sir."

Interesting.

"Ted! I said get me the fuck back to Earth! Oppenheimer isn't even here like I thought he was, and I've got a fucking cabinet meeting in the morning...." Quimby looked at his watch, and tapped it. "Shit. Have I been up all night? What time is it? God, I hate space...."

The tactical officer pointed at the screen again. "Sir! The *Independence* just t-jumped away!"

"T-jump? Meaning we can't track it?"

The officer shook his head. "Sorry, sir."

"Did Volz log in a flight request?"

Another shake of the head. *Damn that Volz.*

"But, sir, the signal ... it stopped. Wait ... hold on...." Finally, the officer looked up, smiling. "It q-jumped away."

Mullins's face mirrored the tactical officer. "And we *can* track a q-jump signature."

The officer nodded. "Earth," he said quietly.

Quimby was losing his shit. "Ted! I said—"

Mullins spun around. "Mr. President, I'm terribly sorry. Yes, we're just leaving now. And when we get there, I think I've got another surprise for you."

That seemed to change the president's mood. "Oh?"

"Yes." He sat down in the captain's chair. "Admiral Proctor's head on a platter, no less."

Quimby seemed mollified by that. At least, he left to go grab an hour's worth of sleep. Enough time to arrange the trap. "Lieutenant Johnson, as soon as we get to Earth and verify that Proctor is indeed there, launch another meta-space-shunt-enabled anti-matter missile."

"Aye, aye, sir."

Mullins watched the viewscreen shift to indicate their q-jumps had initiated. "Time to turn all of Earth against Proctor, and make an example of those who oppose us. And better yet, it'll be the Dolmasi doing the hard work for us. And when we come in to clean up?"

Lieutenant Johnson grinned. "We'll be hailed as heroes?"

Mullins returned the smile. "Exactly."

CHAPTER SIXTY-FIVE

High Orbit over Earth
ISS Defiance
Bridge

"Coming up on Earth," said Liu. "Just one final q-jump."

Proctor nodded. "Thank you, Ms. Liu." She tapped the comm button. "Rayna, are we good to go?"

The comm crackled. "As good as ever. That brush with the Dolmasi did us no favors. Just let me know if you're planning on running into them again."

"If I could read the future, we'd all be billionaires with our own moons."

"I don't wanna moon. I want to tinker with my babies without anyone shooting at me."

"When this is all over, I'll make sure you get your pick of any ship in the fleet. Proctor out." She turned to Whitehorse. "You ready?"

"Yes, ma'am. We should be able to at least partially counter any meta-space pulse. Assuming we detect it in time, of course."

Good. At least they'd have a fighting chance to get the Dolmasi on their side. Or, if not on their side, then at least convinced that war was not in their best interest. But they could only be reasoned with if they weren't driven insane by Mullins's and Oppenheimer's meta-space shenanigans.

Whitehorse continued: "And just in case, mag-rails are ready. Just give me a target."

"Hopefully it won't come to that. Qwerty?"

He shrugged. "I think I'm there. I've incorporated former President Avery's information into everything I've come up with so far. Won't know until I actually shoot the shit with them again. I'll either be telling them we want to sit down and talk, or that we want to hump their camels. Never can tell with a polysynthetic language structured by homophonic lexemes."

"I trust you," she said, before he could continue the jargon. "It'll have to do for now." She turned back to Liu. "Initiate final q-jump."

The former intel officer nodded once and pressed a few buttons on her console. Moments later the infrared image of empty space disappeared to reveal a wavering Earth, cloud-dappled and serene. As luck would have it, they'd arrived directly over the Caribbean, and she was confronted with the water-filled hole in the Florida panhandle where Miami had been thirty years ago, until the first battle of the Second Swarm War had completely annihilated it.

Never again.

"Anything?"

Whitehorse shook her head. "Nothing yet. All meta-space

signals from IDF vessels are normal. Nothing from the surface." She looked up. "They might not be here yet."

"Keep scanning."

Minutes passed, and Liu settled them into an orbit she claimed would let them see all q-jump arrival points at once. Finally, Whitehorse caught Proctor's attention.

"Ma'am, no meta-space buildup yet from any IDF ship, but I am reading something ... odd."

"What do you mean, odd?"

She swallowed hard. "Remember how Titan and the other moons the alien ship attacked started increasing in mass in the days and weeks afterward? Well I'm reading some gravitational anomalies in the vicinity of Earth."

Proctor bolted to her feet. "From *Earth*?"

Whitehorse shook her head. "No, not from Earth itself. I only noticed it because the navigation system's computer had to automatically adjust its course to account for the effect. It's like ... there's extra mass somewhere nearby pulling on all of us. But not in the direction of the sun, or the moon. Hell, I even scanned Valhalla Station, and it looks normal. No idea where it's coming from."

A pit had started to form in Proctor's stomach. "Keep an eye on it. Send a message to Granger, tell him to be on the lookout for—"

"I'm sorry, ma'am ... who?"

Proctor caught herself. Damn. She'd been thinking about Tim too much, what with the conversations with Huntsman and Avery, and the fact that Tim's coffin had essentially been found at the core of an alien ship.

"Captain Volz. Please tell him to keep an eye out for—"

"Admiral!" yelled Whitehorse. "The *ISS Vanguard*. Mullins's ship. It's here."

"How do you know?"

Whitehorse looked up, her face drained of color. "Because another torpedo just launched from nowhere. And ... I'm reading an anti-matter signature."

Proctor smiled, and sat back down. "Time to catch him in the act. For all of Earth to see. If this doesn't convince President Quimby to see reason and sack the bastard, I don't know what will." She turned to Qwerty and Liu. "Tell Ballsy to have the *Independence* stay put, Qwerty. Liu? Once we counter the pulse, we should get into a new orbit, since Mullins will immediately know we're here, and where we are."

Liu smiled. "Counting on it."

CHAPTER SIXTY-SIX

High Orbit over Earth
ISS Defiance
Bridge

"Admiral! Reading massive meta-space spike!" yelled Lieutenant Whitehorse from across the bridge.

"Counter it." Proctor gripped her armrests until the knuckles were white.

Whitehorse nodded. "Analyzing pulse, and matching ours to destructively interfere...." She looked up with a smile. "I think we've got it. Their pulse amplitude has dropped by a factor of about a million."

"Is the shunt still transferring energy from the anti-matter blast?"

After a moment, Whitehorse shook her head. "Not anymore. The reaction is over. They managed to shunt quite a bit of energy into meta-space before I countered it, but not nearly as much as at El Amin."

Proctor smiled, and finally relaxed. "We'll do better next time. Terminate ours, but be ready to re-engage. At least we know now we can counter Mullins's and Oppenheimer's plans to get us into a war." She turned to Liu. "Now, get us out of this orbit before Mullins figures out where that meta-space signal came from."

Liu's smile was off. More like glee than satisfaction at a job well done. "With pleasure, Admiral."

Proctor watched the status of their orbit. At first it seemed Liu projected their course slightly down into a lower orbit, before pulling up and increasing their inclination to a more northerly direction—by now they were over France, and aiming towards Norway. Except....

"Whitehorse, did you fire off another meta-space pulse?" Proctor tapped her console, bringing up the data logs from their meta-space transmitters.

"*I* didn't." She glared over at Qwerty. "Did you do something?"

He shook his head, befuddled. "Ain't me. Looks like it happened right as we were adjusting orbit."

Before Proctor could figure out what had gone wrong, Lieutenant Qwerty caught her attention. "Admiral, the *Vanguard* is calling—they're transmitting a message over ELW radio, coded for us."

"Play transmission, Mr. Qwerty."

A buzz as the decoder managed to scrape the message clean of all but the most persistent static. "I can see you, Shelby. Can you see me?"

"He's bluffing. He can't see us," said Liu. "Look. I can't pinpoint the source, but I can tell that it's moving towards that other orbit I feinted to."

Proctor regarded her. "So *that's* what you were doing. Did you send out a meta-space pulse without authorization? You were trying to lure him into a particular orbit?"

Before she could respond, Mullins continued over the speakers. "I've got President Quimby here with me, Shelby. And he's been a witness to your betrayal. We saw you coordinate with the enemy at El Amin. We've recorded you sending out that meta-space pulse just now. We know you're behind this attempt to summon the Swarm. Yes, we know they never left. We've figured it out. And your plan to re-establish contact with them and help them conquer our world will fail."

Qwerty glanced up at her. "He's no longer transmitting on an encoded channel. This is a general broadcast. Everyone in the solar system can hear this."

"Which means we should be able to track him. What the hell is Quimby doing over there?" she murmured, before flipping the comm receiver on. Proctor chose her words carefully. "Admiral Mullins. I urge you to reconsider your use of the meta-space pulse. I know it was you. I don't know why you're trying to start a war with the Dolmasi, but we will not stand for it."

"Of course you won't. The Dolmasi are still under Swarm control, just like you. Of course you wouldn't like us fighting your allies. But I'm giving you one chance. Surrender. I'll even arrange for you to be officially discharged and there won't even be a court martial. Just give peace a chance, Shelby." His voice had taken on a mock-pleading tone. He was on a stage the size of Earth right now, and they both knew it. And unfortunately, he was an excellent actor.

Proctor, on the other hand, was not. "Oh, please. Everyone knows you just want to be a petty little tyrant. Run your own little kingdom and—"

Qwerty interrupted her. "He's closed the channel."

"And that's not all, Admiral. A small Dolmasi fleet just q-jumped into the outskirts of high Earth orbit. They're holding their distance, but it looks like those six seconds of the meta-space pulse were enough to summon them here."

"Dammit," muttered Proctor. She turned to Qwerty. "It's show time, Lieutenant. Tell them we're not a threat. Tell them we want peace."

Whitehorse had leapt to her feet. "Admiral! The *Vanguard*—it's ... it's suddenly visible on our sensors! It's like they ... I don't get it, but their hull is gleaming like the shiniest silver metal coating there ever was."

"What?"

"It's ... *gallium*. What the hell? They plowed right through a cloud of gallium. And the Dolmasi have changed course." Whitehorse looked up in horror. "They're homing in on the *Vanguard*."

Proctor strode over and rested her hands on Qwerty's shoulders. "Mr. Qwerty, I need you to do this. Now. Tell them to back off."

He nodded. "Working on it, ma'am." He was muttering furiously into his microphone, distorting his voice into strange-sounding diphthongs and almost melodious strings of vowels. Moments later, he nodded again. "I think it's working. I just heard back from them, and ... well ... they sound surprised. Shocked that I can talk to them. Which I suppose is better than them sounding angry."

"Good. Tell them to back off from the *Vanguard*. Tell them we're ready to talk, but that they need to back off from the *Vanguard*. Now!"

Qwerty sang another few lines of unintelligible sentences back into the microphone, and, miraculously, their advance depicted on the tactical monitor halted.

She breathed a deep sigh of relief. Good. War averted. For now.

"Like hell," someone muttered behind Proctor's back. "For you, Danny." Proctor turned, and when she saw Liu's face, she understood. Finally.

"Liu, back away from the terminal."

Liu smiled. An almost frenzied smile. "Too late. It's done."

"Admiral! She fired a torpedo!" yelled Whitehorse.

Proctor motioned at the marine standing by the door. "Arrest her."

Liu's smile deepened, even as the marine secured her arms. Her eyes were as wide as saucers. "You're too late! This is it, Admiral. Finally. Revenge. And yours too. Mullins took our Danny from us. From me. From you. And now I'm taking his life from him."

"Can you disable it?" she shot at Whitehorse, who was shaking her head.

"No, she's done something to it. Modified it. I can't access the—"

And before she could finish, the viewscreen lit up. The *Vanguard*, which had turned into a shining metal ship, its stealth tech apparently overwhelmed by some unknown countermeasure, exploded in a vast, muted fireball, quickly extinguished by the vacuum. Glowing red hunks of shattered hull and a fine mist of molten slag was all the was left to mark the grave.

Whitehorse continued. "And, ma'am, if these readings are correct, there was another active meta-space shunt on the *Vanguard*. Lots of that explosive energy made it into meta-space. More than lots. About a million times greater than the pulse they transmitted earlier. About the same level as the one at El Amin."

Mullins was dead.

President Quimby, newly-elected president of United Earth, was dead.

And the entire solar system probably believed that she killed them. And summoned the Dolmasi to help her do it.

And, to top it all off, the destroyed ship had dumped an untold amount of energy into meta-space, and in the absence of the Ligature, she had no idea what that meant. They'd just announced to the universe, on the galaxy's largest bullhorn: *we're here, come get us.*

Each of those events was, by itself, unlikely. And for all of them to happen at once was…

One in a million, she thought.

She spun around to Liu. "Why? How? How did you…."

Liu was laughing almost maniacally. "I've been planning this for weeks, Admiral. As soon as that fucker did *this* to me," she indicated her ruined face, "as soon as he killed my Danny, he sealed his own coffin. I arranged for that gallium to paint his ship a nice shiny silver for all of Earth to see. Oppenheimer was all too happy to provide the funds when I told him my plan. I tweaked our stealth system so that someone, if they knew *just* where and how to look—especially someone familiar with stealth tech, like Mullins—could see where we were. And I lured him into the path of the gallium. And now Danny is avenged."

Her half-melted face was grinning so widely, it almost looked skeletal. Ghoulish. She was crazy. Absolutely crazy.

She motioned to the marine holding Liu. "Get her out of here."

"Admiral...?" began Whitehorse.

Now what? Proctor sighed, and turned to tactical. "Yes?"

"I think I know the source of that gravitational anomaly from earlier." She hesitated, as if not even believing her own words. "Titan just showed up."

"Titan." She repeated the word, unable to keep the incredulity out of her voice.

"Titan, ma'am. I don't understand how it's possible, but it's here. Less than fifty thousand kilometers away. And ... it's heading this way." Whitehorse finally looked up from her console, her face looking quite dazed. "Really quickly."

CHAPTER SIXTY-SEVEN

High Orbit over Earth
ISS Independence
Bridge

"Captain Volz! The main body of IDF's Earth Defense Fleet is moving to flank the *Defiance*, led by the *Resolute*. Oppenheimer's flagship. Looks like they're trying to hem them in, sir."

Volz seethed, gripping the armrests of the captain's chair until his knuckles were white. "Oppenheimer," he said, bluntly. "How are they tracking the *Defiance*? Is their stealth system still working?"

The tactical officer shook his head. "It was until a few moments ago. Looks like they plowed right through the same cloud of gallium that exposed the location of the *Vanguard*. Their hull is now painted bright and metallic—it's impossible to mask."

How in the hell...?

But there was no time to dig down the rabbit hole of nested conspiracies that was United Earth politics, IDF, GPC, Grangerite maneuvering, and whatever the hell Mullins had been up to. Until the *Defiance* had slagged him.

All he cared about now was what the hell to do about the moon that had just shown up.

He still couldn't believe his eyes. A *moon* had just shown up. It was almost surreal—Volz couldn't take his eyes off the screen. He watched as less than a hundred thousand kilometers from Earth's moon, Titan grew ever bigger, a stark white and sickly yellow orb bearing down on the birthplace of humanity.

Twenty billion people are probably looking up into the sky and shitting their pants right now, he thought. "He actually thinks she did it. Damn you, Oppenheimer. We've got a planet-sized space station flying towards Earth, and you're focused on arresting the one person who can do something about it." He jumped to his feet and approached the tactical station. "Lieutenant, show me the latest scans of Titan. What happened to the hole that the Golgothic ship bored into it? Is it still there?"

He shook his head. "Partially, but when the scraps of the ship crash-landed it basically buried the hole under a few hundred meters of rock and soil."

"What if…" he turned to one of the tactical monitors that showed the positions of the various ships and fleets around Earth, waving Commander Mumford over from tactical science to join him. The *Defiance* was there, shining brightly with its new coating of gallium on the hull. Most of IDF's Earth Defense Fleet was bearing down on it. A large Dolmasi fleet hovered in the distance, apparently trying to make up their minds about what to do given the new developments of both Mullins's ship exploding and a rogue moon showing up at the wrong planet. "What if we can convince the Dolmasi to help us ... reopen the wound, so to speak? Basically replicate what the alien ship did to Titan. Bore down into that hole, and then when it's fully exposed, knock the shit out of ... whatever burrowed its way in there."

Mumford looked skeptical. "Like, launch a nuke down the hole and hope it knocks out the giant moon-sized space station?"

"Something like that, yeah," said Volz.

"Uh, sir, I think that only works in the movies."

Volz shrugged. "Well, it's all we got." He turned to the comm. "Get me the *Defiance*."

Moments later, Proctor's lined face appeared on the screen. "Ballsy? What do you think? Shoot at Oppenheimer? He probably thinks I killed the president and is trying to arrest me. The Dolmasi? Titan? We've got a target rich environment here…."

"I'd say we focus on the one that can take out Earth, Admiral," said Volz.

"Agreed. But I'm fresh out of moon-stopping ideas."

Volz laid out his plan, and to his surprise, Proctor didn't laugh at him. "Ok. I'll get Qwerty on the horn to the Dolmasi and see if we can't convince them that Titan is just as much a threat to them as it is to us."

"And the Earth Defense Fleet?"

Proctor smiled. A defeatist, sad smile. "If they shoot me down as I try to save Earth? Fuck 'em. Yeah, you heard me, Oppenheimer. I know you're listening in—this channel isn't secured. You want to have at me as I try to save our fucking planet? Go to hell. Have at me. But I'm going to die on my feet, saving my people. Just like ... just like Tim. Just try and stop me."

To Volz's surprise, the comm officer caught his attention. "Sir, hail from the *ISS Resolute*. Requesting to join the conversation."

Volz jerked his head up towards the screen and nodded, indicating to the officer to patch the admiral through. Moments later, the Fleet Admiral of IDF showed up on the viewscreen, alongside Proctor's face. "Shelby. You'll pay for what you've done here today."

"Oh, for god's sake, Christian, just hear me out on—"

"Save it, Shelby. Killing the president is one thing you'll never walk away from. But ... we can postpone justice for now. You're right—that moon is an existential threat to Earth. I bet one against a million that it's the Quiassi or Findiri. If you had have gone out and looked for them and neutralized that threat like I'd ordered, maybe we wouldn't be in this position. All the same, they're here, and we need to move fast."

Proctor looked ... surprised. She'd apparently not planned on Oppenheimer to be so ... pragmatic. Neither had Volz. *Anyone can change*, he supposed.

"Yes. Yes, we do, Christian. Did you listen in on our plan? Have anything to contribute?"

Oppenheimer flashed a grim smile. "Just a lot of firepower to open up that hole down to Titan's core." He glanced sidelong off the viewscreen, whispering something to another officer. After a few nods, he turned back to the screen. "Ok, channel's secure—we can speak freely without twenty billion people listening in. Once that hole is open, we've got some leftover firepower thanks to former president Avery. An antimatter bomb she produced for the Second Swarm War."

Good God, does everyone *have one of those blasted things?*

Proctor played coy. "I thought we got rid of all those? The joint chiefs thought they were too dangerous to keep around."

"Most of them were disposed of. But when I came on board after you left IDF I ... intervened. Saved a few for just such an occasion. In case the Quiassi and Findiri ever decided to pop in. Joint chiefs backed me up. Not sure the president knows ... I mean, the *former* president. And it looks like Mullins was able to lift at least one of them off of me. Two, if the reports from El Amin can be believed. I've got one left."

Proctor looked incensed, and her face said she had a million questions and retorts, but to her credit, she buried them all and focused on the task at hand.

Saving Earth.

"Ok." She looked offscreen and listened to a report, giving another curt nod. "Mr. Qwerty informs me that he thinks the Dolmasi are on board. If he's translating them correctly. At least they're not shooting at us yet. Looks like Titan is almost here. Is the fleet ready?"

"Ready as we'll ever be. I'll give the orders to special ops to ready the anti-matter bomb for insertion into the shaft we create in Titan's crust." He turned as if to end the conversation, but glanced back at the screen. "Oh, and Shelby, don't think this means you're not going to be held accountable for your actions. If we succeed today, I'll see you court-martialed for the murder of President Quimby. And if we lose today…" he paused, weighing his words.

He threw caution to the wind. "I'll hunt you down and put a bullet in your head myself for throwing away our planet just to settle one of your petty grudges."

Oppenheimer signed off before Proctor could protest. She turned to Volz, and actually smiled. "Well? At least he's not shooting at me either. Yet. Probably because he doesn't suspect yet that I know he was involved in that gallium cloud. If he did, he'd have killed me by now before I can testify to the inevitable senate panel."

Volz sat back down in the captain's chair. "Think this plan can actually work?"

She looked caught between a sigh and a profane outburst. "Probably not. It's a *moon*. If it decides to collide with Earth, there's nothing we can do to stop it. But at least we're not going down without a fight."

The tactical officer shouted across the bridge. "Sir! Massive power spike coming from Titan!"

Proctor leaned forward, and her expression became resolute. "I guess it's now or never."

CHAPTER SIXTY-EIGHT

High Orbit over Earth
ISS Defiance
Bridge

"Ma'am, Vishgane Kharsa on the Dolmasi flagship confirms they're moving in for their run at the surface of Titan," said Qwerty. "Says he has fifty terawatts of collective power from their ships' antimatter turrets to fire at the target. Also says he'll make us pay for the disruption of the Ligature when this is all over and hang our skins as trophies above his command center. He ... uh, doesn't sound too happy ... but at least he's not shootin' at us."

Proctor nodded. "Good. Payback can wait for all of us." She glanced at her tactical readout. "Looks like Oppenheimer is making good on his promise. The Earth Defense Fleet is turning to bear on target and powering up their terawatt lasers." She turned to Whitehorse. "Power up ours. Let's get this show on the road."

Titan grew larger on the screen, until it filled the entire front wall. Far below, on the surface, she could just make out the site where the pieces of the Golgothic ship had crash landed all around the hole it had bored into the surface, which was now covered by rock and dirt. All they had to do was punch through, and maintain the hole open just long enough for Oppenheimer's special ops team to insert the anti-matter bombs.

Would it be enough? Would just the threat of what they were doing be enough to convince whatever force or intelligence that was steering Titan to back off? And if not, would the destructive power of the bombs be enough to push the moon off course? She checked its trajectory. Still pointed at Earth. Except ... it wasn't pointed *exactly* at Earth. Just slightly above the north pole. What did that mean?

"Ma'am, Oppenheimer's ship reports the fleet is in firing range." On Proctor's tactical screen, she confirmed. A swarm of green dots had closed to firing range on the rogue moon, accompanied by a wash of yellow dots indicating the presence of the Dolmasi fleet, that had, for now at least, put their war on hold and decided that Titan posed as much a threat to them as it did to humanity. Moons shouldn't be able to *steer*, after all, and if it could steer towards Earth, it could steer towards Verdra-dol.

"Fire."

As one, over fifty human cruisers, frigates, carriers, and corvettes, combined with dozens of Dolmasi light cruisers, opened fire on the site of the hole. Rock vaporized away. She could even see it on the screen without any magnification, like a sprout of fire from the surface of Titan, just visible through the tenuous yellow atmosphere.

"Progress?"

Whitehorse tapped her console. "Down one hundred meters. One hundred fifty. Two hundred." A pause. "Going faster now. One kilometer. Two kilometers. Three—"

But that was as far as she got before the screen washed out with a blaze of light, the pixels over-saturating. When it autocorrected the light balance, she gasped.

From the very hole they had created, another beam had erupted. Red. Deadly shimmering red, like the beam that the alien ship had wielded so effectively and terrifyingly against their ship just two weeks prior.

Titan was ... firing.

Firing.

Titan was no longer a moon. It was a space station. "It's a fucking cannon," she breathed. Her mother's voice didn't even chide her for language. "A planet-sized cannon."

"What the hell is it shooting at?" said Volz over the comm.

Whitehorse frantically worked her console, shaking her head in frustration. "It's—it's not hitting any of the ships in the fleet. Neither our fleet or the Dolmasi."

"Earth?"

Whitehorse tapped a few buttons and the viewscreen flipped to show Earth, with the giant red beam disappearing past it, zooming off into space thousands of kilometers above the north pole. "It's missing Earth, too."

The red beam shimmered and pulsed. Almost ... regularly. Was that...

Was that another code?

Holy shit.

"Mr. Qwerty, if you please—"

But he'd already sprung into action. "Translating now, Admiral." He worked, and after a moment, his jaw hung open, slack. "It's not morse code like before, ma'am. It's ... *dear Lord*."

"What?!"

Qwerty's face had gone white. "It's encoded audio."

"Play it!"

The red beam pulsed and shimmered, continuing its destructive path into ... nothingness, far above Earth. And over the speakers, a voice.

An alien, almost robotic, mechanical voice.

And yet, a voice she recognized.

It was impossible.

"Shelby, they're back," croaked the voice. "Shelby, they're back."

Proctor had slowly risen to her feet without even realizing it. Before she could speak, the voice repeated itself a third time.

"Shelby, they're back," it scratched. "And ... so am I. Like a ... like a ... brick wall out of nowhere. I ... I think I was supposed to tell you that."

She grasped for her armrest, feeling her legs about to give out. This was impossible. This was a fantasy.

This had to be a dream. And with the voice repeating Carla's last words—words she'd never told another living soul—it made the whole event even more surreal, even more fantastic. And combining this coincidence with the relevance of the dream to Avery's contribution, it was too much.

But whatever it was, that was unmistakably Captain

Timothy Granger's voice, however robotic or mechanical it sounded. Granger's voice from the grave. From the void. Granger coming, returning—just like the fucking Grangerites predicted—to save them all, again.

Her mind flashed to Carla's hospital bed, where the dead girl lay silent and peaceful and bloody, as a defiant young Shelby yelled her disbelief at her grieving mother. Raging against the unlikelihood of an arbitrary god and the terrible injustice of a mortal life that had ended too soon for an innocent young girl. "*I don't believe, mother!*" she'd yelled. "*I don't believe in your fake magic god!*"

She collapsed back into her chair, staring at the red beam disappearing into the void beyond Earth. The red beam encoding Granger's voice. The red beam originating from the core of a moon that, against all hope, against all reason, now held the body or the consciousness or the essence or the mind of … Captain Tim Granger.

The Hero of Earth.

"I believe," she whispered.

Whitehorse pointed at the screen. "But what the hell is it firing at?"

CHAPTER SIXTY-NINE

High Orbit over Earth
ISS Defiance
Bridge

"Tim," she said. "Tim, is that you?"

Qwerty, jaw still half open, pointed up at the screen. "That's ... that's insane."

"I'm inclined to agree, Mr. Qwerty. But ... facts are facts. Evidence is evidence. Who else could it be?" Indeed, the pieces were starting to assemble together in her mind. And as unlikely a picture as they were painting, as she said, facts were facts. The piece of the *ISS Victory* that was embedded deep within the alien ship, dated to thirteen billion years ago. The original message that read *Shelby, they're coming*, hidden in the alien ship's energy beam using morse code—a method so unlikely and unsophisticated that it was a wonder they even caught it.

And now Granger's voice, albeit ... altered. Different. She supposed thirteen billion years in a black hole wouldn't do one's vocal cords any favors.

Qwerty wasn't having it. "Could be anyone's voice, ma'am. Could be computer generated."

"No. It's him." She couldn't say exactly *why* she knew it was him. She couldn't exactly blurt out *It's him because he's repeating cryptic words that my dying sister said to me that I never told anyone about*. But they needed to believe her. "I don't know how, but it's him. I know it." She reached down to press a button on her comm that would broadcast to the fleet. "All hands, all ships, cease fire. I repeat, cease fire, immediately."

The *Independence*'s and the *Defiance*'s laser turrets all fell silent, and after some hasty translation, Qwerty managed to pass along the order to the Dolmasi, but the Earth Defense Fleet continued its bombardment on Titan, drilling deeper and deeper into the previous hole, though several ships had now retargeted the exact site where the red beam was firing from.

"Oppenheimer, we need to stop. Now."

A sigh over the comm. "Really, Shelby? First you side with the Dolmasi, then kill Mullins and Quimby, and now this? Titan is a direct existential threat to Earth, and now you want to stand back and let it continue on its mission of destruction?"

"We don't know what its mission is! And Christian, I think … I think Tim is on that thing."

Silence over the comm. She held her breath, knowing how crazy she sounded. "Excuse me? Did I hear that right?"

"Yes, Christian. Tim Granger just spoke to us. Encoding his voice into that red beam. He said they're back, Christian. *The Swarm.* They're back."

Another pause.

"He actually used those words? He said, *the Swarm is back?*"

She closed her eyes and held her head in her hands. "Well, no. He didn't say Swarm. It was implied."

Oppenheimer grunted a laugh. "So, the ghost of Granger is ... *implying* ... that the Swarm have returned?"

She swallowed back a lump in her throat that had suddenly appeared. "Yes."

Another pause, this time for nearly ten seconds. "And ... you have proof? Dammit, Shelby, what the hell has gotten into you? You used to be the fleet admiral of IDF. You're a *scientist*, for god's sake. Where's your evidence? Where's the smoking gun? Where's your fucking proof?"

She held her face in her hands. He was right. She had no evidence. Just inexplicable coincidences. Circumstantial evidence that she had assembled into a picture. She was ashamed to admit what she saw—a picture of a dead Granger coming back to save them all. Again.

"I have none. But ... it feels right, Christian."

He guffawed. "Just listen to yourself, Shelby."

"Ma'am," began Whitehorse. "About that beam coming from Titan. It's aiming at some undefined point above the north pole of Earth."

"Yes?"

"We thought it was just heading off into deep space. But ... it's not. It's actually disappearing at a point about fifty thousand kilometers from Earth. And that point where the beam is disappearing ... it's approaching."

Proctor frowned. "Wait. You're saying the beam is simply disappearing at a singular point, and that point itself is approaching Earth?"

"Yes ma'am. And that's not all. You know that gravitational anomaly we detected earlier? The one we assumed was Titan before it appeared? Well from these numbers, Titan doesn't account for all of it. It's why I had trouble determining the source, because there was more than one."

Proctor lifted her head up to talk to the comm. "Did you catch that, Christian?"

"I did. What of it? Still doesn't prove that Granger Jesus has returned from the dead to save us all. Get your head out of the clouds, Shelby."

She pounded her armrest. "Dammit, Christian, look around you. A blasted *moon* just appeared out of nowhere. If Granger returning from a black hole is stranger than *that*, then I don't know how to help you."

Whitehorse's eyes widened and she pointed at the viewscreen. "Ma'am! Something's happening!"

Proctor looked at the viewscreen to watch. There, above and beyond the Earth, the starlight was shimmering. Wavering. Almost like how the *Defiance*'s viewscreen looked when it was stealthed. The starlight ... *stretched*. And when it had stretched to a point where the lines of light were bending and reddening and beginning to blur, something else appeared.

Something massive.

Something bigger than the largest spaceship she'd ever seen.

CHAPTER SEVENTY

High Orbit over Earth
ISS Defiance
Bridge

It felt like a dream. A nightmare. And yet even in her nightmares she'd always known that the horrors she saw or re-experienced were shadows and phantoms, and would soon fade away if she could only wake up. Just wake up, dammit.

But she didn't wake up.

This was not a dream.

Beyond Earth, at a point her console was telling her was over thirty thousand kilometers away, a monstrosity appeared. A behemoth.

A ship.

Easily ten times the size of a Skiohra generation ship. Maybe a hundred. And even though it was far beyond Earth, it looked nearly as large.

Titan's red energy beam slammed into it, raking across its

thousand-kilometer-long surface, spitting great gouts of fire as it tore into the hull, but it continued on its course towards Earth.

"What the hell is it?" she breathed. Though she knew the answer. Granger had already told her.

Through the comm, Commander Mumford on the *Independence* replied, "Ma'am, I'm reading unmistakable ... *Swarm* signatures off this thing. Power levels are far higher than the original Swarm carriers we faced thirty years ago, but the power phase profiles are identical."

Impossible. They couldn't be back. They couldn't be back, bigger, stronger, and more powerful than ever. Tim had stopped them. *She'd* stopped them. But the evidence was staring her in the face, bearing down on Earth, ready to unleash who-knew-what kind of fiery hell on the birthplace of humanity.

Lieutenant Whitehorse seemed to be stunned into silence. The whole crew was speechless. Their mouths hung open. No one knew what to say or what to do—they were all frozen, as if they were stuck in a dream. Or trapped a burning building where every exit was locked.

They needed a leader.

Proctor stood. She planted her feet firmly and clasped her hands behind her back. "Mr. Qwerty, patch me through to ... everyone. Wide band transmission. And translate for the Dolmasi, if you please."

He nodded. "Aye, ma'am. You're on."

"This is Admiral Shelby Proctor. My fellow servicemen and women, my fellow citizens, our enemy is unveiled at last. We do not fight the GPC. We do not fight Shovik-Orion or any other corporation. We do not fight amongst ourselves. We do not fight the Dolmasi, or the Skiohra, or any other living, breathing beings native to this reality. And we most certainly do not fight against the so-called Golgothics—what we now know to be a completely fabricated, made-up, imaginary enemy." She paused, letting the words sink in as she watched the terrible, enormous ship approach Earth. "No. We fight the Swarm. And this time, we don't do it alone. We were never alone," she murmured, watching the entire moon of Titan accelerate towards the massive ship.

Lieutenant Whitehorse caught her attention. "Admiral, power surge coming from the new ship. Off the charts. Similar to the power output of Titan. I think it's readying some type of weapon—"

As if in answer, the screen lit up. From one of the four giant, kilometer-sized ports on the gargantuan, twisted new ship, an energy beam erupted. It lanced out across the tens of thousands of kilometers separating them, and slammed into the surface of Titan. A white fireball blasted out from the moon, billowing up into a distorted mushroom cloud with waves of rock and debris flying up out of the moon's gravity well.

"Tim," she said, her breath catching. The Swarm beam—green and utterly deadly, just like she remembered from the war—was boring into Titan, sending up massive plumes. *He can't die. Again. Not again.* "All hands, and everyone within the sound of my voice ... open fire. Attack!" She glanced back at Whitehorse, and nodded. "Fire."

CHAPTER SEVENTY-ONE

High Orbit over Earth
ISS Defiance
Bridge

As one, the Earth Defense Fleet of IDF—all sixty ships—the *Independence*, the *Defiance*, the Dolmasi fleet, every single ship in the vicinity of Earth, accelerated towards the grotesque, utterly alien ship, and unleashed everything they had into it.

In all of Proctor's memory of the Second Swarm War, she never remembered such a scene. Never had she witnessed so many ships firing so many weapons at a single target.

And it was certainly having an effect. Thousands of explosions peppered the uneven surface of the Swarm ship. Bulbous, kilometers-long sections that hung out from the main body of the ship haphazardly burst into massive gouts of fire before the vacuum extinguished them. On the surface of things, it looked like an almost too-easy victory was imminent.

But the sheer scale of the thing made progress deceptive.

While the fleets were pounding the section of the behemoth ship she could see, she knew that hundreds of kilometers lie out of view, untouched and undamaged.

"Shelby," said Admiral Oppenheimer over the comm, "I'll take *Resolute*'s task force and flank that thing's port—we're reading a power signature over there that indicates it might be the ship's power plant. Maybe if we knock that out—"

She nodded. At this point, it was anyone's guess how to stop this thing. "Understood, Christian."

Titan continued raking its red beam across the surface of the ship, back and forth, almost haphazardly. It was terribly destructive, but as far as she could tell it wasn't having anything more than a superficial, localized effect. She turned to Whitehorse to confirm. "Is that beam doing anything to it?"

"Not that I can tell. It's just burrowing into the surface of Titan," she replied, seeming to misunderstand Proctor's question. "And Titan's weapon is doing pretty substantial amounts of damage to the ship, but its power levels are stable."

Proctor nodded slowly. "We need to help him out." Even a battle station the size of a moon was not quite enough to take out this new, massive incarnation of the Swarm ship. And their own ships batted about around it like gnats. They needed something to tip the scales, to put them over the edge.

On the viewscreen she watched as, in the distance, another deadly green beam erupted off the surface of the ship and slammed into one of the IDF battleships in Oppenheimer's attack wing. Within a second it had bored completely through the hull—its armor and shielding crumpling like tissue paper—and the ship exploded.

"The *Firedrake* is gone," said Whitehorse. "And so is the

Rattler—that was the ship Oppenheimer had the anti-matter bomb on." She looked up, her face getting whiter by the second. "It's picking us off one by one. We won't last another two minutes."

So this was it.

This was how humanity ended.

"Ma'am, it's rotating," added Whitehorse. "One of those weapons spires is now aiming directly downward. Right into the center of North America."

Proctor watched in helpless horror as the monstrosity turned, and the giant, bulbous beam turret began to glow. Given what it had done to the surface of Titan, central North America would soon be a glowing wasteland.

Another ship appeared out of nowhere. This one much, much smaller.

"Ma'am, I'm getting a hail from a ship called…." Whitehorse peered at the screen, "The *USS Elf Owl*."

She let out a breath she hadn't even realized she'd held. "Babu. Zivic." She motioned to Qwerty to patch her into the fleet. "All ships, aim at the base of that turret pointing at Kansas. One spot. Dig a hole. I'll explain later."

The amassed fleet, even the Dolmasi ships, began pounding at a single location at the base of the dozens-of-kilometers-long beam turret. The tip was glowing a fierce green, indicating it was nearly charged to capacity. And the hole they were blasting was minuscule compared to its length.

But it should be enough. It had to be.

"Ensign Babu, you ready?" She tapped her comm to make sure she was talking to the newly-arrived missile frigate, which was hopefully carrying a full inventory of the anti-matter missiles that President Avery had stockpiled and hidden all these years. "Launch ... five, no, ten—" The sheer size of that turret, and the size of the beam leaping off another of the turrets targeting Titan boggled her mind. "Shit, just launch *all* of them. Straight into that hole we opened up for you."

"Ma'am ... uh, we have a problem," came Babu's voice.

Damn.

"What is it?" she barked at the comm receiver.

"The launch mechanisms. They've all deteriorated. It's been twenty years since they've been serviced."

A pit formed in Proctor's stomach.

"Ensign?" She took a breath. "Are the detonators intact?"

"Yes, ma'am."

She looked down, and tried to keep her voice steady. *Earth. Remember Earth.* "Then, *Captain Babu*, deliver those missiles into that hole. Whatever it takes. Even if that means...."

She couldn't even finish the sentence.

Everyone on the small bridge was looking at her, the meaning clear in their faces. They were horrified, but they understood the need.

"Admiral," Babu began. "Was that ... was that ... *a promotion?*" His voice was light and breezy, but it had an edge to it. He knew. He'd understood her. But, being Babu, he was going to go out with a grin, however much it hurt.

She swallowed. "Yes. Yes it was, Captain." She watched the tip of the turret begin to crackle with energy. Earth's destruction was imminent. "Captain, godspeed. I'm sorry, we're out of time. Go. Now."

She stood up.

Everyone else on the bridge stood up.

"Batshit, time for you to actually earn your callsign," she said.

"Just give me a target, ma'am," his voice crackled through the comm.

"I hear you're trying to break your father's record. Look out your window. Swarm fighters. More than you could ever ask for."

"Apples to apples," he replied, distantly.

She frowned. "What?"

"Sorry, ma'am. What's the mission?"

"Escort Babu in. Get him into that hole at the base of the turret on that ship. Then get out before it blows. Understood?"

"With pleasure, ma'am. Batshit out."

The missile frigate accelerated away towards the hole. Zivic and his wingman, Bucket, shot out of its tiny shuttle bay and swarmed all around the thing, shooting aside any stray Swarm bogeys that got in its way. She trusted that they'd pull away, but she was almost too numb to even say anything. Not a word, not a breath as she watched them swerve, veer, barrel roll, hard six, blasting bogey after bogey that darted after the frigate.

"Admiral," continued Babu, even as his ship was just a few kilometers from the hole, "by my new authority as Captain, I'm renaming this bucket of bolts. This is Captain Babu, signing off from ... the *Plunger of Doom*."

Even as her vision blurred with the tears, she let out a laugh that she stifled with a fist.

The frigate plunged into the hole, and a second later the viewscreen washed out in a blaze of white. When it readjusted, she watched as the entire turret broke off from the grotesque, giant ship, its jagged end still crackling with kilometer-sized

explosions from the residual anti-matter build-up.
"Godspeed, Captain Babu," she whispered.

CHAPTER SEVENTY-TWO

High Orbit over Earth
Lieutenant Zivic's Cockpit

The counter on Zivic's dashboard monitor ticked higher and higher. Sixty-seven. Squeeze trigger. Sixty-eight. Hard six, roll, squeeze trigger, miss, tap port thruster, squeeze trigger, sixty-nine. Seventy. Warning lights, puncture in the port fuselage. Squeeze trigger, seventy-one.

He was in the zone. He knew, instinctually, that this was it. This was the endgame. This was showtime.

Finally, after far, far too long, his father's record was going down.

"Bucket, watch your four!" He spun up and around, the sudden g-force throwing him against his restraints, but managed to finger the trigger just in time to relieve Bucket of his tail. Bucket, returning the favor, swerved hard left and spun, raking another fighter homing in on Zivic.

His eyes still hurt from watching Babu's ship explode

inside the hole the fleet had carved into the monstrous ship looming in the background, its hull sprawling away into the distance like the mutated, gnarled surface of a planet that looked like it had rheumatoid arthritis and a bad case of leprosy.

"Batshit, get your ass back to the *Defiance*, now!"

He did a double-take. The voice was not Admiral Proctor's, or Jerusha's.

It was his father.

"What, worried that your record's about to fall, dad?" Seventy-three. Loop, squeeze trigger, seventy-four.

"Ethan," his father began again, this time, his voice sounding ... pained? "Ethan, listen to me. Let it go."

Let it go? Swerve, hard dive and left, squeeze trigger, seventy-five.

"You've got to be kidding me, Ballsy. Let it go?"

"Please, son."

"Dad, you fucking left me and mom when I was fucking three! I didn't see you for fucking fifteen years, you never called once. Not a hint of interest. Not a fucking glimmer of you wanting to even know me. Not until mom dies do you even say hello, and that's at her fucking funeral, and you're telling me to fucking *LET IT GO?*"

A round clipped his right wing and he spun out before regaining control by a last-second reroute of auxiliary propellant. He yelled again in frustration, and peppered another bogey with dozens of rounds. Seventy-six.

"Ethan, I'm sorry. I'm so, so sorry. I fucked up. Big time. But please, listen."

Seventy-seven.

Seventy-eight.

Bucket yelled over the comm. "Batshit, watch out!"

He swerved away from a bogey he was about to collide with, flipped a six, and blasted it and its partner to hell. Seventy-nine, eighty.

"Yeah, dad? Listen to what? What the hell could you possibly say to me after all that?"

The sigh came through loud and clear. "Son, just that ... I messed up, and lost your mom. And lost her permanently before I could make good. And I messed up again, and lost you too. Please, I can't lose you again without making good. Please give me another chance."

The giant ship started turning again.

Give me another chance.

He'd thought those same words, over and over again in the past few weeks, waking up in cold sweats after nightmares where Sara Batak died again and again and again, and always, Zivic was powerless to stop it.

"Batshit," began Bucket of the comm, "you're venting propellant. One more minutes and you're a sitting duck."

He shrugged. "Better than a shitting duck," he said, squeezing off another few dozen rounds. Eighty-one. Eighty-two. *God, that sounded funnier in my head.*

"What's it going to be, Batshit," Bucket continued. "We've already pulled off our heroic shit. We going down in blaze of glory?"

Squeeze trigger. Eighty-three.

"I'll let you know in about eighteen bogeys," he said, raising his voice over the klaxon that had started screeching in the cabin. Pressure loss. He was at vacuum. Propellant almost gone. Fuselage riddled with holes.

He looked down and saw a billowing white stream coming off his leg. One of the bogey's rounds and clipped his suit and he was venting oxygen.

"Time's up," he said to himself.

CHAPTER SEVENTY-THREE

High Orbit over Earth
ISS Defiance
Bridge

More shimmering green light illuminated the screen as the Swarm ship lashed out at other IDF cruisers and battleships from its other, smaller turrets. Even as part of it burned with secondary explosions ripping through its hull, over three quarters of the massive ship looked to be completely untouched.

"It's not enough," she murmured. "We can't beat this thing."

Captain Volz's voice erupted over the comm. "Shelby, that thing is just not stopping. And … it's turning again. Pointing one of the smaller turrets at Earth. Might not be as big as the other, but we're looking at extinction-level shit here if it fires."

"How bad would it be?" said Proctor. But she was already doing the math in her head, and it wasn't pretty.

"You know Chixlub? The dinosaur-killer?" Qwerty held his thumb and forefinger out a few centimeters apart. "Child's play. Multiply Chixlub by a million. The end. Earth is uninhabitable for a thousand years, ma'am."

Whitehorse nodded. "Detecting a massive power buildup. Looks like it's readying another beam."

It couldn't be, she thought. After all that had happened. The series of unlikely events, only to culminate in the Swarm finally hitting their target. Finally destroying Earth. Why couldn't the unlikely events favor humanity? Just once? Just one more one-in-a-million shot.

Just like Carla. It was happening just like with Carla. The disease had flared—the so-called Golgothic ship had appeared out of nowhere like a cancer. Then the threat had abruptly disappeared, only to be replaced by the horror of something even more abrupt and deadly. A speeding car out of nowhere mowing down the innocent.

And they were powerless to stop it.

Except this wasn't a dream, and they still had the most powerful weapon she'd ever seen defending humanity. Titan continued pummeling the Swarm ship, little by little chipping away at the thing. Perhaps, given another hour, it could completely destroy it.

But they didn't have an hour.

"It's finished turning. Power levels are rising," said Whitehorse.

Tim, we need you, she thought. *We need you to do more. We need that brick wall out of nowhere. We need the bricklayer.*

"Oh my God. The bricklayer."

"Ma'am?" said Qwerty.

She'd just done it with Babu. He was young. A full life ahead of him.

Now she needed to do it to Tim. Again. Whether he was still sixty-five or ninety-five or thirteen billion, it was his time.

This was why he'd come back.

He came back to die.

She spun to face him. "Mr. Qwerty, can you open a channel to … to Titan?"

He shook his head. "Honestly, ma'am, I've been trying here in the background the whole time. Seems whatever is down there in the core either is too shielded to pick up our transmission, or they're not equipped to receive it."

"Fine. Then we use his own language. Lieutenant Whitehorse, prepare to fire a terawatt laser. Any target. But Mr. Qwerty is going to patch in a phase pattern that matches what Tim used to talk to us. Can you do that, Mr. Qwerty?"

"Yes, but … what in God's green Earth are we going to say?"

"Leave that to me."

CHAPTER SEVENTY-FOUR

High Orbit over Earth
ISS Defiance
Bridge

"Ready, Admiral," said Whitehorse. Qwerty nodded too.

"All right. Message as follows," she began, watching as Qwerty readied to encode her words into the phase of the laser beam. "Tim, it's Shelby. I'm stealing your nickname, Tim. I'm hurling a brick. And it's you. I'm ordering an Omega Protocol. I repeat, Omega Protocol is hereby ordered. And you, Tim Granger, are the brick."

Everyone on the bridge waited, not even breathing, not even moving. Staring at the screen, waiting for an answer, or an acknowledgement.

"Anything?" she asked.

"Titan's still firing at the Swarm ship. No change in the beam. And the Swarm ship looks like it's about to fire on Earth," said Whitehorse.

She nodded towards Qwerty. "Again. Tim, this is Shelby. We're on our last leg here, Tim. All we've got left is you. I hate to…" she bit her lip. "I hate to get you back after all these years, only to throw you away. It's … it's a miracle that you're here. I believe that. But we need you to do it again. To sacrifice yourself for us. Again." She bit her lip harder. "My god, I don't want to lose you. Not again. But it's Earth. It's our home. I imagine, even after thirteen billion years, it might seem like a distant memory—I won't even begin to understand what you've been through. But it's our home. Mine. Yours. And only you can save it. Please. Omega Protocol, Tim. It's the only way."

"Admiral! Something's happening," said Whitehorse.

Indeed. On the screen, she saw that Titan's beam had shut off. On her console she saw a massive power spike originating from Titan's core, and moments later she saw that translate to movement.

Somehow, against the very laws of physics, Titan visibly accelerated. A hundred kilometers per second. Two hundred. A thousand. And before she knew it, the collision was imminent.

She mashed a hand on the all-hands comm link she'd held on standby. "All ships! Get out! Stand clear!"

The fleet was already on the move, accelerating out of the way as fast as they could go. Several q-jumped away, disappearing in white flashes, apparently knowing they'd never get away in time before Titan was upon them. One ship was too damaged to move, and was smashed into nothingness as Titan plowed right through it, erasing any trace of its existence.

The two enormous masses connected in a piercing, white flash. Yellow-gray Titan, and the somewhat smaller gray monstrosity that was Earth's oldest and most persistent enemy, disappeared in the glare. The viewscreen oversaturated with the glow of the blast, and by the time it adjusted, she saw that most of the bulk of the Swarm ship was a molten mass on the ruined landscape of the moon, covering over half of the surface.

And just as fast as it had started, it was over.

"Admiral, Titan's crust pretty much vaporized where it hit the ship. That entire hemisphere is molten, and spewing out mass like a giant moon-sized volcano. Atmosphere is gone. Earthquakes all over the entire surface," Whitehorse looked up. "I don't know if the moon itself is even stable anymore. It could just break up."

Proctor scowled. "Surely its gravitational mass will hold it together."

"Of course, Admiral. But not before it breaks apart from the acceleration stresses, and then recollapses back in on itself. The hull of that Swarm ship penetrated pretty deeply."

Proctor watched the viewscreen as the yellow moon, still on its previous trajectory, soared away from the Earth. At its speed, it would be well beyond the orbit of the Earth's actual moon within a few minutes.

"It's still not slowing down, ma'am."

He'd saved them. Again. And again, he'd be lost to them forever.

"Still no sign of slowing. Could be that the collision disabled whatever ... propulsion ... that thing has."

Titan grew smaller as the minutes passed, the angry red glare on the side of the moon where it had crashed into the giant Swarm ship still glowing like a giant eye.

And then it disappeared.

"It's gone, ma'am. No sign of Titan anywhere on passive or active sensors." Whitehorse scowled at her console. "I suppose if it's jumped a short distance away we'll know soon…."

Proctor could finally breathe. "It's all right. It jumped. That's enough for me." She turned to face Whitehorse, the marine who'd replaced the one that had removed Liu, and Qwerty. "It means he's alive." She glanced back up at the screen to stare at the empty space where Titan had been. Half its surface had been molten—who knew how deep the destruction had penetrated into the core? "But for how much longer?"

Epilogue

Earth
Lower Manhattan
United Earth Presidential Mansion

"Mr. Vice President?" the aide leaned into the room.

John Sepulveda closed his mouth. He'd been mid-kiss. Hadn't even gotten to start the foreplay yet. His wife rolled her eyes and pushed her shirt back down, giving him the look that said, *so this is how it's going to be now?*

"It's *President*, now, son. And this better be really, really good."

The young aide, the assistant to the late President Quimby, cleared his throat awkwardly. "I'm sorry, Mr. President, it's been ... a wild few hours. It's just that, Mr. President, Admiral Oppenheimer wants to talk to you immediately."

Sepulveda reached down to pull up his pants. "For God's sake I was just sworn in ten minutes ago. Can't it wait another twenty?" *You don't interrupt celebration sex*, he added in his mind.

"He's here now, sir. And he has someone with him he says you need to meet. Says it's quite urgent and—"

DEFIANCE

"Ok, ok, ok, fine," Sepulveda grumbled, fastening his belt buckle and straightening his shirt. His wife had already retreated to the bathroom of the presidential suite, a set of opulent rooms that were still full of the late president's possessions. Hell, it still smelled like rum and body odor. For all his charm, Fred Quimby was not known for his personal hygiene.

He went through the door and into the president's office—*his* office—where Oppenheimer was pacing back and forth. Another man was sitting in one of the plush chairs near the desk.

Sepulveda stopped dead in his tracks. "You've got to be kidding me. What the hell is that fanatic doing here?"

Oppenheimer stopped pacing, and smiled, extending his hand to Sepulveda. "Mr. President, congratulations on your recent swearing in." They shook hands, and the admiral swept his free hand over to the man seated, who slowly rose. "Allow me to introduce you to Patriarch Huntsman."

"The Grangerite," said Sepulveda, with a sneer, as if it were an epithet.

"The one and only," said Huntsman, with a smile.

Oppenheimer waved the patriarch over. "Mr. Huntsman, in addition to being a leader of the faithful on dozens of worlds, is also one of IDF's most valuable intelligence assets. He's infiltrated the GPC at the highest level. Has for years now. And he's here now to help us solve our biggest problem."

"The Swarm? They've returned?"

Oppenheimer nodded. "Yes. It appears they have. Maybe. But the problem I was referring to was that the murderer of President Quimby is still out there. And she has openly collaborated with the Dolmasi, who we are in a current state of war with. And she is on the run, having stolen one of our most advanced warships, equipped with stealth, and refuses to return to face a court martial."

Sepulveda shrugged. "She also saved Earth. What's your point?"

"She did *not* save Earth. She nearly destroyed it. Titan nearly collided with Earth, and she was there, cajoling and encouraging it on. And don't forget the plain fact that *she killed your predecessor.*"

President Sepulveda sat down at his desk. "And what about Titan? The head of IDF Intel just briefed me, right before the swearing in, that there's a chance that ... *Granger*, is down there. Is that true?"

Oppenheimer shrugged, and thumbed towards Huntsman. "That's part of why he's here."

Both turned to the patriarch, who looked dour. "Mr. President, how do I say this...."

"You say it quickly and waste as little of my time as possible."

Huntsman's eyes flashed with what Sepulveda thought might have been fear. But maybe it was annoyance. "All the major religions have a messiah figure. Mine included. But in all those religions, it is a commonly held belief that, before the messiah, comes the false messiah. The harbinger of doom. The servant of the destroyer."

Sepulveda snorted. "And you Grangerites believe that Granger is your messiah?"

Huntsman's eyes were unreadable. "More or less. He will save humanity in the end."

"And so what you're telling me is that ... *whatever* is on Titan, it's not Granger?"

Huntsman's eyes went cold. "Most certainly not. It is the anti-messiah. The anti-christ, if you will. It has come as the harbinger of doom. It is from *that* danger that Granger will save us all. I'm sure of it."

Sepulveda held his head in his hand. *Religious fucking fanatics.* "And ... you have proof?"

Huntsman only laughed. "Mr. President, *Titan* just q-jumped in from nowhere, apparently summoned a deadly Swarm ship from the void, and then perhaps destroyed it. Who's to say Titan can't summon another ship? You saw it with your own eyes. Everyone on Earth saw it. It fired some mysterious red beam across Earth's bow. The beam disappeared into nothingness. And from that nothingness came the destroyer. The facts are on my side, Mr. President. Believe what you want about who or what is inside Titan, the fact remains that it is a grave threat. I believe it to be the anti-messiah. The anti-Granger. But whatever it is, it must be stopped—that much I'm sure we can agree on."

Sepulveda glanced at Oppenheimer, who nodded, indicating his grudging agreement.

"Ok, fine. Titan's gotta go. If we can find it." He started to turn around, ready for this meeting to be over. Oppenheimer shook his head.

"And not just Titan, Mr. President. Admiral Proctor was in contact with Titan just before it escaped. Just like she was in contact with the Dolmasi. She killed Quimby. It's clear to me ... that she needs to be taken out as well. I tried once, a few days ago on her own ship. She ... eluded capture."

Sepulveda's mouth hung open slightly. *Unbelievable.* "You're her superior! Why didn't you just order her back and arrest her?"

Oppenheimer looked like he was suffering a fool, and Sepulveda hated him for it. *He'll pay. Eventually.* "I had this conversation with your predecessor. President Quimby believed the ... *optics*, would not look good if I relieved her. So I had to use more ... subtle means at my disposal."

Sepulveda snorted. "So, in a way, *you're* responsible for Quimby's death, are you not? If you hadn't failed, he'd be alive."

"And *you'd* still be in the most useless office on Earth," retorted Oppenheimer.

Sepulveda chuckled. "Touché." He kicked his feet up on the desk, definitely starting to feel the gravity of the office, and the moment. He snorted. "So? What do you propose?"

"Simple. I propose we give Mr. Huntsman here the third stealth ship that we've got in dry dock. He lures her to a specific location, and when he has her in his sights, he terminates her. Since he'll be stealthed, we get to chalk it up to a q-jump accident or a collision with a fragment of El Amin, or something."

"El Amin? You're planning on terminating her there?"

"Yes. The only place I know we can lure her to." He produced a data pad from his pocket and tossed it on the desk. Sepulveda pulled his feet off and leaned forward to pick it up, thumb it on, and stare at the image displayed. A figure lay still in a hospital bed, tubes sticking into him, racks of monitors behind him.

"So, you're going to get in the third stealth ship, lure her to this asteroid field, and … pow? Are you sure this third ship is up to the task? We already saw first-hand what happened to Mullins and Quimby."

Oppenheimer nodded. "I am. I personally piloted it just last week. Out to Vilasha-dol in Dolmasi space to attempt to speak to them to avert this war." He smiled. Sepulveda wasn't entirely sure that the admiral wasn't speaking ironically. "I was not successful, apparently. But regardless, Mr. Huntsman here can lure her in to El Amin, and deal with her there. Once and for all."

"I don't understand. Why would she care?"

"Read the caption. The identity of the man in the hospital bed."

Sepulveda read the text underneath the image of a man with breathing tubes stuck down his throat, with needles taped to his arms. A breathing apparatus stood off to the side. Sepulveda couldn't even recognize any features under the charred skin on the patient's face. "Daniel P.," he read, and looked up. "Who the hell is that?"

Oppenheimer smiled. "The key to Admiral Proctor. The perfect lure."

Sepulveda stared at the charred young man in the hospital bed. So young. And finally it clicked. All the news reports, the snippets of intelligence he'd gleaned from the redacted presidential briefs. "This is the instigator of the Sangre de Cristo incident."

Huntsman and Oppenheimer both nodded. "It is."

"He survived the fall through Sangre's atmosphere."

"He did. Barely. He was one of our best intelligence assets within the GPC. He played his part well, and he'll eventually be rewarded. But first, I need your authorization. For the mission."

Sepulveda continued staring at the prone, broken body lying in the bed, barely clinging to life. He thought of Quimby, who never even got the chance to cling to life. He thought of that moon firing into the void, and that Swarm ship, half as big as North America itself. And that woman, that damn, reckless woman, who was at the root of it all.

The Motherkiller. The Companion of the Hero of Earth. Now the Bane of Earth.

"Do it."

Sepulveda looked up at Oppenheimer, who looked relieved.

"Do it now."

Thank you for reading *Defiance*.

Sign up to find out when *Defiance*, book 5 of *The Legacy Fleet Series*, is released: smarturl.it/nickwebblist

Contact information:
www.nickwebbwrites.com
facebook.com/authornickwebb
authornickwebb@gmail.com

Printed in Great Britain
by Amazon